Johanna Lifted Her Chin and Confronted the Angry Man Facing Her.

"Why are you here? Isn't there a barn dance going at your place?"

There was just enough light in the cabin for Tyler to glimpse the outline of her feminine curves beneath the thin wrapper. It was the first time he had seen her in anything other than male clothing, and he halted his advance.

"There is," he answered.

"I'm not going."

"Yes you are, Johanna. I want to see you in a dress, and have some excuse to hold you in my arms."

"You never needed an excuse before."

"I've tried to stay away from you but . . . I need to be with you."

"Well, I don't need anything from you, Tyler Kendall!"

Dear Reader,

We, the editors of Tapestry Romances, are committed to bringing you two outstanding original romantic historical novels each and every month.

From Kentucky in the 1850s to the court of Louis XIII, from the deck of a pirate ship within sight of Gibraltar to a mining camp high in the Sierra Nevadas, our heroines experience life and love, romance and adventure.

Our aim is to give you the kind of historical romances that you want to read. We would enjoy hearing your thoughts about this book and all future Tapestry Romances. Please write to us at the address below.

The Editors
Tapestry Romances
POCKET BOOKS
1230 Avenue of the Americas
Box TAP
New York, N.Y. 10020

Fields of Promise

Janet Joyce

A TAPESTRY BOOK
PUBLISHED BY POCKET BOOKS NEW YORK

Books by Janet Joyce

Fields of Promise
Libertine Lady

Published by TAPESTRY BOOKS

An *Original* publication of TAPESTRY BOOKS

A Tapestry Book published by
POCKET BOOKS, a division of Simon & Schuster, Inc.
1230 Avenue of the Americas, New York, N.Y. 10020

ISBN: 0-671-49394-9

First Tapestry Books printing February, 1984

10 9 8 7 6 5 4 3 2 1

POCKET and colophon are registered trademarks of Simon & Schuster, Inc.

TAPESTRY is a trademark of Simon & Schuster, Inc.

Printed in the U.S.A.

*For those first names
written in the family Bible,
and to Kate,
who made it possible
for their story to be told.*

J.J.

Fields
of
Promise

Chapter One

THE DIAMOND-SHAPED STACK OF THE LOCOMOTIVE spewed clouds of black smoke and showers of orange sparks into the vivid blue Nebraska sky as the Western National train pulled out of the small station. A shrill blast of the whistle proclaimed the train's departure from the city of Omaha, but the sole passenger who occupied the opulent private Pullman at the end of the train didn't hear or react, his long muscular form lying sprawled amidst the plump satin pillows scattered across a red velvet divan. The empty proof of the amount of whiskey Tyler Phillips Kendall had consumed the night before rolled in irregular patterns across the colorful threads of luxurious Persian carpeting.

A fetid odor of cigar smoke clung to heavy gold-fringed drapes that sheltered the unconscious man

1

from the first morning rays of the spring sun. The engine gathered speed, generating a rhythmic sway that guaranteed his continued slumber.

It was almost an hour later when the train rounded a sharp bend in the track that Tyler was nearly flung from his make-shift bed. Instinctively, he made a grab for the tufted back of the divan, holding on until he was sure he wouldn't be thrown onto the floor. Gradually coming up out of his stupor, he opened his eyes but quickly closed them again, emitting a loud agonized groan as everything in his sight began swirling. A dull pain throbbed in his head, keeping time with the sickening sway of the car and the harsh clanking of the train's metal wheels upon the narrow tracks.

Grimly acknowledging that it would be hours before he could expect some relief from the colossal hangover he had brought upon himself, Tyler ran a shaky hand down his stubbled cheeks, smoothing his full brown mustache as he muttered a self-derisive expletive under his stale breath. It took several more seconds before he tentatively ventured to open one bleary gray eye, stifling the burning bile that rose in his throat. He attempted to stretch his cramped legs, wincing as the stiffened muscles protested painfully. Eventually, he was able to prop himself up against the plump cushions, but his rough awakening made him aware of more than the physical tortures he was suffering.

He prayed for a swift return to the peaceful oblivion of the last few hours when no memories had plagued him. He had drunk himself into a mindless stupor to

2

block out the events of the previous day, but those precious hours were now being painfully paid for. It was questionable whether that brief tranquility was worth the cost, for it was still all too easy for him to recall the part he had been pressured into playing during yesterday's statehood celebration in Omaha.

With a sardonic grin twisting his lips, he eyed the dried mud on his expensive leather boots, the limp creases in his tapered doeskin trousers and the damp whiskey stains on his gray superfine frock coat. Certainly, he no longer fit the image of a dignified banker's son from Boston and even less a heroic veteran of the Civil War. Nevertheless, it was also true that he didn't look any more like a farmer today than he had yesterday, when he had been introduced as one to a group of homesteaders commemorating Nebraska's admittance to the Union.

Intent on making the purchases and arrangements that were necessary before completing the last leg of his journey, he had thought to pass unnoticed through the crowds he encountered as he made his way along Omaha's main street. Unfortunately, his considerable height plus his expensively tailored clothing made him stand out in a crowd, and Oliver Barthold, the main speaker, had immediately called attention to him.

The pompous, white-haired president of the Western National Railroad had introduced Tyler to the gathering and invited him up to the podium, but Tyler had declined, uncomfortable with the attention being given him. He had acknowledged the introduction and then attempted to melt back into the crowd but Barthold would not be denied. He began extolling the virtuous decision Tyler had made in joining the hundreds of other farmers and veterans who believed Nebraska to be the "promised land," dramatically portraying him as a war hero who had heroically led the men under his command as they valiantly fought to preserve the Union. Against his wishes, the assembled dignitaries had drawn Tyler up the wooden stairs of the gaily draped platform and given him an honored seat behind the podium—the last place Tyler wanted to be.

Since the war, he had heard more than enough rousing speeches from well-fed politicians who had never glimpsed the carnage of a battlefield, and even though Barthold was the major shareholder in a private company instead of a candidate for public office, the meaningless promises he delivered sounded much the same. It had taken all of his self-control not to jump back off the platform when Barthold told the roughly clad crowd not only that Tyler had been a captain in the Twelfth Massachusetts Dragoons and earned a medal for his bravery but also that he currently represented the Kendall Bank of Boston, an institution that—hand in hand with the railroad—held a vested interest in the future prosperity of the new state.

Running a restless finger inside the starched collar of his shirt, Tyler had scanned the crowd for its reaction to Barthold's announcement and read the disdain in several leather-brown, taciturn faces. Tyler had hoped to fit in with the hard-working people who would soon become his neighbors, but knew that if word got around that he was associated with the railroad and an affluent Eastern banking family, he might never be accepted as one of them. He had been immensely relieved when Barthold switched the emphasis away from him to the Western National's intention to lay several additional spur lines. Although Tyler noticed that Barthold had carefully managed to avoid any mention of the increased freight costs the farmers could expect to be charged, he could see that the homesteaders had contemptuously noticed the lapse. As the silver-tongued older man took his seat beside Tyler, giving way to a new speaker, several surly comments about the railroad's steadily increasing rates had filtered through the frigid spring air.

"Barthold, you were damn lucky they didn't run you out of town on one of your own rails," Tyler proclaimed gruffly, wincing as the sound of his own voice echoed painfully inside his aching head. After the renewed throbbing had somewhat subsided, he again braved opening his eyes and silently studied the ornate gold patterns stamped into the ceiling of Barthold's private car. His mind began drifting back in time and he could not stop the memories that seemed to mystically unfold across the etched surface above him, as if it were a stage where a painful melodrama was being enacted for the hundredth time . . .

"You can't be serious!" blustered his father. Edward Kendall's face darkened to a mottled red as he fixed his son with a steely gaze, a look that had always quelled any rebellion in Tyler when he was a boy.

"I am," Tyler insisted, returning his father's gaze with identical intensity. "I have already purchased the land and secured my transportation to Nebraska. I will be leaving in a week."

"Tyler, you are a Kendall! Kendalls are not farmers. Your father is the president of one of the largest banks in this country." His mother, Amanda Phillips Kendall, the elegant matriarch of the family, nervously patted one perfectly manicured hand across her bosom as if the very idea of her younger son turning to such a life was enough to cause heart failure. A Kendall did not dirty his hands in common labor.

Tyler looked across the expanse of the expensively furnished parlor of his family's Boston townhouse to where his parents sat together on a rosewood-framed settee. His fists clenched at his side, Tyler attempted to control his anger and convince them that his reasons for emigrating to Nebraska were sound. "Mother," he said quietly, reminded that the graceful woman across the room had adored him since birth and understanding that she could not comprehend his desire to turn his back on the society where, by virtue of his name alone, he would be assured a position. "Boston society and . . . all of this"—his hand swept in an arc to include the physical evidence of immense wealth contained in the fashionable parlor—"it's closing in on me."

"You just need to rest. The war and all those terrible months in prison have exhausted you. Take some time, go to the beach house, sail, relax," his mother suggested with a placating smile. "Take all the time you need, and when you're ready your father will find a position for you at the bank." She rose from the settee and crossed the room to place a hand gently on his arm. "You have a responsibility to this family and to society to maintain a certain position. It's time you settled down, married. Why, just last week Dorothy Marshall implied that her niece, Felicity, was quite impressed by you. Felicity Marshall is a beautiful young woman, well bred and educated at the finest schools. Her background is impeccable. She would make the perfect wife for you."

Tyler turned pained eyes on his mother, shaking his head from side to side in frustration. "You just don't understand, do you? More time won't change anything. I've tried for two years. I just can't put off the inevitable any longer. I'm no longer suited to this sort of life, if I ever was. Felicity Marshall is a very attractive young lady and she will make someone a perfect wife—but not me. I'm thirty years old and it's time I made some sense out of my life. I need space. I'm going to Nebraska—with or without your blessing."

"What will you do for money?" Edward Kendall's words were delivered in a disdainful sneer. "Surely even *you* have realized that you will see little or no profit for years."

"I have my mustering-out money. That's more than most farmers have to start out with."

"A few hundred dollars?" Edward snarled. "Why, you spend more than that in one night's drinking and gambling. You won't last a month out there, boy."

"I'll make it last."

"Humph!" his father grunted in total disgust. "You

have that inheritance from your grandfather, I suppose, and I made some good investments for you during the war that you could draw upon."

"I don't want it. I don't want any money I haven't earned myself. Give it to my brother. James can put it in trust for his firstborn!" Tyler shrugged his arm away from his mother and started toward the parlor door, no longer trusting that he could control himself and not wanting to explode in the stifling atmosphere that permeated the room.

"Oh Tyler, you can't mean that!" his mother cried.

"Your mother and I won't stand for it. When you insisted on serving in the army we put aside our arguments, though God knows it was ridiculous. You could have bought your way out of the draft. Remember what happened then? It was Kendall money that bought you your commission and later arranged for your release from that Rebel prison. You owe this family!"

Tyler paused at the door, his hand tightly clenched around the heavy brass knob. Setting his jaw, he slowly turned back. "I don't owe this family anything," he said with quiet deliberation. "While young men lay on a battlefield with their guts spilling onto the ground, this family got richer. The respected Kendall bank invested in companies that sold spoiled food, threadbare blankets and inoperable munitions to the war department.

"Sure, Kendall money made it possible for me to go in as a commissioned officer and what good did it do? Your ne'er-do-well son led his patrol right into an enemy ambush! Then I was the one released from prison while good officers were left there to die."

"You were a good officer too, Tyler," his mother argued. "What happened could have happened to anyone. After you were released, you served with great honor. General Grant presented your medal himself."

"That piece of brass won't bring back the lives lost because of my ineptness in the beginning!"

The arguments had continued until, in the end, Tyler had stormed out of the parlor, packed his belongings and vowed never to return. The last words his father had said to him as he stood consoling his wife's heartbroken sobs were, "You'll fail at this, son. It won't be very long before you find that this is the greatest mistake of your life and that your place is back here!"

Running his long fingers through his tousled brown hair, Tyler tried to arrange his six feet, three inches, more comfortably upon the velvet-upholstered couch, still hearing those words as the recurring doubts began to assail him. Indeed, what did he know of farming? Of a future without the luxuries he had enjoyed since birth as the son of a wealthy Bostonian financier?

In the five days it had taken him to cross the country by rail, he had managed to skim through a few pamphlets he'd picked up from the "boomers" who proclaimed the fruitfulness of Nebraska soil to anyone who would listen, but he was beginning to wonder if the realities were anything like the lofty statements he'd read. Only a fool could believe that one need only "tickle" the surface with a plow to assure that a bounteous crop would be produced. Even the gardener who tended the splendid grounds surrounding his family's mansion worked harder than that to coax the plants into lush growth.

As a child, Tyler had toddled at the heels of the quiet-spoken Negro freeman who nurtured the tiny patches of soil in the midst of the city. "They's the Lawd's promise in every seed, Mastah Tyler," Samuel had explained as he patiently showed the little boy how to prepare the soil and place the seeds at the proper depth in the kitchen garden, then instructed him in the cycle of cultivation as Tyler tended the corner patch given over for his exclusive use. It had been a source of great pride to him when the promise in each tiny seed coupled with his labors had yielded a fragile living plant.

Trying to remember every bit of knowledge the gardener had conveyed to him, Tyler muttered aloud, "Thanks, Samuel, but I have a feeling I need to know more. Much more."

Oliver Barthold, a long-time friend of the family, had been of little use to him, other than by insisting on providing the luxurious accommodations of his private car when he learned of Tyler's presence on the train. While Tyler had been enjoying a smoke at the back of his car the first evening of the trip, a porter had moved his belongings without his knowledge or permission. Upon learning of the change, Tyler had been furious but Barthold had overridden his heated objections by suggesting that he could be of some help to him, supply useful information about the new state—help, Tyler learned, too late, was worthless.

Barthold's knowledge of Nebraska was as negligible as that of Tyler's aristocratic parents. All he could supply was the location and number of miles of railroad track laid across the new state. Though this overweight, verbose friend of the Kendall family thought it strange that Tyler was turning to farming, he had the decency, after his initial surprised reaction, to keep his opinion to himself.

Upon several occasions during the trip, Tyler had wandered into the passenger cars to escape Barthold's lengthy dissertations. When he attempted to strike up a conversation with other farmers who might tell him what he needed to know about the land, he had managed to glean little useful information. After one look at the expert cut of his clothes, his uncallused hands, coupled with the clipped Bostonian sound of his voice, their suspicions had been aroused and their responses had become stilted. All he had actually achieved was confirmation that his future life as a farmer wouldn't be easy, but as the train carried him steadily closer to the acreage he had purchased northwest of Omaha along the fertile banks of the Elkhorn River, he had stubbornly clung to his dream—peace in bountiful plenty would soon be his.

There wouldn't be endless reminders of the war wherever he turned. Surely, the maimed bodies of the survivors of that horrible war wouldn't be stationed on every street corner he passed. He looked forward to the physical exhaustion he would no doubt feel at the end of each day laboring on his land—an exhaustion that would ensure dreamless slumber.

The continual sway of the car lulled him into a pleasantly drowsy state, his hazy brain barely registering the train slowing to a stop as he mentally pictured himself looking out across the vast fields of green crops he had planted with his own hands. A beautific smile curved his lips and his gray eyes closed on the idyllic fantasy he had finally devised to escape the shallow chatter at the constant round of social affairs he had been forced to attend over the past two years.

The fantasy was a far more positive method of escaping than that which he had employed for most of the months since the war. All the whiskey he had consumed had dulled his senses and brought on the oblivion he sought, but only temporarily. Nor was the oblivion any more permanent after the frequent nights he'd spent losing himself between the white thighs of faceless women, women he visited after escorting the Felicity Marshalls of the world home at a respectable hour. Fragments of those nights inserted themselves in his dream and Tyler frowned.

"This here's a holdup, mister!" A harsh, raspy whisper cut into his pastoral dream. Tyler's eyes flew open. The black barrel of a smooth-bore rifle was aimed at his face.

"Don't move less'n you want a hole clean through that fancy vest you're wearing."

"What the . . ." Tyler was abruptly forced back into a startling reality, his scattered thoughts instinctively focusing on the ivory-handled service revolver that lay uselessly out of his reach on Barthold's desk. "Damn!" He cursed his own negligence, but the lethal authority of the gun aimed point-blank at his chest kept him immobile. He waited in silence while a second assailant, who had already begun searching the car, removed his only visible means of defense, jamming the revolver somewhere beneath the voluminous folds of his tattered coat.

With steadily mounting frustration, Tyler eyed the three armed figures who had entered silently through the back door of the car. Although their features were concealed behind wide woolen mufflers wrapped about their faces and roughly fashioned fur hats pulled low over their foreheads, he gained the impression of youth. Only the tallest one, who kept his weapon aimed at Tyler's heart, could be described as full-grown. The other two were much shorter, their slender bodies lost in enveloping over-coats.

In other circumstances, he would have attempted to overpower them, but he sensed a reckless determination in their manner that made him hesitate. During the war, he had faced desperate young men almost half his age and had quickly learned not to underestimate their capabilities. He could almost smell their fear and that made them highly unpredictable adversaries.

"Where do ya keep the money?" the stripling who stood over him questioned, exchanging nervous glances with the smaller figure who had stationed himself near the connecting door to the other cars, guarding against any intrusion.

"What money?" Tyler stalled, his furious gaze

moving to the one by the door, whom he had already sensed was the group's leader.

His assumption was proved correct when his gaze was met by two penetrating blue eyes. Without wavering, the smaller youth gave a slight nod of his head, a silent order for his cohort to proceed.

As he stared into the icy blue eyes of the group's leader, Tyler felt that the young man was curiously satisfied with Tyler's helpless fury. The thought angered him even further. Swallowing the nausea that threatened, he forced himself to sit up, making sure he made no sudden moves that might startle his over-tense assailants. "You've hit the wrong car," he tried. "There's no money in here."

"Don't fool with us, Barthold." The break in the adolescent voice did not lessen Tyler's caution. "We know who you are and we plan to take some of that gold you drain from the farmers in these parts."

Tyler was unwilling to take any chances with the gun held on him by an increasingly unsteady hand. He sought and gained unspoken permission from the leader, then slowly swung his long legs off the couch until his booted feet rested upon the floor. A stab of pain shot through his head and, wincing, he brushed a shaking hand through his brown wavy hair, again aware that the leader was inwardly laughing at his unsteadiness.

Taking a deep breath, he announced, "Goddammit, I'm not Barthold. You boys are making one hell of a mistake." He forced his aching head to remain erect and fixed the leader with a riveting gaze.

His announcement was followed by a taut moment

of silence. The nervous youth who had evidently been assigned to do all of the talking swiftly sought advice from the calmer lad who remained standing by the connecting door. The leader's curt negative nod indicated his disbelief of Tyler's claim as he stepped across the car and joined his companion who still stood guard over Tyler.

Lifting his gloved hand, the leader attempted to calm the third member of their band, whose quaking figure had not moved from his position at the back door. When he had assured himself that the much smaller youth was in control of himself, the leader returned his attention to Tyler and they fought a silent visual duel, with Tyler returning the piercing blue regard intent on his face, but his challenging stare didn't sway the young man in charge. A harsh whisper, muffled by the heavy woolen scarf wound around the lower half of his face, broke the tension only slightly. "We're not that dumb, Barthold." His blue eyes were iced with deadly determination that immediately prompted his taller companion to reenter the conversation.

"We know you were s'posed to be in Omaha yesterday and this here's your own fancy train car. Says so all over the side."

As if to hasten Tyler's surrender to their demands, the leader poked his shoulder with the barrel of his gun, stepping back far too quickly for Tyler to make a grab for the weapon. "Move!" he ordered. "Now!"

Gritting his teeth, Tyler shrugged resignedly. "I'll give you what little money I have with me, but I repeat, you're making a mistake. I'm not Oliver

Barthold. I know this is his car but I'm merely a guest. Barthold's still in Omaha."

A finger coiled tightly around the trigger of the rifle and Tyler heard the click of the hammer being cocked in readiness. "Get the money." The leader's hollow whisper was backed up by a menacing wave of the rifle barrel, and Tyler realized he could no longer delay the inevitable if he didn't want to be shot.

With his hands clenched into fists, Tyler stood up slowly, willing his limbs to stop shaking as he was ordered to raise his arms. Grudgingly following orders, he carefully made his way across the car toward the elaborately carved mahogany desk but paused behind it, attempting one last token argument.

"Since I'm not Barthold," he declared, "whatever fortune you were expecting isn't here. Do you want to risk years in prison for the small amount of money I've got with me?"

"Get on with it," the leader ordered, glacial blue eyes following the movement of Tyler's hands as he finally extracted a set of keys from his trouser pocket. He hesitated before inserting one of the keys into the locked desk drawer, hoping to find some weakening in the rigid stance of the leader but there was none. A steady finger on the trigger of the black-barreled Sharps rifle was his indication to proceed more quickly.

Tyler unlocked the desk drawer and removed a small metal box, then unlocked it with another key. He placed a stack of bills on the polished wood surface, then turned the cash box upside down to show there was nothing else contained inside. The hammer of the gun trained on him slowly returned to its resting place, and Tyler couldn't prevent his audible sigh of relief, furious with himself when he again sensed the leader's secret amusement over his small show of fear.

Shifting the gun to his other arm, the leader reached out and scooped up the stack of paper money. While his taller companion kept his lethal buffalo gun aimed at Tyler, the leader stuffed the money into a pocket of his coat. Suddenly, there was a loud clatter from the doorway and all eyes turned to see the third robber picking his weapon up from the floor.

"Sorry, Joe," the slight figure hastily apologized in a breathless high-pitched tone.

Again Tyler wondered about the age of his assailants. Judging by the high pitch of his voice and slight stature, the clumsy one by the door couldn't be any more than twelve or thirteen. Hoping that the moment's distraction would provide him with an opening to reach for the small derringer lying tantalizingly close in the open desk drawer, Tyler kept his eyes riveted on the two figures standing by the desk as he stealthily moved his hand.

The leader's attention returned far too quickly and he raised his rifle. "Don't try it, Barthold."

"Come on around the desk away from that peashooter," the tallest youth decreed.

Tyler stemmed his rising temper and did as he was told. His head was pounding, his hands were shaky, and his brain was still too befuddled by alcohol to function very well in the situation. "I'll make sure you boys live to regret this," he gritted thickly. "I'll track you down and that's a promise." Glancing from one of his assailants to another, he saw that his words had little effect. They were determined to follow through with their crime.

Knowing he was being given no other choice, he sat down in the chair indicated by the leader, frowning as the tall gunman carefully eased his large weapon onto the desk, then pulled a short length of rope from his pocket. Tyler's hands were jerked behind his back, the rope wound tightly around his wrists and soundly tied, effectively securing his arms behind him. Another rope was withdrawn from the youth's pocket and Tyler's feet were tied together in front of him.

"Aren't you carrying this a bit too far?" he protested, but before he could close his mouth, the leader stuffed a kerchief into it and swiftly knotted the corners behind his head.

"It's been my pleasure, Barthold," the leader assured in a husky whisper, his penetrating blue eyes twinkling with enjoyment as Tyler glared impotently back at him.

There was nothing he could do but go on staring while the trio prepared to leave. "We're only taking what's owed us," the leader declared, contemptuously tossing a paper bill on the floor as they backed out of the car, leaving him tied to a dainty gilded chair.

A few minutes later, the train lurched into motion, and briefly Tyler feared the teetering chair might tip over. Somehow he managed to keep himself upright, trying to relax, but rage waved like a red flag in front of him and he began to struggle furiously.

How had that damned unlikely-looking threesome managed to stop an entire train? Or had they enough intelligence to time their attack to a regular wood-and-water stop? Reluctantly, he admitted that their dispassionate leader had probably done exactly that, which meant no one would be coming back to check on his welfare. He cursed himself for having left explicit instructions with the conductor that he wasn't to be disturbed under any circumstances until they reached the end of the line—Hemmington, Tyler's destination.

Squirming helplessly, he felt his anger mount as the train picked up speed. Silently, he berated himself for a fool. It was apparent that the young leader of the robbery had considered him amusingly inept. He would not soon forget the mocking blue eyes of the one called Joe. If he hadn't gotten himself falling down drunk, maybe he wouldn't be in this ignominious position. He might have outwitted and overcome his youthful assailants if he had been in any condition to think straight.

Vowing never to take another drink, he tried slipping his wrists through the ropes but they had tied his bonds too tight. When he realized he couldn't get loose, he forced himself to relax, finally resigned to completing his journey bound to the spindle-legged chair.

The thieves had lightened him of over five hundred

dollars. Other than the few coins that remained in his coat pockets, it was the only money he had ever earned that wasn't connected to his family.

Damnation! He had wanted to prove himself out here without begging his family for any kind of assistance. He certainly didn't want to confess that he was already in trouble before he had set one foot on his land, nor was he willing to admit defeat.

Having little else to do but think, Tyler inventoried what possessions he had left, a saddle horse, blankets and a small army tent. While in Omaha, he had purchased all he would need to begin farming, but now he had no funds left to pay off the drivers of the wagons. He had over a week to wait before his supplies were delivered and unless he earned some money, he'd have to swallow his pride and wire for more funds.

As far as his personal needs were concerned, he still had possession of his rifle, mess kit and canteen but had planned to purchase foodstuffs at the settlement before heading out to his property.

"Well, Tyler, old boy," he mumbled against the gag, "you've done it before."

He'd learned how to forage for provisions when he'd needed to during the war, perfecting the talent while in prison, and now he was being forced to do so again. He admitted to himself that he probably would be starting with as much as most of the people who homesteaded the land. It would have been more if he hadn't been so impatient to get to his property, had waited in Omaha until his wagons were ready and driven one of them himself—then he'd still be in possession of his money.

Venting his anger on the ruffians who had stolen his stake, he shouted, "I'll find you one day, you damned young scoundrels!" but the gag muffled his angry outburst to an ineffectual garble of muted sound.

Chapter Two

"YOU WHAT? HOW COULD YOU!" BERDINE HEINSMAN'S voice raged above the wind howling outside the sturdy walls of the small log cabin. Lifting her arm in an angry gesture that included the other members of the Heinsman family, she fixed them all with a formidable blue-eyed glare.

The four heads of varying shades of blond hair, gathered around the worn oblong table, were raised to her in subdued silence as she directed furious words at her nineteen-year-old sister, Johanna. "You risked your lives! You could all have been killed."

"None of us were even hurt," Johanna pointed out, striving for calm though beneath the surface of the table her hands plucked nervously at the coarse material of her brown canvas overalls. "Now we have enough money to pay the back taxes and the second mortgage Pa had to take out last year. We were going to lose the farm, Berdine!"

She returned her elder sister's glare with a determined glower. "Dang it! Pa worked too hard for this land to let it be claimed by some Eastern bank that doesn't want it in the first place. If it'll make you feel any better, think of it as a favor to the bank. This way they'll get back all the money they loaned us plus considerable interest. It wouldn't do them any good to own a piece of empty farmland. There wasn't any other way if we're going to meet that note when it's due. We did what we had to do."

"Robbing a train?" Berdine screeched, losing the final ounce of her composure. "We shall all be hanged! All of us! And if not, we shall surely suffer eternal damnation! Lord have mercy on our souls!"

Turning her gaze on the only male member of the family, sixteen-year-old Frederick, she railed on. "Johanna may have lost her mind, but you, Fritz? You've always had a cooler head. How could you have gone along with her idiotic plan? Placed the children in such danger?"

"I'm not a child. I'm fourteen, Berdie, and a woman growed," Cordelia interrupted, her fair complexion blotched with embarrassed color when she realized that all eyes were upon her. In a quieter voice, she continued, "And I can decide things for myself."

"But I'm the head of this household and I make *all* the decisions for this family." Berdine punctuated her fury by pounding on the table with the flat of her small, workworn hand, causing all but Johanna to flinch at her uncustomary show of fury. "You'd best understand that, young lady!"

Somewhat mollified by Cordelia's chagrined expression, Berdine was unaware of the obvious fallacy in her statement until she noted the stiff smiles exchanged between Johanna and Fritz. Knowing that her family had made a momentous decision without even consulting her, she went white and sank weakly down on the end of the bench, lowering her face into her hands. "How could you?" she repeated despairingly, tears escaping from between her fingers. Her bowed head with its glistening braided coronet of dark gold shook as she moaned, "Oh merciful heavens, how could you have done this despicable thing?"

"Don't cry, Berdie." Eight-year-old Amy, the youngest member of the family, rose from her place at the table and went to comfort her sister. Placing a thin arm around Berdine's quivering shoulders, she tried to console her. "No one will ever know it was us."

"We will know and none of us will escape God's judgment," Berdine cried bitterly, dropping her hands away from her face and into her lap. "I'm glad Mama isn't alive to see the day when a Heinsman would stoop to thievery."

"The railroad owed us," Fritz defended hastily, his adolescent voice fluctuating between high tenor and resonant baritone. "Je-ru-salem, Berdie! We've only gotten back a little of what the Western National took away by charging farmers the highest rates. If you could've seen the inside of Barthold's rail car, you'd know the man won't miss the money we took off him."

"That's true, Berdie," Johanna stated firmly, not a trace of guilt showing on the smooth, rosy cheeks of her oval face. "The man is a drunken wastrel, if I ever saw one. The kind who lives off the life's blood of people like us. You know that both Pa and Karl would be alive today if greedy men like Barthold didn't exist."

Her vehement words provoked a long thoughtful silence as each member of the family recalled their father and brother, who should have been seated with them at the table. Karl, the firstborn son, had gone to work for the railroad in order to subsidize the family's meager income, but his life had been unnecessarily lost in a poorly planned detonation of explosives.

The railroad's determined drive to lay track across the country came at the expense of the men it employed. To the wealthy owners of the railroad, residing safely back East, and the callous construction foremen who heartlessly drove the workers that were slaving to meet company demands, labor was plentiful and therefore expendable. Consequently, each mile of iron rail was paid for with the sweat and blood of men and all too often with the needless loss of their lives or limbs.

When Axel Heinsman had learned of the death of his son, something had dried up inside him, the laughter that had always lurked so close to the surface dying out in his eyes, the musical lilt in his German-accented voice going flat. Despite last year's having been a good one for the crops, he had been forced to take out another mortgage on his land in order to support his family and pay the outrageous freight charges the railroad demanded to transport the excess grain he had produced. The old strength that had carried him through droughts, locusts, the death of his beloved wife and the backbreaking drudgery of taming the virgin Nebraskan soil was no longer there to sustain him.

During the years following Karl's death, he had begun to mutter with growing incoherency, his despondency multiplying in direct ratio with his bitterness and hatred toward the railroad. Eventually, he had convinced himself that the railroad would not be satisfied until it had robbed him of all he had worked for. Axel Heinsman had wrestled with the forces of Nature for more than a decade, but the increasing power of the railroad finally broke him and he succumbed to a stroke, moaning Karl's name as he passed away.

Since Axel's death, Berdine, the eldest surviving child, felt she must shoulder the dual role of father and mother to the remaining Heinsman children. She had years ago assumed the role of mother. At the time of Helga Heinsman's death, shortly after giving birth to Amy, young Berdine had solemnly promised her mother that she would provide moral guidance for her brothers and sisters and raise them to be dutiful, God-fearing Lutherans.

"I have failed," Berdine moaned in anguish, her shoulders sagging in defeat. "I promised Mama I'd teach you to follow God's laws, and even though Papa hated the railroad, he was an honest man. He would never have condoned stealing."

"It wasn't stealing, Berdie!" Johanna cried. "The

railroad never paid us Karl's back wages or one penny compensation when they killed him. They didn't even have the decency to return his body to us. You know that grave out there is empty." Her lush soft lips thinned and she hissed between her teeth, "We're even now!"

Straightening her shoulders, Johanna wiped away the bitter tears that burned beneath her thick lashes. "Pa always said that God helps those who help themselves. This is Heinsman land and will stay Heinsman land no matter what it takes."

"A man is nothing without his land," Fritz said, echoing his father's well-remembered sentiments. "Pa brought us from Ohio to fulfill his dream, and none of us can blacken his memory by letting a money-grabber like Barthold steal our property."

Seeing the conflicting emotions crossing Berdine's strained features, Johanna pressed, "Don't waste your pity on that slovenly drunk we waylaid. The money he spent on his boots would have fed this family for months, maybe years."

Swinging her long legs over the bench, Johanna stood up from the table and went to her sister's side. Taking both of Berdine's small hands in her own larger ones, she knelt down, her blue eyes as cold and condemning as her father's had been when referring to the railroad and the men who ran it. "You should have seen Barthold, Berdie. It was no disgrace to rob the likes of him. He reeked of whiskey, took the Lord's name in vain and . . ."

"And I'll wager he's a fornicator too!" Amy interjected exuberantly, sensing that Johanna was beginning to sway their righteous sister into seeing the justice of their actions. Although Amy hadn't actually seen their victim, she was too excited by the adventure to let that important fact prevent her from joining in.

"Amy!" Berdine cried, appalled. "Where did you learn that word?"

Johanna leveled her youngest sister with a forbidding scowl, silently warning her that she had gone too far, but Amy's childish innocence shone from wide blue eyes as she announced self-righteously, "Pastor Braun condemned all fornicators in last Sunday's sermon. You stayed home with Cordie 'cuz she was feeling poorly, but the rest of us heard him say that fornification was a vile abomination in the eyes of the Lord." Her last words were said in such an authentic imitation of their stalwart pastor that Fritz began snickering.

"As well he might," Berdine agreed hastily as she gave Fritz a quelling look that immediately sobered him. "But we do not use such language in our home."

"But Pastor Braun said that word and more. He said hell and damnation. He said . . ."

"Amy!" Johanna stopped the girl's emotional reiteration. "That's enough."

Amy wilted. Unused to being chastised by Johanna and confused that her use of their minister's very words had brought about her sister's censure, she bent her head. Her shining silver-gold braids fell forward over her slight shoulders and her little hands shook in her lap as she tried unsuccessfully to hide the tears that slid from the corners of her large blue eyes.

After muttering a soft apology to Amy, Johanna

strove to bring the conversation back to the practical matters at hand. Standing away from Berdine, she shoved her hands into the wide pockets of her overalls and began to pace. With her long flaxen hair free from the confinement of the single braid she oftimes wore, falling about her shoulders, her expression was hidden as she stared at the floor.

"What's done is done, Berdie. If we tried to return the money, we'd have to pay for the crime." The tall slender figure, clad in baggy overalls and an old shirt that had once belonged to Fritz, came to a stop by her older sister. Impatiently tucking her silken hair behind her ears, she bent and placed her hand on Berdine's softly rounded shoulder. "Is that what you want, Berdie? Shall we turn ourselves in and let that rich railroad tycoon send us to prison?"

"Of course not, Jo." Berdine reverted to the familial nickname that told her sister the argument was nearly over. "But what do we do? We cannot use stolen money to pay off our debts. It wouldn't be right."

"We can and we will," Johanna vowed fervently. "I am taking that money to Hemmington as soon as I can and posting a draft to the Kendall Bank of Boston. That way, this farm will be all ours again. God willing, we'll have a good crop this year and we'll never have to remortgage again."

Stalking to where their outer clothes were hung on a row of wooden pegs next to the door, she lifted down her coat and reached into the pocket. Clenching a thick wad of crumpled paper money in her fists, she crossed the room and threw the bills upon the table.

"Barthold will never miss this money. Count it, Berdie. We only took what we needed."

At first, Berdine simply stared at the money, her hands clutching and unclutching the thin material of her bleached calico apron. With a deep sigh, she smoothed her palms down her skirt, then slowly reached out for the money. Her hands shook as she carefully counted the wrinkled bills into a tidy stack.

"I hope the good Lord will forgive us for this," she announced quietly when she had finished. Then a tiny smile pulled up the corners of her generous mouth. "Even He once cast out the moneylenders, and according to you Barthold is a far worse scoundrel than those scurvy ancients."

After Berdine's yielding, there was a noticeably lighter atmosphere in the cabin. Resuming character, Amy tucked her long blond braids up under her knitted cap and giggled. "Oh, Berdie, I was so clever. The engineer thought I was surely a boy. And Mazie was wonderful—that ol' cow did exactly what I told her to do. Just stood there jawin' her cud while I acted like I was trying to pull her off the tracks."

Not to be outdone, the more reticent Cordelia mustered her courage and chimed in to describe the daring escapade from her point of view. "I had the varmint in my sights the whole time so's he daren't move a muscle."

"Shur 'nuff, Cordie," Fritz teased, a wide smile breaking across his broad freckled face. "You had him so scared, it must have been the ripples of his trembling that pulled the gun clean out of your hands and made Pa's old musket fall right on the floor!"

Now that the danger was over, the robbers could afford to laugh and all of them took part as they related the details of their adventure to a wide-eyed Berdine.

"He had the beady red eyes of a weasel, but was so influenced by drink that the cowardly skunk could scarcely stand on his own two feet when we ordered him to open the money box." Johanna dramatically mimicked their victim's shaky gait as he had stumbled across the opulently appointed Pullman. "He was quaking in his hundred-dollar boots, almost drooling with fear."

Although she knew she was grossly exaggerating the picture she was painting for Berdine, Johanna was enjoying herself too much to feel the least bit guilty. Berdine would never know that the man they had robbed was young and good-looking, with a powerfully virile strength, even if he had been so much the worse for drink that he could hardly stand. Johanna would never admit to anyone that when she had looked deeply into the man's dark gray eyes, she felt an immediate and completely alien pull on her feminine senses. Maybe it was an unfamiliar awareness of herself as a woman that had made her react so strongly to him. She had relished his humiliation, savored his defeat at her hands and almost wished she could have told him that he had been held up by three young girls and a stripling boy.

"What did he look like, Jo?" Berdine asked.

Fortunately, Cordelia jumped in before Johanna was forced to stretch the truth even further. "He was an old and grizzled geezer. His eyes were red like a

mad dog's." The delicately thin youngster straightened her spine and beamed with youthful bravado,
her coronet of strawberry-blond hair becoming a halo
as it caught the dim light. "We knew we were up
against a bad villain, but the stakes were high and we
persevered."

"Took his gun before he knew what had struck
him," Fritz gleefully announced. "He had one of
them fancy-handled pistols that I'll wager he cheated
some poor starving soldier out of after the war.
Don'tcha think so, Jo?"

"Prob'ly so, Fritzie!" Johanna more than matched
her brother's eagerness to exaggerate even more of
the details of how they had overpowered their dangerous victim. "I had that thing tucked safely away
before he could make a move toward it."

With a wide smile of satisfaction, she patted her
waist, but immediately her smile turned to an expression of horror when she felt the hard barrel of the
service revolver still tucked in the bib of her trousers.
"Oh no," she breathed as she carefully removed the
heavy weapon, staring with widened eyes at the object
she held with both hands.

All the excitement that had carried her through the
robbery, the ride home and the confrontation with
Berdine had camouflaged the weight of the ivory-
handled revolver she now cradled gingerly in her
palms. "I've still got his gun." She raised her eyes to
meet the shocked expressions on her siblings' faces,
then returned her gaze to the gun, carefully turning it
over and studying it as if for the first time.

She ran one fingertip along the cold barrel and onto

the warmer ivory of the handgrip, her eyes narrowing when she discovered a small silver plate. Holding the gun higher to catch the flickering light from the smoking lard lamp that hung over the table, she was able to read the engraving. "It says 'T.P.K., Capt. U.S.A.'"

She turned to the family, filled with relief that their victim, who had certainly been young and fit enough to have served his country, was not the original owner of the gun. "You were right, Fritz. This gun belonged to some poor veteran of the war—or worse, his widow who was probably down to her last penny and forced to sell it to Barthold."

Somehow the initials being different from Barthold's provided added ammunition against the man and further justification for her possession of the weapon. She carefully placed it on the table, then shoved her hands back into her pockets. "I didn't mean to keep it, but I'm not sorry. A man like Barthold doesn't deserve to have it."

"We don't either, Jo," Berdine announced quietly, her hands fluttering over her ample bosom.

No one spoke for several moments, sobered by the certain knowledge that their crime was now greater than originally planned. It was Fritz who finally reached for the gun, respectfully studying it as he held it in his large hands. "It's one of those high-caliber cap-and-ball revolvers used mostly by officers. This one must have been custom-made for the poor devil. Captain T.P.K. sure had a mighty fancy and expensive piece.

"If Karl had lived, he might have gotten into the

war. Might even have had one of these." He stood up. Scraping the bench back, he stepped over it and walked slowly toward the mantle that graced the wall of stone forming the fireplace. After reverently placing the revolver on the thick slab of oiled walnut, he turned to his sisters and announced in a quiet voice, filled with the authority he felt as the only Heinsman male, "We'll just keep it right there until we decide what to do about it. Until then, it can serve as a reminder of all the brave men who fought in the war."

"Better as a reminder of this family's folly," Berdine mumbled beneath her breath. Brusquely, she stood up and crossed to the iron cook stove, busying herself stirring a bubbling pot. "There are chores to do. They won't get done if we sit here all day. Being away half the day, you'll have to work fast to get finished before dark." Raising her head, she listened to the rising wind. "We're in for a storm, and we'd best prepare for it in case we're stuck inside for a spell."

Without arguments, each Heinsman went about his assigned duties. As Fritz and Johanna bundled into their outer clothing and opened the heavy door, a strong gust of chilling wind and swirling snow entered the cabin's main room before they could secure the door behind them. Trudging side by side through the deepening snow with the family's shepherd dog trailing close at their heels, they leaned into the wind. Tucking their faces down into their mufflers to protect them from the driving icy snow, they turned the corner of the cabin and picked up the axes by the woodpile.

After splitting a good supply of wood and carrying it into the house, they filled a pair of buckets apiece at the well and made their way toward the sheltering walls of the stable. Neither Fritz nor Johanna attempted any more speech than was necessary above the sound of the rising storm until they were safely inside the half-timber and half-dugout structure built into the side of a small hill.

"The crows were flying crazy all morning, Jo, and the wind's picked up some since we got home. We'd better make sure everything's tight before we leave the barn. There's a howler coming for sure," Fritz pronounced as he struck a flint and coaxed a spark to ignite the wick of the lantern. Holding the lantern fueled by precious kerosene high in one hand, he reached for the wooden bucket that hung by its rope handle on a peg near the door and handed it to his sister. Grinning down at her, he said, "You can milk our partner in sin while I see about the rest of the stock."

Johanna returned the grin, her dark-fringed, corn-flower blue eyes sparkling as she took the bucket and picked up the low, three-legged milking stool. She patted the shaggy brown hide of their docile accomplice before settling down on the stool, then blew on her cold hands to warm them before wrapping her long fingers around the cow's teats. "Suppose old Mazie knows she's wanted by the law, Fritz?" she called to her brother, the image of their slow-moving cow's part in the escapade causing a gurgle of laughter to erupt from her generous mouth.

The sound brought an immediate hoot of responding mirth from her brother, who had climbed to the loft and was pitching forkfuls of sweet hay down to the family's pride and joy—a pair of mixed-breed draft horses their father had acquired by trading a yoke of oxen to a family who were heading west on the Oregon Trail, only a few miles south of the Heinsman farm.

"Aw, Jo. You know what Pa always said about cows being so dumb they don't hardly know nothing but to stand still when they shouldn't. All we had to do was lead her to them tracks and the rest came natural, especially with Amy pulling on her." He paused and leaned against the handle of the pitchfork. "You know," he said thoughtfully, "that was so easy, maybe we ought to try it again, so's we could get enough for one of them new McCormick gang plows and another team of horses."

"Don't even think it!" Johanna ordered sharply. "I'd never admit it to Berdie, but we were lucky and you know it. Besides, we're even now and if we did it again, we'd really be the criminals destined for the fires of hell that Berdie's so blamed sure of."

Warmed by the heat emanating from the patient cow swishing her tail back and forth, Johanna stopped milking to unwrap her muffler and pull off her cap, letting her long hair spill around her shoulders. "The way that snow is piling up, you'd best toss enough straw down to keep the animals warm. Maybe some extra feed and water, in case we can't get back out to the barn for a while."

Her hands returned to their rhythmic task of extracting milk from the cow's full udder, and Johanna let her mind wander over the events of the day. The four fellow conspirators had met in the barn as soon as the morning chores had been completed, having convinced their eldest sister that they were all needed to bring in the sheep from the far field as well as check the fences. Though most of their fields were enclosed by the thorny Osage orange bushes Axel had planted continually since the first year they began claiming the land, it had been easy to convince Berdine that the few wood fences might need repair. Fences, like almost everything else on the farm, were always breaking or falling down, and having done some of the spring plowing and planting during the first thaw, Berdine had known it was as good a day as any to see to them. Broken fences could mean loss of livestock, something they certainly could not afford. Berdine had cheerfully packed some food in a basket for them so they wouldn't have to return to the cabin for the noonday meal.

Spiriting the guns out of the house had been quite another matter. Boldly, Fritz had removed them from the hooks beside the fireplace and handed them to Johanna, announcing calmly that they might be able to bring back some game to supplement the dwindling salt pork remaining in the barrel and that he'd give Cordie a few pointers in shooting. Seeing the practicality in his reasoning, Berdine had nonetheless strongly cautioned them all to be careful. Johanna had managed to conceal Cordelia's guilty blush by stepping in front of her and wrapping a muffler around her face as she shoved her younger sister firmly out the door.

Leaving Berdine busily carding a pile of wool, sure she wouldn't be glancing out the only glass window their cabin possessed, they'd made their escape from the house. The horses and even stubborn Mazie had allowed the foursome to lead them quietly out of the barn and quickly away from view. They'd mounted the broad backs of the docile draft horses, riding double and leading Mazie on a rope as they crossed their fields. Carefully skirting the rutted trail that led to Hemmington, they made their way to the railroad track without incident.

Their confidence in the success of their plan had never wavered. Everything had gone perfectly except they'd all had to coax and shove Mazie to the middle of the track to await the approaching train. Leaving Amy with the cow, the others had hidden themselves and the horses in a thicket of cottonwood that grew near the tracks.

As soon as the train had stopped, Fritz and Johanna gingerly leaped to the platform at the back of the Pullman with Barthold's name emblazoned in gold letters on the side, Cordelia following closely behind. Johanna had been first and, with her slender body flattened against the wall beside the door, had stealthily peered through the glass and seen the long muscular body sprawled unconscious on the velvet-upholstered couch.

Johanna finished milking and carefully lifted the bucket of steaming milk from underneath the cow before standing up. She shivered not from any cold drafts that blew through the cracks in the timbers but from the memory of the gray-eyed man on the train.

He hadn't been at all what she'd expected, and there had been a brief moment of hesitation on her part before she signaled Fritz and Cordelia to follow her aboard.

After pouring some of the foaming milk into a small wooden trough, she set the bucket near the door, covered it with a flat piece of wood and anchored the makeshift lid with a rock to protect the remaining milk from the waiting family of cats. Shep sat by the door, his soulful eyes expressing regret at her caution. Johanna laughed aloud and playfully scratched behind his silky ears. "Sorry, fella, you'll have to wait for your supper just like the rest of us."

Going on with the chores, Johanna moved mechanically to complete the tasks she and Fritz undertook every day, but always the image of an angry male face with unsettling gray eyes swam before her. The husky rasp of his voice had sent shivers down her spine and she'd been thankful for the concealing bulk of her long overcoat, sure that he wasn't able to detect her shaking knees. Anger over her foolish reaction to the man had finally stilled her quaking limbs and kept her voice steady, her hands still on her gun. She resorted to that anger again to settle her racing senses as she went about seeing to the animals, especially the valuable horses and the remaining oxen whose good health and strength were so essential to the plowing, planting and eventual harvesting of what just had to be a good crop.

The snorting and squealing of the hogs as they jostled for position at the feed trough in their pen at the back of the stable brought her out of her troubled thoughts. The familiar sounds and pungent scents of the animals soothed her nerves, and before long she joined her brother for the trek back to the house, having convinced herself that she'd never lay eyes on Oliver Barthold again.

Chapter Three

"END OF THE LINE," THE CONDUCTOR ANNOUNCED FROM the other side of the connecting door between cars. "Hemmington, Mr. Kendall. We'll be unloading your horse in another few minutes."

Tyler mouthed his reaction to the news through the thick gag, his words completely undecipherable but loud enough to keep the conductor from moving away from the door.

"What's that, sir?" the man inquired solicitously, a distracted but curious note entering his discordant voice.

Tyler's increasingly loud grunts, accompanied by a rapid but muted thumping of the legs of his chair upon the carpet, finally brought the response he was seeking and he heard the welcome sound of the door being pushed open. Seconds later, the incredulous conduc-

41

tor was removing the gag and untying the ropes that had kept Tyler prisoner in the small chair. "I've been robbed," Tyler grimaced, rubbing his wrists to restore circulation.

"Robbed, you say?" The barrel-chested conductor raised bushy gray brows, pushing his cap off his creased forehead and scratching his bald head as he watched Tyler stand up. "Tain't likely. Naw, tain't possible."

Stabbing the phlegmatic man with a contemptuous glower from his gray eyes, Tyler pointed to the empty cash box turned upside down on Barthold's desk. "Curse it, man, I didn't tie myself up. I've been trussed up since the last water stop. They made off with my whole damned stake."

"No water stop since Fremont," the older man muttered sluggishly, his perplexed expression fueling Tyler's temper to the point where he was hard put to keep from throttling the man, if for no other reason than to exhort more of a reaction. Ignoring the vitriolic expletives directed at him by his overwrought passenger, the conductor offered obligingly, "S'pose it could've happened when we stopped for that young sprout and his fool milk cow."

"Could have been," Tyler agreed sarcastically, placing both hands on his hips. "So what do you intend to do about it? For God's sake, man, one of your passengers has been robbed!"

With unhurried movements the conductor walked to the safe, bent down and tried to open it by twisting the handle. "'Pears to me they didn't get no company money. Guess you'd best report it to the stationmaster, though. Made off with all your cash, you say?"

Again shaking his head as if the whole idea confounded him, the man pointed out the window toward the red frame building at the side of the tracks. "Barney can wire the news back to Omaha for you, if that's what you want to do, but those fellers who stole your money will be long gone before the law steps in. Couldn't 'ave been from around here. No sir, they's probably high-tailed it back to wherever they come from, by now. I'm sure nuff sorry, mister."

"Sorry," Tyler repeated grimly, wondering pessimistically if the simple-minded conductor was any example of the kind of people he could expect to meet in Nebraska. If so, he was going to have a difficult time holding on to his temper. The man behaved as if the robbery were a minor inconvenience that Tyler would be wise to put behind him. However, Tyler Kendall was unused to being taken advantage of and wanted to make it clear that he expected something to be done about it.

"It's those scallywags that stole my money who'll be sorry," he shouted angrily. "If the local authorities don't investigate this matter, I'll locate those cursed thieves on my own."

"Good luck, mister." The conductor politely tipped his hat and stepped back to the door. "S'pect you'll be wanting to change clothes and such, won'tcha? Take all the time ya need. This here's the end of the line and we'll be here for a spell. I'll tie that big bay of yours at the hitching post by the side of the station.

He's a fine-looking animal, darn lucky they didn't make off with your horse, too. Now that would be somp'n to get riled about."

Feeling a bit foolish that his angry pronouncement had been met by little more than the conductor's calm instructions for disembarking the train, Tyler shook his head and issued a derisive laugh that was in the main self-directed. "You're a lucky man, Kendall," he smirked at the reflection of himself in the small brass-framed mirror that hung on the wall behind Barthold's desk. "Got your horse, got your clothes. What else do you require?"

It seemed that the only good thing that had happened to him all day was his rapid return to sobriety. Evidently being robbed, tied up, and having a gag stuffed between one's teeth was a rapid cure for the torturous wages he had paid for his excessive drinking.

It was while he was replacing the money box inside the desk that he remembered his handgun. He searched the top of the desk, then the floor, but couldn't locate his service revolver anywhere. He tried to recall if he'd seen the leader of the young culls who robbed him put back the gun but knew he had not. That blue-eyed varmint had taken it with him and that was the final insult.

Tyler shoved in the desk drawer with a vicious push of his hand, then stormed across the car and pulled his saddlebags from beneath the bed. He threw them across the red velvet spread, and unbuckled the flaps. Shrugging out of his frock coat, vest and shirt, he crammed them into the bags, then sat down on the bed and pulled off his low dress boots. Unbuttoning his trousers, he let them drop to the floor and swiftly stepped out of them, kicking them onto the bed with a disgusted flip of his stockinged foot. "I'll find that little filcher and his band of fledgling thieves if it's the last thing I do," he vowed aloud as he stuffed the rest of his clothing into the saddlebag.

A set of heavy riding clothes was packed in a separate valise he'd stashed in the tall narrow cupboard at the back of the car. He quickly dragged them out, along with a pair of more serviceable boots. Clad in only his union suit, Tyler was uncomfortably aware of the chilling temperature inside the car, the fire having long since died out in the small ornate stove that occupied one corner.

Swiftly, he pulled on a pair of heavy woolen breeches. The image of himself with his hands around the throat of a blue-eyed stripling took his mind off the cold as he fastened the buttons along the off-center placket of his wool tunic. Sitting down, he struggled into his boots, cursing as the stubborn Wellingtons proved as difficult as always to place on his feet. As soon as he had stamped around long enough for the boots to feel comfortable, he returned to the cupboard and withdrew his rifle, shoulder-caped greatcoat and wide-brimmed felt hat.

Smashing the hat down on his head, he dropped the coat over his arm, picked up the rifle and strode back to his saddlebags. Hoisting them over his shoulder, he stalked to the door and stepped outside the car onto the narrow platform. He didn't bother using the single step between himself and the ground but jumped off the platform, holding his hat on his head so the blustering wind wouldn't blow it away.

"Lovely weather we're having," he grumbled, squinting up at the boiling gray-white clouds that obscured the sun. "All I need right now is a good drenching rain!"

"No rain in them clouds, mister." A thin white-haired man was peering out a window of the station. "By nightfall, we'll be under a mountain of snow, mark my words."

Ignoring the man's forecast, Tyler asked, "Are you the stationmaster?"

"Barney Holcomb," the man introduced himself, warm brown eyes almost matching the deep coppery tan of his leathery face. "What can I do for you?"

Nodding at the weather-beaten door a few yards away, Tyler stated, "I'll come in. Didn't the conductor tell you the train had been robbed?"

"Nope," Holcomb returned, his face disappearing from the window as Tyler shouldered open the door and went inside.

"This kind of thing happens so often around here that nobody cares anymore?" Tyler inquired testily, dropping his saddlebags onto the floor as he approached the old man seated on a stool near the small black stove.

"Hemmington don't condone thieving, mister," the man replied, sounding offended. "This here's a God-fearing community. Good people. Too busy seeing to their own selves to steal things off'n others."

"Well unless I've imagined the whole thing"—Tyler

had almost reached the point where he was considering that possibility—"some of your good people have lightened me of over five hundred dollars."

"Tarnation!" Holcomb exploded, scraping back the stool and hurrying to the paper-strewn desk. "That's a whole lot of money. Who you say stole it?"

"I don't know who stole it." Tyler tried to keep his voice calm. "That's why I want to contact the law. The conductor told me that you would send a wire to the authorities in Omaha. Will you?"

"Will if you want." Holcomb pulled a nub of pencil from a desk drawer, placing it on a small scrap of paper. He shoved the writing materials across his desk toward Tyler, waiting expectantly for him to compose the message he wanted to send. "Don't s'pect it will do much good."

"And why not?"

"Don't recall any lawmen from Omaha ever coming out this far," Barney informed. He frowned, then cast his gaze up at the rafters as if there might be some information to be found there. After a long moment's pause, he scratched his chin and elaborated, "Course I ain't recalled the need for one, neither."

"Good people," Tyler repeated sarcastically, beginning to sense that he wasn't going to gain any more satisfaction in his dealings with the stationmaster than he had with the conductor.

"Nobody who'd take even a penny off'n another man. That's for sure."

"Let's send the wire anyway, Mr. Holcomb." Tyler stepped forward, swiftly writing his message on the scrap of paper. "A man who's just lost every cent to his name needs the satisfaction of telling someone who might be able to do something about it."

"S'pect so," Holcomb agreed, swiveling in his chair. "You know your letters real good," he complimented, then started tapping the key on the telegraph transmitter and sent the message.

"Thank you," Tyler responded belligerently, then swept his hand down over his mustache, impatiently waiting for the signal that his message had been received but resigned to the fact that he shouldn't expect much help, not even from the authorities in Omaha, who presumably admitted the existence of thieves. "If you get an answer to that, I'll be back in town next week, when my goods should arrive from Omaha."

"You planning to settle near here?" Holcomb asked, surprise evident on his lined face.

"I've bought some land on the Elkhorn," Tyler admitted. "Can you point me to the land office? I need directions to my property."

"You ain't going out there now, are ya?" Holcomb seemed more agitated by that prospect than by Tyler's previous announcement that he'd been robbed. "Not with a blizzard blowing in?"

"I've seen snow before, Mr. Holcomb." Tyler grinned, experiencing an irrepressible urge to show the old man that he wasn't afraid of severe weather. "I should be camped on my land before the day is done. I'll find a place to escape the elements."

"A man can't escape a howler, son," Holcomb advised sagely. "Won't know what hitcha." He shook his head from side to side and repeated the warning. "No sir, won't stand a chance agin a blow like this'n."

"Let me worry about that." Tyler lifted his saddlebags across his shoulders. "Tonight I'll sleep on my own land. Nothing else will do."

"What's your full name, son?"

"Kendall," Tyler replied, a quizzical expression lighting his gray eyes. "Tyler Kendall."

"Got a middle initial?"

"P." His frown grew deeper. "Why did you want to know?"

"For the marker, son," Holcomb declared solemnly. "When we lay you out it's only proper to have your full name put on the grave."

"Grave?"

"After the thaw, we're sure to find your body," Holcomb said, not a spot of humor in his voice. "Seems only fitting somebody should get your name 'fore then. Any kin we should notify?"

Nonplussed, Tyler didn't quite know what to say. During the war, he'd endured several storms with little but his greatcoat to protect him. He'd considered some of them severe, but had never once thought he might die in one. The old man had to be exaggerating. After a moment's pause, he dismissed Holcomb's chilling speech. "The land office, Mr. Holcomb?"

Shaking his head at the stubborn thrust of Tyler's chin, Holcomb muttered, "Short stretch down the road, inside Meeker's place. Miz Meeker'll help you. You can get most anything you might need at the mercantile." He fixed one last look at Tyler and offered a final warning, "You're welcome to stay here in the depot till this thing blows over. Going away from shelter's nothing but foolhardy, boy, mark my words."

"Much obliged, Mr. Holcomb," Tyler drawled, then a bit more hastily than he would have liked, he ducked out the door of the station. Rounding the corner of the building, he found the horse he had purchased in Omaha, saddled and tied to a post. A blast of wind sent shivers down his spine and he drew on his calf-length greatcoat, no longer doubting that the heavy clouds overhead contained snow, not rain. After positioning his saddlebags across the bay's broad back, he tightened the cinch and adjusted the stirrup leather to accommodate his long legs, then spoke aloud to the large animal.

"Been calling myself a fool all day, fella." He reached out to stroke the horse's soft muzzle, grinning when the animal playfully shoved him aside by swinging his head into Tyler's shoulder and whickered softly as if they had shared a comradely joke. "And I'm naming you Sergeant, just so you'll know which one of us is in charge."

With the fluid motion of long practice, Tyler grasped the pommel and swung up on the horse's back. Holding the reins between his teeth, he pulled a pair of leather gloves from his pocket and drew them on his hands. "Move out, Sergeant," he ordered. As if the big bay had understood the soft-spoken command, he turned his head toward the small row of buildings farther up the muddy, deep-rutted road that was Hemmington's main—and only—street.

As he traveled the short distance between the train

depot and the village, Tyler took in the crude, weather-worn assortment of buildings. One of several board-and-batten structures sported a rustic cross, identifying it as the church. Directly across from it stood another building of similar style and size but with a crudely lettered sign, "Meeker's Mercantile." There was a handful of houses of varying types of construction, their only similarity being that they were small and rude by Eastern standards. At the far end of the street and all alone, as if the citizens of the tiny community weren't any too happy about its existence, stood a saloon that advertised whiskey and rooms.

It was late afternoon before Tyler had completed his business in Hemmington. Luckily, he had discovered that the small saloon in the village offered meals and he'd eaten his fill of a stew made of some unidentifiable variety of meat. Knowing it might be days before he'd get anything better, Tyler didn't question the ingredients, but rather savored the hearty concoction and the thick slabs of bread served with it. At the land office that occupied one corner of the store, he'd presented his deed and, with the help of the storekeeper's wife, located his land on the surveyor's map pinned to the wall.

"You'll be next to the Heinsmans' farm. They're good honest folk, Mr. Kendall. You could do worse for neighbors," Mrs. Meeker predicted.

"It's a shame their Pa died last year, but the family has carried on without him." She reeled off a list of names of the surviving Heinsmans but Tyler was unable to commit them to memory. He did notice that the list was predominantly female and ignored the twinkling gleam he saw in Mrs. Meeker's eyes as she warmly welcomed him to the community. It was the same gleam he had seen on many a society matron as she introduced him to a young debutante. There seemed to be a universal need in all married women, no matter where, to find a wife for a bachelor.

Recognizing that the garrulous Jenny Meeker was about to start regaling him with the attributes of the numerous Heinsman females, he turned the conversation toward the town and the surrounding countryside. By the time he'd spent his last nickel being outfitted with a week's supply of foodstuffs, he'd been apprised of the residents of Hemmington and warned by both Meekers about the approaching storm. So dire were their predictions that as Tyler headed out of town, he began to at least half-believe that he was riding toward his doom.

It hadn't started snowing yet and he convinced himself that the kind people in the village were worrying for nothing, especially since Mrs. Meeker was basing her forecast on the fact that she'd heard a rooster crow during the middle of the night and her cat had washed behind its ears that morning. The wind had picked up during his time in the store, but since it seemed to be coming from the southwest, he was sure it would probably blow itself out by sundown. By then he would be comfortably installed in the sturdy canvas army tent rolled around his blankets and secured behind his saddle.

He was about a mile out of town when he located the first landmark the Meekers had described to him. A deep ravine lined with cottonwoods veered off to the right and Tyler guided his horse in the opposite direction. A growing sense of excitement gathered inside him as he viewed his untamed surroundings. Soon he'd be riding across his own property and in the near future would occupy a cabin built with his own hands.

He could hardly wait to get started and decided to spend the time before his supplies arrived locating and clearing the area where he'd build his home. That is, if he had any time to devote to his own land, he reminded himself bitterly. Since he had to find some means of earning money to pay off the drivers, his halcyon plans might have to be delayed. Refusing to dwell on the loss of his funds and determined to consider it only a temporary setback, he concentrated on studying the surrounding countryside. So far, he liked everything he'd seen, from the thick groves of tall oak, ash and box elder to the wide swatches of tall prairie grass to the west that were cut by numerous streams of clear water.

He had almost dismissed the townspeople's admonitions when, without warning, a dark rack of clouds rose up on the horizon. Bracing himself for an increased velocity in the wind, he was still not prepared for the violent bluster which almost succeeded in pulling him out of the saddle. Before he could catch his breath, another mighty blast came at him from another direction, and he felt as if he'd somehow ridden into the swirling fury of an invisible cyclone.

Reining in beneath the shelter of a willow copse, he swiveled in the saddle and opened one saddlebag, pulling out a neckerchief. He barely managed to keep it from being torn from his fingers as he folded it, then used it to secure his hat on his head, tieing the ends under his chin after he had pulled the brim down on each side of his face as far as it would go. "Better hurry on, Sarge. This wind cuts like a knife."

He soon discovered that the wind was nothing like the sharp particles of ice that began pelting him. Each cloud unleashed blinding bursts of snow, seemingly from every direction. He managed to make out the craggy rock in the shape of a bear's head that he had been told to expect, indicating he was only a short way from the Elkhorn River, but after that he was hard-put to see more than a foot in front of his face. He pressed on, hoping to locate some sort of shelter to protect him until the weather cleared, but suddenly it appeared as if the land was barren of rocks, of trees, of anything that could stand in the way of the sweeping onslaught of snow coating everything in its path.

Tyler couldn't tell if he'd gone blind from repeated attacks of wind-driven snow upon his face, or if there really was nothing in sight but a vast blanket of white. Completely disoriented, he could find no fixed point to guide him and was shocked by the continual drop in temperature.

He sensed the fear in his animal, felt it in himself, but knew they'd both perish if they stopped without finding shelter. "Come on, boy," he crooned, urging the powerful animal to greater speed. "We'll find someplace soon, someplace out of this monster wind."

He was rapidly losing all feeling in his hands. His face was numb with cold, and he knew his horse fared little better as they plunged through the mounting drifts of snow that seemed to build out of nothing into heights half a man tall. With chilling certainty, Tyler knew that if he fell off the horse, or if the animal stumbled and fell, he would be swiftly buried in the snow with no hope of rescue.

No man would be foolish enough to have ventured out in this if he'd truly known what was meant by the term "howler." Tyler could never have imagined such an awesome spectacle without experiencing it first-hand and feared he'd never have cause to do so again. He fought against acknowledging the station master's prediction and the depressing thought that the only thing that would show he'd ever passed this way would be a crude grave marker bearing his name.

More than likely his family wouldn't find out about his death for months. He could almost see them, hear them repeating the arguments they had presented when he announced his plans to leave Boston. "You're a fool to go out there. They don't call that whole area of the country the Great American Desert without cause. As usual, you're going off to try some scheme for which you have no background. You won't last a month."

How naive he had been to dismiss their opinions so readily. He was more than a fool; he was a demented idiot, too damned stubborn to listen to advice from anyone, not from his parents or from any of the well-meaning people who had tried to tell him what he'd be letting himself in for if he left town. He wasn't aware that his mind was drifting, that he was no longer giving any direction to his horse, which courageously paced on without his guidance, carrying him into the light gray swirl that appeared to have no end.

A colorful pageant appeared before his eyes, tableaux that brought both agony and joy. The bright red blood gushing from the wound of a fallen soldier who had died so close to him that he felt the man's final gasp for breath. The pastel-colored ballgowns of young women who stood waiting for him to choose one of them for the next dance at a summer cotillion. The yellow eyes of rats, greedily waiting to feast on whatever crumb a prisoner was too weak to lick off his fingers. And finally, the rolling green swells of the Atlantic surging into Boston Harbor, as he and his brother James manned the sails of their family's schooner. Pleasures and pains he would not experience again.

He lost track of time, a soothing lethargy creeping over his body. He no longer felt any urgency to find shelter, only the need to sleep, to close frozen lashes over his tearing eyes, shut out the gray nothingness closing in on him, which seemed almost alive, even carnivorous. It was better to recall the past than admit his part in the present, and eventually he slumped over the neck of the horse, his boots frozen in their stirrups the only thing keeping him on the struggling animal's back.

It was not he but the horse that discerned a familiar sound through the rushing of the wind. With an instinct for self-preservation apparently stronger than that of the man he carried on his back, the stallion turned toward the sound. Yet it was the man who decreed that the perilous journey was nearly over.

"See it?" Tyler didn't know what caused him to force open his eyes one last time. He groaned, tightening his stiff fingers on the ice-coated reins. "A light, old boy. Come on, before we lose sight of it." As if experiencing the same resurgence of strength that Tyler was feeling, the stallion valiantly obeyed the command, his senses detecting the scent of other animals and a warm stable. Head down, nostrils flaring, he plummeted through the drifts, not stopping until he felt a weak pull on his reins.

"If we kept in the right direction, this has to be the Heinsman farm. Someone has to be in there," Tyler murmured, forcing his legs away from the horse's sides, then sinking to his knees, his numbed legs giving way when his feet touched the ground.

Never once taking his eyes from the small glow of yellow that beckoned faintly in the swirling snow, he staggered toward it. Something blocked his passage, something made of wood. After a few moments of frantic searching, Tyler realized that he had found the cabin. Even though his fingers were frozen, he could feel the shape of the logs, laid one on top of the other. He knew it would be useless to shout, for no one could possibly hear him over the roar of the wind, so he saved his little remaining strength and attempted to find the entrance.

Fighting a sense of panic greater than any he'd ever experienced, that he'd somehow lose touch with the rounded timber, his progress was slow but finally he felt an indentation, a flat expanse of wood that had to be a door. It had to be.

Raising one arm, he pounded on the wood, praying

there was someone inside who would hear him, who'd rescue him from the ice-driven whips that lashed his body in a continuous beating. "Help," he shouted, hope mixed with desperation as he huddled against the sheltering side of the building, beating on the door with unfeeling fists. "Please, somebody, help."

Chapter Four

"SOMETHING'S OUT THERE!" AMY INSISTED, CLINGING TO Berdine's arm as she stared at the door.

"It's probably just the wind, 'fraidy cat," Fritz decreed, nonetheless moving toward the fireplace and taking down a gun, while Shep's low growl became more sinister.

The thumping sound they had first noticed when the dog began whining at the door had grown weaker by the time they decided to investigate. Johanna copied Fritz's action, removing the buffalo rifle from its hooks and cocking the hammer, as together they walked cautiously to the door. "Berdie, don't open it too far. Not until we know who or what's out there."

"Hold the dog, Cordie." With the care of long custom, Berdine lifted the heavy wooden bar over the door. "It may be David," she warned. "Don't be too hasty with those guns."

"He's got more sense than to come out here on a night like this," Fritz said, taking aim with his weapon. "He may be sweet on you but he ain't that big a fool."

Fighting back her embarrassed blush, Berdine slowly pulled open the door, immediately tucking her head against her shoulder and bracing her body against the heavy gust of snow-laden wind that robbed her of breath. A freezing blast of arctic air rushed into the cabin and Berdine leaned heavily against the inward push of the door as she peered outside, gasping with surprise when she spotted the large white mound sprawled across their threshold.

A muffled groan emitted from the snow-covered heap at her feet indicated that she was dealing with a helpless human being and, throwing all caution aside, she swiftly bent down. "Help me," she ordered over her shoulder as she attempted to drag the heavy body through the open door. "It's a man and he's near froze to death."

Both Johanna and Fritz put their guns aside, coming swiftly to Berdine's aid. Each taking hold of an arm, they dragged the man's inert body into the warmth of the cabin. Cordelia let go of the dog, then she and Amy combined their weight to close the door while their brother and sisters struggled to pull the unconscious man closer to the fire.

"Get his wet clothes off," Johanna instructed, dropping to her knees. She cradled the man's head against her breast, leaned over his shoulder and started working at the frozen knot of the neckerchief that held his hat fast to his head. "Cordie, you and Amy get his gloves off and start rubbing his hands. Fritz, get his boots. We have to get him warm. He could die if we don't act fast."

Now that the man had been dragged inside and Johanna had taken over, Berdine stood immobile, her face anxious and her hands tightly clutching and unclutching her apron. Her eyes searched the shadowed features of the man's face, fear tugging at her heart. She visibly relaxed when the ice-coated felt hat was removed from the man's head—he was indeed a stranger. The moment's guilt she felt at being relieved that the storm's victim was not her beau fled as she went back into action.

As her sister struggled to remove the man's wet and frozen garments, Berdine extracted an armful of quilts from the storage chest beneath the settle's hinged seat. Dumping them on the floor beside Johanna, she went to the stove and began filling the kettle. "Get him wrapped in the dry blankets and I'll bring a pan of hot water for his feet."

Having finally succeeded in untying the stiff neckerchief and removing the man's hat, Johanna tore at the last frozen button on his coat. Since his shoulders lay across her lap, she could feel the shivers that wracked his body and she tried to work faster. "You'll be all right, mister," she assured softly. "We'll take care of you."

With Fritz's help Johanna heaved him forward. They pulled off his coat and exchanged worried glances as they noted the cold dampness of his tunic. Even the heavy melton greatcoat had been inadequate in warding off the ravages of the blizzard. It took both of them to pull his wet tunic over his head, and even though they moved his arms for him, the action seemed to exhaust him. When they peeled his light woolen undergarment down to his waist, his shoulders sagged heavily back across her thighs like a dead weight. But, Johanna knew he was very much alive, and over his shoulder could see the tense outline of his jaw as he bit back the pain. "Go easy," she instructed her younger sisters, who were briskly rubbing his hands between their own. "His blood's starting to move again and he's hurting."

The man was trying to speak, trying to tell them something, but none of them could understand the syllables he stuttered through violently chattering teeth. It was Amy, leaning over him and brushing her small hands over his frozen cheeks, who finally grasped what he was saying. "There's a horse out there, Jo. He's fretting 'bout his horse."

"I'll see to it." Fritz leaned back on his haunches. "Hope the poor critter stayed close or I'll never find him." Standing up, he quickly dressed in his outer clothes and left, promising everyone that he'd make use of the rope tied between the house and the barn while he searched for the man's animal. "If he's wandered off, I'll have to leave him go."

The grim reality of Fritz's words came as no surprise to the Heinsmans, but Johanna immediately felt their strong effect on the stranger, even though she couldn't see his face. It took all of her strength to hold him down, her sharp admonition finally quelling his agitated movements. "There's nothing you can do, mister. Trust us, we'll do all we can."

Necessity nullified respect for propriety, and the four Heinsman females stripped off the stranger's few remaining garments. Johanna supported his back as they wrapped a quilt around him, then asked the others' aid in helping him to his feet. Taking most of his weight on her shoulders, Johanna assisted him into a chair by the fireplace, swiftly tucking another quilt around his bare legs as soon as he was seated. "I think he could take some broth by the time you get it ready," she said to Berdine, then bent down and lifted his feet into the pan of steaming water her sister had just placed on the floor.

Knowing the man was having a difficult time enduring the pain without crying out, when the warm water brought the blood rushing back to his frozen feet, she ordered Amy and Cordelia to go help Berdine, while she turned her back, stoking the fire to a roaring blaze. When she was satisfied that the fire would burn hotly for some time, she waited until she heard the man's harsh breathing return to normal, then stood up and turned around, astonished to find a pair of steely gray eyes studying her.

Sympathy turned to shock and she paled to the color of chalk, stupefaction paralyzing every bone. It was Barthold! Their gazes locked and she was unable to move as she took in the bold male features she had thought she'd never see again.

"Is your n-name H-Heinsman?" he asked slowly through chattering teeth, each word taking an incredible effort.

Standing before the hot fire, Johanna couldn't back any farther away from him and was far too frightened to respond. How had he found them? How had he discovered their identity so quickly? And Barthold not only knew their name but also where they lived!

She recalled how angry she had made him during the robbery and now knew what force had driven him out into the rampaging blizzard. How they had underestimated him and the extent of his fury! She and her family might soon be forced to pay the price for their crime against him.

A cold prickle of fear snaked its way down her back. Her hand fluttered to her throat and her conscience placed a noose around her neck that tightened painfully. The blazing fire behind her became the fires of judgment licking at her flesh, condemning her soul to eternal damnation.

"Let's get some of this broth into you," Berdine suggested kindly, elbowing Johanna aside as she knelt down by the stranger's chair. Smiling radiantly at their visitor, Berdine patiently forced spoonfuls of broth between his blue shivering lips as she carried on a friendly one-sided conversation.

"We *are* the Heinsmans," Berdine confirmed, totally unaware of the alarmed expression on Johanna's deathly white face and oblivious to her sister's frantic gestures. "I'm Berdine Heinsman and these are my sisters, Johanna, Cordelia and Amalia. Our brother, Frederick, has gone out to see to your horse."

Between swallows of the warm broth, the man attempted a weak smile and finally stuttered, "You will n-never know how h-happy I am to have f-found you."

To Johanna's ears the words sounded prophetic. Wildly searching the room for the nearest means of defense, her horrified gaze froze on Barthold's ivory-handled revolver resting in its place of honor on the mantle. If he had any doubts about who had robbed him, the revolver would give him instant proof of their guilt. Her throat constricted in panic, as if a diamond-back rattler were coiled on the mantle poised to strike. Quelling her fear, she knew there were only two options—hide the incriminating weapon or be prepared to use it.

Trying not to call attention to herself, she edged in front of the fire, her fingers sliding cautiously along the oiled wood until they reached the gun. As Berdine blithely chattered on, Johanna curled her fingers around the smooth handgrip of the weapon. She did not know how long it would take Barthold to regain his strength, but when he did—she would be ready for him.

"Neighbor . . . I'm your new neighbor." Tyler's teeth continued to chatter as he pulled the blankets closer around his shaking shoulders. "Name's Kendall. Tyler Kendall."

"Neighbor?" Berdine queried happily, replacing the spoon in the empty wooden bowl. "Well, that's highly welcome news. We heard someone had bought the land next to ours. Do you have a family who will be joining you, Mr. Kendall?"

"'Fraid not," Tyler admitted through his clenched

jaws. "I'm unmarried, Miss Heinsman." He was puzzled by his own sense of regret that he could not supply a wife and family for this pleasant-looking young woman, whose momentary wistful expression revealed her disappointment. A wife and family were the last things he needed. He had left Boston to escape emotional involvements.

Johanna didn't know what to think. He was indeed the man they had robbed, but he sounded completely honest when he introduced himself as Tyler Kendall. Could a man who had barely recovered from being lost in a blizzard put on such a convincing act?

During the robbery, the man had claimed he was not Oliver Barthold but she hadn't believed him. What if he had been telling the truth? What if they had robbed an innocent victim of circumstance? Another farmer like themselves? But he couldn't be! Why would a farmer be riding in Barthold's fancy private car?

Barthold or Kendall, it didn't matter what he called himself—he was still the man they had robbed. Had he come to accuse them of the crime? She had to know. Clearing her throat, she gathered her courage. She tried to speak calmly, hoping she'd be able to tell if he was being truthful with her by the look on his face when he answered her question. "You said you were glad to have found us, Mr. Kendall. Why is that?"

Trying to locate the owner of that soft husky voice, Tyler knew he would find the tall, slender woman he had beheld when he first opened his eyes. In the dim light, he was unable to discern her features, but her silhouette against the fire displayed the shapely curves of her womanly body, despite the ill-fitting men's garb she wore. He was awed by the gleaming splendor of the cloud of long hair, fallen over her shoulders like a shimmering cascade of pale gold. Some indefinable current was passing between them, and he'd felt oddly disappointed when the woman with the broth, a smaller softer version of the other, stepped between them, blocking his view. "According to Mrs. Meeker, you are my closest neighbors. When I realized I wasn't going to survive much longer out there, my last hope was to find you."

"It was God's will," Berdine nodded, as if that explained everything.

Johanna's fingers on the gun handle felt the silver plate embedded in the ivory and she immediately recalled the initials engraved there—T.P.K.! He was Tyler Kendall. They had robbed the wrong man!

Taking advantage of Berdine's position in front of the man, Johanna quickly slid the gun behind the mantle clock before he could see and recognize it. Her heart was thundering so loudly she was afraid he might hear it, but she tried to keep her expression bland as she slowly sidestepped away from the fireplace. She knew what she had to do but was terrified that she wouldn't be able to accomplish it before Kendall grew suspicious.

Hoping Berdine would keep him occupied, she crossed to the stove, where Cordelia was heating a large pot of coffee. "Don't say anything," Johanna whispered, taking Cordelia's arm in a fierce grip and pulling her into the farthest corner of the lean-to addition that enclosed the cooking area.

"What's the matter?" Cordelia queried softly, a perplexed frown furrowing her brow.

"Don't make a sound!" Johanna threatened under her breath. "Not one!" Glancing quickly back at their visitor, she saw that he hadn't moved from the chair and couldn't see her. Taking no chances, she placed one hand over Cordelia's astonished mouth, then whispered, "That man is the one we robbed this morning. Says his name is Kendall, not Barthold. I'm not sure yet if he's on to us, but we're not going to do anything that might give ourselves away. Stay clear of him, Cordie. Let me handle it, all right?"

Cordelia's expressive face showed abject horror, the exact look Johanna was afraid the man would see if she had allowed Cordelia to find out for herself who their visitor had turned out to be. "Get a hold on yourself," she breathed fiercely, taking another covert glance over her shoulder. "Stay by the stove and keep your face hidden. Don't look at him. I have to warn Fritz. Do you understand, Cordie? I have to go outside and warn Fritz."

It took several moments but finally Cordelia nodded her head and Johanna removed her hand. Looking deeply into her young sister's frightened eyes, Johanna tried to impart some of her own waning calm. "It will be fine, Cordie. Just follow my lead and try not to draw attention to yourself."

None too sure of her own ability to continue behaving naturally, Johanna left Cordelia by the stove and strode to the door. Deliberately pulling down different outer clothes than the ones she had worn that morning, she dressed to go outside.

"Where are you going?" Berdine rose from her kneeling position by Tyler's chair.

"To help Fritz," Johanna replied in an abnormally feminine voice.

Before Berdine began the arguments Johanna was fully prepared to ignore, the door to the cabin pushed open slightly and Fritz edged himself through the crack. "Found his horse," he announced proudly. "Got him brushed down and a blanket throwed over him. Once he warmed up some, he started taking feed. He's a big strong bay stallion, probably'll be fine."

Fritz flung a set of leather saddlebags on the table. "Brought these in. 'Spect he might be wanting 'em."

Hurriedly, Johanna snatched Fritz's hat off his head and pulled the heavy woolen muffler from around his neck. Stepping in front of him, she unbuttoned his coat and dragged it down his shoulders. "Smile," she encouraged in a whisper, her blue eyes boring into his face, warning him of some danger he had not yet seen and could not have expected.

"Come here, Fritz," Berdine called. "Meet our new neighbor, Mr. Kendall. He's bought the next section over."

Having no luck trying to decipher Johanna's strange behavior, Fritz brushed off her restraining hand and walked toward the fireplace, rounding the man's chair. "Nice to meetcha, Mr. Kendall." He offered his hand and a broad friendly grin.

"Fritz! You're getting snow all over the floor!" Johanna cried, hoping her irate observation might explain why Fritz's grin had faded so swiftly, why his hand was quickly retracted before the occupant of the chair had a chance to grasp it. "Come back here right now and get out of those boots!"

Fritz stumbled back to the door as if all the demons of hell were behind him. As Johanna explained the situation to him in hushed tones, Berdine's tinkling laughter covered the awkward moment. "Can't say he's ever moved that fast before. Of course, no one can deliver orders like our Johanna."

Staying out of their visitor's line of vision, Johanna still experienced a strong urge to scream when Amy chimed in, "It's best to do what Jo says though. None of us likes to cross her temper."

The low male chuckle she heard prompted a convulsive shiver of apprehension to dart up her spine. She found herself staring at the back of the man's head. The flickering light from the fire was spraying pale copper sparkles through his thick brown hair. Still damp, the dark strands curled at the ends, slightly separating at his tanned neck.

Although the quilt was drawn up over his broad shoulders, from her vantage point behind him, Johanna could see the place where his neck joined his back, a strong expanse of muscle she knew would be smooth and lightly bronzed, the same evidently natural color as the long, soft-haired, well-muscled lengths she had glimpsed when she'd tucked the additional quilt over his bare legs. She pulled herself up short, feeling smothered by a sudden wave of heat that rose up inside, flushing her cheeks and flooding her large eyes with the brilliant blue of a late summer sky.

As a member of a large family living in this small cabin, she had naturally learned the difference between a male and female body, but she'd never experienced any such feelings when she'd accidentally witnessed her father or brothers without all of their clothes. On hot days she and Fritz often swam naked in the river, but she had never felt this wrenching sensation in the pit of her stomach at the sight of his bare body. As she recalled her part in undressing Kendall, she was overwhelmed with heated sensations at the memory of his naked flesh, sensations that were making it quite difficult to breath.

"Jo?" Berdine questioned, then getting no reaction, inquired more sharply. "Johanna?"

Johanna jumped, snapping out of her reverie with a jolt. "What?"

"Your coat, Johanna," Berdine reminded, her gray-blue eyes revealing both annoyance and curiosity. Johanna wasn't usually one to lapse into daydreaming. "You don't have to go outside any longer. Why don't you take off your coat?" Switching her attention from Johanna to Cordelia who lingered by the stove, she inquired, "Good heavens, Cordie, what *is* taking so long with that coffee?"

"I'll get it." Johanna surprised everyone by volunteering for the domestic task. Half running, she shrugged out of her coat and replaced it on the peg, then swiftly crossed to the lean-to, stumbling in her haste and cracking her shin on the bench by the table. "Hell's bells!"

Berdine covered her sister's colorful oath by asking their guest if he required sweetening with his coffee, but she was well aware from the slight twitching of the man's mustache that he had heard Johanna's unlady-like epithet.

"No thank you, ma'am," Tyler replied, swiveling in the chair in an unsuccessful attempt to glimpse the commotion going on behind him. He had ascertained that the girl called Johanna was the one who had pillowed his head against her soft, full breasts. Since the moment by the fire, when they had stared into one another's eyes, he hadn't been able to get more than a glimpse of her. He was beginning to think she was deliberately avoiding his field of vision. His curiosity about her was growing with every passing moment, but even stronger was the urge he had to sleep.

As it became increasingly difficult to keep his heavy lashes from closing over his eyes, only the thought of another glimpse of the lovely golden-haired girl with the intriguing voice kept him from giving in to the lethargy that was rapidly overtaking his body. Not realizing that he had indeed drifted off for a short moment, he was startled awake by Berdine's gentle voice: "Here's Johanna with your coffee, Mr. Kendall."

At first he had difficulty focusing, but then a slender pair of trembling hands holding out an earthen mug swam into view. When he reached for the cup, the quilt slipped off his shoulder and, at the startled feminine gasp he heard, he quickly pulled back his hand to grab for a fold in the heavy material. In the back of his mind, he was aware that someone had removed his wet clothes, but it suddenly dawned on him that he was completely naked beneath the quilt and that it had been largely the girl called Johanna who had accomplished the feat.

Although Tyler was not overly modest, the indignity of having a young, pretty woman strip off his clothes when he was too helpless to do so himself struck him full force. His shame increased as he felt a blush steal up the back of his neck and spread along his jaw. He hadn't blushed since he was a boy and his gray eyes darkened with annoyance. Looking up, he glared defiantly at the shapely vision he had intended to charm with a practiced smile. "I'm at a disadvantage, miss," he growled, a curl of his lip lifting his mustache.

Neither Tyler nor Johanna was expecting Berdine's flustered interference. "Oh, I am sorry, Mr. Kendall. Johanna, you'll have to hold the cup for him."

"But I . . . I . . ." Getting this close to her victim was the last thing Johanna wanted to do, but she was left with no choice as her family deserted her, removing themselves to the table while Berdine strung up a rope behind the cook stove and draped Tyler's soggy garments over it. She caught Fritz's eyes, pleading for him to rescue her, but he was concentrating on adding a generous amount of milk and molasses to the cup of steaming coffee Cordelia had poured for him.

Deciding she must finish the task Berdine had unwittingly assigned to her as quickly as possible, Johanna resignedly lowered the cup but her hands were shaking badly and some of the scalding liquid splashed onto the quilt. Without thinking, she nervously reached out with her free hand, frantically brushing at the drops of liquid that rolled down the quilt. As soon as her fingers touched the material, she was aware of her mistake for a strong hand clamped around her wrist.

"Be careful, Miss Heinsman," Tyler warned in a tone only loud enough for Johanna to hear, perversely enjoying the rosy blush that instantly burned in her cheeks.

Refusing to be completely cowed by the man, Johanna spoke tartly, keeping her voice down so their conversation remained private. "You seem to have found a way to free one hand, Mr. Kendall. If you will take this cup, I will join my family at the table."

"My hand is not free, Miss Heinsman," Tyler grinned, deliberately pressing her palm more firmly against his chest so she could feel the warmth of his body through the quilt. "We seem to be confronted with a precarious situation. If I release your hand, I must also let go of the blanket, and we wouldn't want that to happen, now would we?"

Knowing he toyed with her, a spark of temper gleamed in her eyes. She had no idea how to deal with this man who mocked her, appearing to enjoy making her blush. "What would you suggest, Mr. Kendall?" she asked shortly, sounding far more sure of herself than she felt.

"I will try not to offend your modesty by retaining my hold on this blanket while you carefully remove those pretty fingers of yours."

"I would be happy to do so, sir, but first you must let go of my wrist," she reproved, annoyed with herself for feeling flattered over his compliment to her hand. No one had ever called her fingers "pretty" or smiled at her the way this man was doing. Indeed, no man had ever even tried to hold her hand.

"If I do, will you still help me drink that coffee, Miss Heinsman?" Tyler scanned her flushed face. "Or will you scamper away from me like a frightened deer?"

"I'm not afraid of you, Mr. Kendall. Berdine asked me to assist you and I shall," Johanna was stung into retorting. She wished she had swallowed the words when she saw the triumphant glitter in his dark eyes.

With a quick motion that belied the exhaustion he was feeling, Tyler let go of her hand without relinquishing the quilt, his expression challenging her to keep her promise. Resting his head back against the chair, he waited for her to raise the cup to his parted lips.

"Would you care for more coffee, Mr. Kendall?" Berdine called from the table. "It would be no trouble for Johanna to bring another cup."

"We are still working on the first, Miss Heinsman," Tyler called back, lifting his thick brown lashes so he could catch Johanna's eyes. "Your sister's been bothered enough."

Only the two people by the fireplace were aware of the double meaning of his words. To Johanna's relief, Tyler appeared to tire of the game he was playing with her and quickly drank the contents of the cup she tilted to his lips, his long frame relaxing against the chair. When he had finished, she unhurriedly straightened her back, preparing to walk away, not run as he had mockingly predicted. "Would you care for anything else, Mr. Kendall?" she asked politely, forcing herself to look full into his face.

At first he didn't answer, his expression blank, but then he roused himself. "I'm too tired for more tonight, Johanna." Her name coming from his lips sounded like an endearment and Johanna sucked in her breath, shock dilating the pupils of her eyes until there was hardly any color left in them but the wash of vivid blue. He seemed about to make some comment as he looked into her eyes, but soon his lashes drifted over the gray and his lips parted without uttering a sound.

Unable to shake off the lingering effects of his mesmerizing gaze, Johanna silently watched his dark head fall forward, and his chin drop to his chest. Right before her eyes, he had fallen asleep and she hoped the slow regular movements of his chest meant that it was the deep dreamless slumber of total exhaustion.

"Mr. Kendall?" she whispered. There was no response. Tentatively, she reached out her hand and touched his shoulder, giving him a slight shake. "Can you hear me, Mr. Kendall?"

He did move then, but it was only to burrow his head against the back of the chair, unconsciously searching for a more comfortable position. She knew it was the perfect time to confront the others with his identity, and decide how they were going to proceed, but something held her in place. A great curiosity welled up inside her and she took advantage of his unconscious state to study him. No longer having to withstand the steely challenge in his dark eyes, she could take her time.

The sheer physical magnitude of the sleeping giant seated before her made the greatest impression. She was a tall woman, but that morning he had made her feel small just by getting to his feet. She had never felt such relief as when she realized he was so befuddled by alcohol that he'd mistaken her for a dangerous man. The thought of confronting him as a woman had terrified her, a fear she was still suffering, even though she had come through their encounter without injury, at least not one she could easily define.

Without fear of any reprisal from him, she tried to discern the outline of his body, but the heavy quilts made such inspection nearly impossible. Only the considerable width of his shoulders was discernible and the strong column of his throat stretching above the folds of multicolored patchwork. Her gaze traveled to his face, tracing the stubborn angle of his jaw and lingering on the full brown mustache that added a rakish touch to his firm mouth. In sleep, that mouth fell slightly open and she was intrigued by the half smile that tugged softly at one corner. After such a harrowing experience, it was amazing that the man could sleep so peacefully and enjoy a pleasant dream.

When he grinned, the deep grooves in his cheeks added a boyish mischief to his angular face and even though his features were completely relaxed, she could still detect the two dimples that formed a slashing groove on each cheek. His lashes were dark brown and thick, the spiky tips brushed with gold.

They were almost the same color as his hair, except that among the brown locks streaked with highlights of gold were a few glinting touches of copper. Now that it was dry, his hair looked thick and springy, the crisp waves cut long over his nape, shorter at the ears. She was moved by a compelling urge to see if it felt the way it looked, and since there was nothing to prevent her from doing so, she threaded her fingers through the stubborn dark wave that had fallen over his forehead and brushed it back. He didn't move a muscle and she was about to take an even bolder step when Berdine's voice halted the motion of her hand in midair.

"Good heavens, Johanna! Whatever are you doing?"

Chapter Five

"I . . . I'M MAKING SURE HE'S REALLY ASLEEP." JOHAN- na whirled around to face Berdine, a blush rising in her cheeks as she saw the doubting expression on her sister's face.

"It appears to me like you had something else on your mind," Berdine teased. "He's a mighty good- looking man, wouldn't you agree?" she continued relentlessly. "And he's a bachelor." With a twinkling light in her eyes, she grinned conspiratorially at the others. "Looks like our Jo has finally been smitten, wouldn't you say, Fritz?"

Expecting Fritz to take advantage of the opportuni- ty she had given him to tease Johanna, as he often did, Berdine was surprised when he said, "This ain't no time for funning, Berdie. We've got real trouble here." Fritz was suddenly not acting like the mischievous, teasing younger brother Berdine was used to. His face was drained of color and his words had been delivered in a low husky whisper.

"Trouble?" Berdine frowned, completely at a loss. "What do you mean?"

"Will you two stop jawin' and get over here and help me?" Johanna demanded from her place beside Tyler.

Having begun to nod and weave in his chair, Tyler was now leaning so dramatically to the left that she feared he would fall on the floor and wake up. Johanna was forced to wrap her arms around him in order to keep him sitting upright. His head was lying heavily on one of her shoulders and most of his weight was against her body. She didn't dare let go for fear he would go crashing to the floor. "He's fallen dead away. Get over here. I can't hold him up much longer."

Fritz, Berdine and Cordelia came quickly to her aid, and between the four of them they managed to carry Tyler into the one and only bedroom of the small dwelling. He murmured something unintelligible as they struggled to ease his long body onto the wide four-poster bed normally shared by Berdine and Johanna. When Johanna loosened her arms from about his shoulders and started to slide his head onto the plump pillow, his brows knitted together in an unconscious frown. He snuggled his head closer against her, a faint smile softening the line of his mouth when he found the comfort he sought—her soft, full bosom.

Johanna felt a gush of billowing heat envelop her

body at the feel of the heavy weight of his head against her. His mouth was slightly open in the relaxed pose of deep sleep and was positioned a scant distance from the very peak of her left breast. She experienced a sudden tautening of her nipples and an increased fullness in her breasts. His warm breath fanned rhythmically against the material of her shirt, heating the tender flesh beneath with each expulsion of air.

Her fear of waking him was overridden by her need to get away, and she quickly slipped out from beneath him, pushing his head onto the waiting pillow. Catching her breath, she glanced covertly at her siblings, who were still hovering around the bed. She hoped they would interpret her rapid breathing as a consequence of her strenuous efforts in moving the man, not as the result of feeling his head against her bosom.

Fritz and Cordie stood at the foot of the bed, frozen in place, their eyes wide in their pale faces as they stared at the man wrapped like a mummy lying upon the feather-filled mattress. It was only Berdine whose mind functioned with any kind of order as she pulled more quilts over Tyler and tucked them snugly in around his feet. Once finished, she walked back into the main room and returned with the man's saddlebags, dropping them on the floor near the bed so he'd be able to find them the next morning.

Arousing herself from her stupor, Johanna managed to pull the edges of the bedding up to his neck, carefully tucking it around his shoulders. When the top of her hand brushed against his chin, she jumped back as if she'd been stung, quickly fleeing the room.

Fritz and Cordelia followed closely on her heels. More slowly, Berdine came after them, silently pulling the door closed behind her before joining everyone around the table.

"Now, what's all this foolishness about trouble?" Berdine queried. "What is the matter with you? You all look as if you've seen a ghost."

"Worse" was Johanna's low response, which got Berdine's immediate attention. Pausing to take a deep breath, Johanna motioned for Berdine to take a seat. "Brace yourself, Berdie. There's no easy way of telling this. Turns out, Kendall's the man we robbed this morning. God knows what he was doing dead drunk in Barthold's railroad car."

"Oh dear God!" Berdine gasped in shock, slumping forward to rest her face in her hands, much as she had done hours before when they had initially admitted their crime. Slowly shaking her head back and forth in total despair, she moaned hysterically, "What's to become of us? I knew we wouldn't go unpunished. Lord help us."

Responding to Berdine's guilt-ridden panic, Cordelia began sobbing and there was a distinct quiver to Fritz's lower lip. Johanna looked to see how Amy was taking the news and was thankful to see that at least one member of the family was not in a state of total abjection. Amy's blue eyes were completely dry. Though the color in her cheeks was not quite as high as normal, an animated smile tugged at the corners of her small pink mouth as she suggested optimistically, "We can sneak the money into his saddlebags."

"Shure nuff, Amy," Fritz grumbled sarcastically, crossing his arms over his chest as he stretched out his legs beneath the table. "He'll just think a good fairy up and brought his money back to him. He'd never guess in a million years we're the ones who put it there."

Still glowering at the noticeably wilting eight-year-old, he groaned. "What else should we expect from a dumb kid? Je-ru-salem crickets! If we did that, we might as well confess. If he hasn't already figured out we're the thievin' rascals that took his money, he'd sure know then."

Amy's optimistic expression fled and her face crumpled, a tear sliding out of the corner of one eye, making its way down her pale cheek. "Stop it, Fritz!" Johanna spoke sharply as she placed a comforting arm around the shoulders of her little sister. "It won't help if we turn on each other. We're all in this together. I don't think Kendall knows who we are yet, and we've got to make sure he never does."

"More deceit?" Berdine wailed loudly, looking at Johanna as if she'd become a stranger. "For shame! Two wrongs never make a right. You know that, Johanna. We have to give the money back and pray that Mr. Kendall will find it in his heart to forgive us. He's a veteran, plus being a farmer like us! We can't take money from someone like him!"

"No!" Johanna shouted. Like Berdine, she had momentarily forgotten the need for quiet. Instantly, everyone turned to stare at the closed door. After several moments of listening for some indication that they had awakened their visitor, they breathed a collective sigh of relief when the only sound to break the silence was the soft ticking of the mantle clock.

Even though she knew she would share the blame if Tyler awakened, Johanna warned everyone to keep their voices down, then in a hushed voice stated her arguments for keeping the money. "Your righteous ways won't keep the roof over our heads, Berdie. He can afford a setback. He's not homesteading, he bought his land outright. He might be a veteran, but that's a half section of prime land he's talking about. You don't get railroad land with military scrip. The man has to be rich."

"He ain't the forgivin' kind neither," Fritz interjected. "He was riled, Berdie. Mightily riled. Said he'd track us down." A glimmer of fear stole into his eyes. "He finds out we stole his money and he'd just as soon shoot us as look at us."

"How many other lies have you told today?" Berdine demanded. "You all claimed he was old, fat and a drunkard." She shifted her gaze to the closed bedroom door, then back to deliver a condemning look that included them all. "Tyler Kendall doesn't quite fit the picture you were all painting earlier today."

Inwardly squirming, Johanna stared unblinkingly at Berdine. "Doesn't matter. I tell you he doesn't need it as much as we do for the mortgage. I'm still going to post that money to the Kendall Bank in . . ." She placed a hand over her heart to still its frantic beating and sank slowly onto the bench. "Jumping Jehoshaphat! You don't suppose it's the same Kendall?"

"Gotta be," Fritz answered in dejected resignation. "Who else could afford that land? Probably paid for it with money stole from us and others like us. No wonder he was riding with Barthold."

"Bet so," Amy chimed in, glad that there might be some justification, no matter how weak, for their nefarious activity. "Wanna return our hard-earned money to the likes of him, Berdie?"

The family argued back and forth for hours, until it was resolved that they could neither risk admitting their crime nor return the money. In recompense, each promised Berdine they would do anything they could to assist Tyler Kendall. Wearily, they sought their beds for what little remained of the night. Fritz, Cordelia and Amy climbed the ladder to the loft as usual, but Berdine and Johanna were forced to sleep on a makeshift bed arranged before the fireplace.

Johanna could not fall asleep, her stomach fluttering with anxiety every time she heard the creak of the mattress in the next room. As Berdine had said, Tyler Kendall was not an old grizzled drunkard but a fine figure of a man, and right now he was sleeping in her bed. Images of him with his dark head nestled against her pillow warmed her more than the blaze from the fire. An uncomfortable and totally new tension built in her lower body, seemingly centered in the secret parts that proclaimed her womanhood.

At first she thought she was imagining it when she heard a pained groan coming from the bedroom, but soon it was repeated. It was a harsh sound unlike any she'd ever heard and she responded to the agony of it without thinking. Throwing off her blankets, she sat up, listening until she heard the mournful sound again.

Not wanting to wake up Berdine, she gingerly edged herself off the mattress and silently crossed the dark room until her hand found the leather-thonged latch of the bedroom door. Unmindful that her underwaist and drawers provided scant covering for her curvaceous figure, she slowly pushed open the door. She could hear the agitated movements of the man who rolled about on the bed, but could see nothing. The piteous moans he emitted wrenched at her heart and without thinking of the consequences, she shut the door behind her and groped her way closer. The man was obviously suffering in the grip of some terrible pain, and she had to help him, no matter what kind of threat he posed to her and her family.

"Water . . . please . . . for God's sake, man . . . dying." The garbled plea rasped through the darkness, paralyzing her for a moment before she flew into action. Moving swiftly to the chest of drawers, she felt for a candle, lighting it with the matches always placed close by. When the small glow flickered to life, she used it to locate the water pitcher, breaking the thin layer of ice on top, then pouring the cold liquid into the small cup kept by the washbasin. She returned to the bed, setting the cup on the table and the candle in a holder.

The man was still mumbling incoherently, but now she could not only hear him but see him. He had thrown off the quilts and his only covering was a corner of a sheet twisted around his loins. Although the room was so cold that she could see her own breath, Tyler's nearly nude body was covered with perspiration, his brown hair sticking damply to his head. A cloud of copper-tipped brown ringlets spread across his massive chest, curled tightly around his dark, flat nipples, then hazed lightly down his taut abdomen before disappearing beneath the edge of the sheet.

Unable to help herself, Johanna's eyes were drawn lower, hesitating on the barely concealed bulge beneath the thin muslin sheet, then guiltily darting away to swiftly travel down his long-muscled thighs. Her breath caught as she fought the urge to run her hands across him, feel the silken, curling hair that covered the smooth skin stretched over those hard muscles. Forcing herself to remember why she had come into the room, she wiped her damp palms down her drawers.

She had come to see if he was in pain or had developed a fever since they'd put him to bed. She placed her palm on his forehead, yelping with surprise when his hand shot up and snaked around her wrist. Pulled off balance, she landed hard on his chest, the quick movement fanning the candle, which flickered and died.

"What the hell!" Tyler exclaimed in a dry whisper, fighting for the breath that had somehow been knocked out of him.

"Let go of me," she whispered hysterically, not daring to talk louder for fear of waking the others and having them find her in this ignominious position.

"Who . . . what . . . ?" His hands groped in the dark, his fingers closing on a soft mound of flesh that pressed against his chest. Before he had time to register anything more than that he was feeling the tender curve of a woman's breast, she broke away from him and scrambled off the bed. Still not completely conscious, he tried to focus in the dark, but saw nothing, as if the soft, warm body had been part of his dream.

Moments later, he was reclaimed by the overwhelming exhaustion that made it too difficult to think, to do anything but sleep. He didn't see the trembling figure that opened the bedroom door and slipped out, returning to her makeshift bed on the floor.

Johanna stared sightlessly at the ceiling as hot shivers wracked her slender frame. Her right breast felt as if it had been branded with a hot iron, the nipple tingling with pleasure-pain. The tension quivering in her loins was almost unbearable and she curled herself into a tight ball of shame. All the sermons she'd ever heard about the sins of the flesh rang in her ears, and although she wasn't sure what she was feeling, she knew the racing excitement that danced through her veins was just cause for prayers of forgiveness.

It had to be a sin to react as she had to the sight of a man's body, to ache for his touch. When his hand had closed over her breast, the exquisite pleasure had frightened her far more than the unexpectedness of it. When judgment day came she would have more on her conscience than the sin of stealing. Too distraught to close her eyes, she was almost grateful when she began to discern the outlines of furniture in the dark room, for it told her that it was past dawn, time to rise and start the morning chores.

She crept out from beneath the warm robes. Needing fresh clothes, she went to the heavy settle and lifted the lid of the storage bin beneath the seat. The family stored a variety of cloth items in the multipurpose piece of furniture, each garment or blanket scrupulously saved to be used over and over again in many different ways. Nothing was wasted. Even worn shreds or tiny scraps were put to some use.

Johanna rummaged around until she found an old pair of Fritz's breeches and a shirt. Shivering in the cold, she stoked the embers of the banked fire, then crossed to the lean-to and quietly went about starting a fire in the cook stove. She worked noiselessly, not yet ready to share the early morning solitude with anyone. Shep trotted to her side and pushed his damp muzzle into her hand, cocking his head as if he were expressing surprise that it was Johanna and not Berdine who was the first human riser.

Absentmindedly, Johanna stroked his shaggy head as her mind struggled with the thoughts that had tormented her most of the night and tried to form a plan that would take her and her family safely through the day. If Cordie and Amy appeared in skirts, perhaps it would dispel any suspicions Kendall might form about them. Yesterday, he had mistaken those who had robbed him for boys. Today, she would have to make sure he couldn't make a connection between them and the ruffians who'd held him up.

Finding a brush, she began with her hair. Instead of pulling it back from her face and braiding it, she left it unconfined, curling over her shoulders. Removing a wide pink ribbon from a drawer in the sideboard, she lifted her hair off her neck and drew the ribbon beneath the shimmering flaxen waves, tying a pretty bow at the top of her head. She wished she could put on a dress to further her own feminine image, but there was no power on earth that could get her into that bedroom while Tyler Kendall was still in there!

Resigned to making the most of what she had, she tucked her shirt into her pants, then cinched the waist so tightly that there could be no mistaking her feminine figure. For once, she was grateful for the full breasts and tiny waist that proclaimed her femininity and unbuttoned the shirt far enough that a hint of cleavage could be seen above the last fastened button. Her fingers hovered over the curve of her breast, remembering the feel of Tyler's hand upon her skin. She prayed he would have no memory of what had happened in the bedroom, almost positive that he had not come completely awake before she managed to escape from the room.

When she heard her young sisters waking up in the loft, she quickly climbed up the ladder, making sure they put on dresses instead of overalls. When Tyler Kendall came out of the bedroom, he would find four young females and only one adolescent male. Fritz overheard their hushed conversation and, understanding her motives, didn't tease her about her looks as he climbed down from the loft to join her in the kitchen lean-to. "I'd best get to the barn on my own, Jo. You don't look too girlish when you come back in from chores."

"Look outside, Fritz." Johanna pointed to the window. "We'll have to dig ourselves out of here. It'll be past noon 'fore we get to the animals. By then, I'll have made the impression I want."

"Sure he'll wake up 'fore noon?"

"He's a strong man, Fritz. He'll be up," she stated grimly.

Nodding in resigned agreement, Fritz pointed to Berdine, who was just coming awake. "I don't think I can act all that friendly towards the man, Jo. Berdie made us promise to show kindness but I'd be better off keeping my distance. He could recognize my voice. I didn't disguise it like you did." He ran a shaky hand through his reddish-blond hair. "Tarnation! I sure didn't expect to lay eyes on him again!"

"Me neither," Johanna agreed fervently, then remembered the shameful pleasure she had experienced last night, when she had "laid eyes on him" for quite some time.

"Why are you two standing around doing nothing?" Berdine queried in annoyance, smoothing her skirts over her hips as she joined them. Her gray-blue eyes widened noticeably when she viewed the changes in her sister's mode of dress. "Johanna Lynette Heinsman, do up your blouse! It's indecent! Any God-fearing man would be shocked by such a show of immodesty. Those pants are skin tight. You won't impress Mr. Kendall by such an unseemly display."

"Impress Kendall?" Johanna was so incensed she could barely contain the urge to shout. "How can you be such a ninny, Berdine? I'm making blamed sure that gray-eyed devil can't mistake me for a boy."

Defiantly pulling back her shoulders, she declared fiercely, "I want to make sure any suspicions he's got about us being the gang that robbed him pass clean out of his mind."

Berdine clasped her hand over her mouth, gaping at Johanna with undisguised shock. Evidently not certain how to respond to her sister's declaration, she looked to Fritz, only to find him nodding like a wise old sage. "No doubting she's a woman, Berdie," he vowed gruffly. "We got more to consider than being seemly. Kendall's got to be pushed off'n our trail." Then as if noticing how much Johanna had developed without his being aware of it, he hedged, "Course, we don't want him sniffing round you like a bear to honey, neither."

"He does any sniffing and he'll sure 'nuff get stung!" Johanna snapped, nearly jumping out of her skin when she heard a loud noise from the bedroom as if something heavy had fallen to the floor. Her defiant words covered her reaction to Fritz's comment. What would she do if Tyler came "sniffing," as Fritz had put it. "Sound's like he's awake," she announced nervously, pacing up and down as she pondered how the family should behave once he entered the room. "Everyone act natural and go about your business."

"I declare, Jo, it's you who's acting powerful strange," Berdine judged, bending over to set fire to the wood in the stove. "Cordie, get some plates on the table. Amy, why haven't you broken the ice off the water bucket?"

There was a loud scrambling from the loft, and

seconds later Amy and Cordelia were down the ladder, meekly following Berdine's orders as she prepared their breakfast. Johanna, who usually didn't take part in the domestic chores, wanted it to appear that she was completely at home in the kitchen. She pulled down one of Berdine's aprons from a peg on the wall, tying it around her waist. "What can I do?"

Berdine's brows rose but she made no comment, other than suggesting rather tartly that Johanna could get some meat from the barrel and carve some slices for the pan. "Wish we had eggs this morning," she declared sadly, glancing at the bedroom door. "I'll bet he's used to a finer breakfast than fried corn mush and salt pork."

"He's lucky to get anything," Johanna decreed. "If I didn't think he'd freeze to death, he'd be set on his way as soon as he shows his face. To think you don't want to offend a man who has the power to place a noose round our necks!"

Before Berdine had the opportunity to respond to that, the subject of their conversation opened the bedroom door, ducking his head beneath the frame as he entered the room. All activity came to an abrupt halt and every eye darted to the tall masculine stranger who strode to the fireplace, warming his large hands before the blaze. Dressed in dark pants and a navy wool tunic that were almost identical to the wet clothes they'd stripped off him the night before, he looked like the devil incarnate to Johanna. While the family watched in tense silence, he lifted one stockinged foot, then the other, to the warmth of the fire.

"Cold morning, isn't it?" Tyler asked the room in general, feeling a bit uncertain in his new surroundings but finally turning around to offer a lopsided smile. "My fingers nearly froze up again while I got dressed." He rubbed the back of his neck, switching his curious gaze from one Heinsman to another. "Did I sleep late? You all look as if you've been up and about for hours."

"Not at all," said Berdine, finally breaking the silence, and wiping her hands on her apron, she walked out of the kitchen to greet their visitor. "How are you feeling this morning, Mr. Kendall? No lasting ill effects from battling that howler?"

Tyler placed his hands on his hips and slowly rotated his torso, flexing his shoulders. "Just a little stiffness, and I've never been more tired," he relayed, raising both arms over his head as he attempted to get out the kinks in his spine.

Dropping his arms to his sides, he continued, "You folks saved my life. How can I ever thank you?" He searched for Johanna, separating her from the others, his flashing white grin seemingly meant for her alone. "And especially you, ma'am." His voice dropped lower, a drawled intimacy in every word making her fear he remembered her being in his bed the night before. "You were the first one I saw when I opened my eyes, and I thought Saint Peter had sent a golden-haired angel to greet me in his place." Raking her shapely figure with assessing thoroughness, his eyes lingered on the enticing shadow between her breasts, then slowly rose to capture her eyes.

Johanna gulped, completely unprepared for the dangerous power of his gaze, his uncanny ability to paralyze her while standing yards away. Unable to stop the rosy blush that crept up her neck and spread across her face, she tore her eyes away from his visual snare, trying to appear unaffected by his boldness.

Of all members of the family, Amy seemed to be the only one who was undaunted by the presence of the tall, dark-clad man. Curiosity radiated from her large blue eyes as she edged her way across the cabin, followed closely by Shep. She and the dog came to a halt in front of him. Tilting her head back, she stared up into his face. "Gee whillikins, you sure are a tall'n, mister."

Tyler only hesitated for a moment before he went down on one knee so he could speak with the child on her own level. "My name is Tyler and, since you helped save my life, I would be greatly honored if you would call me by my given name." He extended his hand. Without pause, Amy reached out her tiny hand, which was immediately enveloped in his. When he brought it to his lips and brushed the top with a brief kiss, her face broke into a wide smile.

"Miss Heinsman, it is indeed a pleasure to meet you," he said gallantly. "I am sure your name was mentioned last night, but I am at a loss this morning." His smile was assuring, his gray eyes twinkling warmly as he waited for the child to respond.

It took Amy a little while to grasp the meaning of his words. "I . . . I'm Amalia Brigetta Heinsman, sir, but mostly folks call me Amy."

"That's a very pretty name, for a very pretty young lady, Miss Amy." Reaching his free hand toward the dog beside her, he waited for him to sniff it before scratching behind the shepherd's silky ears. "Who's your friend?"

Amy's face brightened even further, her blue eyes twinkling with pleasure and pride. "This here's our dog Shep. He's the best dog in this whole county—maybe even in all of Nebraska."

Fearing their awestruck youngest sister might disclose more than her name and an amplified estimation of Shep, Johanna decided it was time to intercede. "Amy, breakfast is ready." There was a noticeable hint of ice in her tone as she added reluctantly, "Will you join us, Mr. Kendall?"

"Of course," Tyler said, his distinct accent more pronounced as he disengaged his hand from Amy's and inquired, "Where would you have me sit?"

Although he didn't understand it, he felt like a leper when at his approach the Heinsmans swiftly shifted their positions at the table, leaving him much more space than he required at the far end.

Afraid they were arousing his curiosity too much by their barely concealed nervousness, Johanna took it upon herself to offer him the place next to hers. "You can sit here, Mr. Kendall."

She didn't dare look at anyone as first one long leg, then the other, stepped over the bench and disappeared beside hers beneath the table. His shoulder brushed against hers as he adjusted his large frame on the narrow bench. "Since there are so many Miss

Heinsmans at the table, would you mind if I called you by your given names?"

"Nope, I guess not," Johanna replied grudgingly, refusing to meet his eyes as she and everyone else waited for Berdine to serve up the plates.

Taking his cue from the others, Tyler waited until they had finished the short heartfelt prayer Berdine said over the food, before attempting to speak again. Evidently, the family was uncomfortable in his presence, and even Berdine, who had seemed so friendly the night before, appeared to be unaccountably highstrung this morning. "Is it usual to have such a fierce storm this late in the year?" He hoped a harmless comment on the weather would put them at ease.

Again Johanna answered for the family, "Nope." The curt negative precluded more questions. Tyler got the message and began to eat, a perplexed frown creasing his brow as he glanced from one pale face to the next.

When his eyes met Amy's, the child grinned shyly and he grinned back. "Aren't you all a bit young to be on your own? Isn't there someone who helps take care of you and the farm?"

Berdine was the first to take exception to his concerned question. "Papa died last year and so far we've been managing just fine, Mr. Kendall."

Johanna was not so polite. "This is our home. We may be young but we don't need anyone's help. Folks out here are raised to rely on themselves not others."

"I've been relying on you and your family ever since I arrived on your doorstep," Tyler returned quietly, entranced by the vibrant blaze of blue in her dark-fringed eyes. "Perhaps you regret taking me in last night, Johanna."

Appalled that he could think such a thing, Berdine quickly assured him that that was not the case, but Tyler noticed that Johanna didn't offer any such assurances. He felt her withdrawal as his attention was claimed by her sister. Deciding he should direct his remarks toward the one Heinsman who was willing to talk in words of more than one syllable, he engaged Berdine in conversation.

For Berdine, the longer she talked with Tyler, the more comfortable she felt with him. Thinking their fears of his revenge were unfounded, she deemed him a gentleman who would never see harm come to women or children. Almost convinced they could confess their crime and that he would forgive them, she ignored the warning glares from Johanna and Fritz and extended the hospitality of their home as long as he needed it.

"We'd be proud to help raise up your barn as soon's you're ready. We'll round up the neighbors and you'll be beneath your own roof before you know it." Berdine poured Tyler another cup of coffee and offered the platter of fried mush.

"A barn raising is the best of fun," Amy enthused.

"I'd be more than grateful, but before that can happen I'll have to find work. My wagons are arriving next week, but I had the misfortune of being robbed on the train coming out here, and I won't be able to pay off my drivers unless I can raise some money."

"Ain't nobody around here who's hiring," Fritz

declared much too hastily, his voice ranging from bass to high tenor. "Folks in these parts barely have two coins to rub together, let alone enough to pay somebody to do their work for 'em." With visible effort, he controlled his voice and stood up from the table. Crossing to the pegs by the door, he pulled down a heavy coat. "I'd best see if I can make some headway outside. You coming, Jo?"

Chapter Six

"COMING," JOHANNA ANSWERED. BECAUSE OF THE weather, Tyler Kendall was going to be staying with them for several days. There was no way she could keep up the impression of being a female homebody for that long, when there was so much work to be done in the barn. She couldn't risk losing one of their precious animals in order to convince him of her femininity.

Standing up from the table, she did have the presence of mind to choose outer clothes different from those she'd worn for the robbery, pulling on a heavy leather coat, boots, leggings and mittens. She wrapped a long woolen muffler around her head and neck, tucking her long hair inside as she joined her brother by the cabin door.

Together, she and Fritz pulled it open, staring

wide-eyed at the gigantic spill of hard snow that blocked the frame. There was only a small gap at the top of the drift that let in about ten inches of daylight and new snow was whirling through that, dusting their feet.

"Je-ru-salem! Would ya look at that! Hope we can dig faster'n it can blow." Fritz reached up and attempted to enlarge the opening.

"Bring some buckets, Cordie," Johanna ordered, both hands on her hips. "Berdine, drag the water barrel over here. When this melts, we'll have enough water to bathe for Sunday meeting and still have some left to do up the washing."

At first, since he had the decided impression that no one wanted his help, Tyler stayed where he was at the table until he saw how even the smallest Heinsman was pitching in to help clear the door. Seeing his boots drying near the stove, he crossed to them and struggled to push his feet into the stiffened leather. By the time he got them on, the Heinsmans had filled several buckets and the large barrel with snow.

"Let me help." He grasped the edge of the barrel, pulling it across the rough puncheon floor as Amy and Berdine pushed from the other side. Returning to the door, he relieved a struggling Cordelia of the two heavy buckets she was dragging toward the fire. On his way back, he got a flashing image of his mother, dressed in a long silk gown, trying to shove a heavy barrel of snow across the floor of the elegant parlor in her Boston home, and he chuckled out loud.

"Something you find amusing, Mr. Kendall?" Johanna asked, breathless from exertion and irritated that he should laugh at the strenuous task they had undertaken in the only way they knew how. "Do city folk have a better method of doing these things?"

Taken aback by her hostility, Tyler lifted the last snow-filled bucket and took it to the fireplace before answering. "City folk?" he inquired, "I don't recall telling you where I'm from, but let me assure you that city folk wouldn't have the first clue what to do about all this snow."

His eyes narrowed when she quickly turned her back on him and returned to work, using a short-handled shovel to widen the slope they were angling upward to the top of the drift. "Sticks out all over you," he heard her mumble, but she didn't address him again until later, when Fritz suggested he hoist her up so she could crawl out the hole they'd enlarged.

"She's too heavy for you," Tyler decreed, putting down his shovel and inserting himself in Fritz's place. "Let me."

"No," Johanna declared sharply. "I'm not relying on a man who's just crawled up out of a sickbed."

"I won't drop you, Johanna." Tyler eyed the stubborn thrust to her chin and the strange expression in her blue eyes. "You're not afraid of me, are you?"

"You're exhausted," she hedged.

"I'm fine."

They went on staring at one another, neither giving in, until Tyler broke the impasse. "Come here."

There was no doubt in anyone's mind that it was an order meant to be obeyed. Angry with herself for being the least bit cowed by the threatening look on his face, Johanna hesitated, finally stepping forward at the very time he reached out and placed both hands at her waist.

"Turn around," he instructed in that same commanding voice, and she swiveled in his grasp until she was facing the tall bank of snow. Even through the heavy leather coat, she could feel his hands as he effortlessly lifted her off her feet. She sucked in her breath with surprise when he threw her upward, then easily caught her around the thighs, leaving her no choice but to sit down on one broad shoulder if she didn't want to fall headfirst into the snow. With her free hand, she grabbed for his hair to keep her balance, but her wet mittens kept slipping so she couldn't manage a good hold.

Raising one arm, Tyler pushed her cold mittened hand from over his eyes while he grasped her tightly around the thighs with the other. "You're a lot of woman," he teased, pushing her hipbone from his ear as he halted before the doorframe. "Bet you're not known to skip many meals."

"Oh!" Johanna gasped, unable to retaliate for the insult without inhaling a mouthful of snow. With all possible speed she reached out with her shovel and dug at the top of the drift until she was ready to be hoisted through it. She could feel the surge of his muscles as he leaned forward, half-lifting, half-pushing her up the slippery slope.

When she landed like a flopping wet fish on the ice-crusted surface, she scrambled to her feet. Looking around, she saw that no one could make it to the barn without snow shoes. Going down on her knees, she found the rope tied to the house, then called back, her voice rising above the howling wind, "Lift up my snowshoes, Fritz. I'll make sure the animals are all right, then start digging from the other end. The wind has died down enough to see a few feet and I think it's stopped snowing."

"You're not going out there alone," Tyler's terse male voice informed her from the cabin. "You'll wait for one of us men."

"Suffering animals don't wait for nobody, mister!" Johanna shouted back, "Dang it, Fritz! Where are those shoes?"

"Right here, Jo," Fritz shouted, tossing one broad caned shoe up the slope, then the other.

"Are you going to let your sister walk around out there?" Tyler's voice boomed, and although Johanna couldn't see what was going on, she knew Fritz was likely the recipient of a gray-eyed scowl that could chill to the bone.

"She'll be fine, Mr. Kendall." Berdine's voice joined the two others before the cabin door. "She knows what to do. This is not our first howler, and everyone must pitch in and do what they can."

"Then give me a pair of those shoes. *I* have no intention of letting a woman stay out there alone."

After hearing that request, Johanna stopped listening and quickly tied the snowshoes' leather thongs around her boots. Confident that Berdine and Fritz would be able to convince Tyler to stay in the cabin where he belonged, she set off for the barn. She certainly didn't need some Boston banker, who was stupid enough to have gotten caught in a blizzard, to help her get to the barn. She doggedly made her way across the frozen drifts of snow. Nor would she need his help when it came to caring for the animals.

Inside the barn, Tyler would only get in her way, and she hoped those left with him in the cabin had told him so. She wondered why he wanted to be a farmer. Recalling the expert cut of the fancy suit she'd first seen on him, she doubted he'd ever gotten his hands dirty, let alone the rest of his body. He'd probably die from the calluses he'd get on his soft hands the very first week.

Luckily, the wind hadn't deposited another deep drift before the barn door and she was able to open it with a minimal amount of digging. Once inside, she untied the cumbersome snowshoes, then lit the lantern. It was amazingly warm in the barn, the close proximity of the animals evidently providing enough body heat to ease the frigid cold outside the small enclosure, and she peeled off her muffler and mittens. Being dug into a hill also helped insulate the building, and Johanna was glad to see that none of their stock was suffering from the cold.

The first order of business was to milk the cow. "Sorry I couldn't get to you sooner, Mazie. Hang on, darlin'," she crooned, "I'm here for you now." Picking up the three-legged stool and a bucket, she walked to the stall, almost sitting down on the floor when Tyler's deep voice broke the silence.

"Does she ever talk back to you?"

Caught off guard and feeling extremely foolish at being discovered conversing with a cow, Johanna snapped angrily, "What in blue blazes are you doing out here?"

"Making sure you don't get lost in the snow," Tyler replied easily, hiding the amused twitch of his lips by removing his hat and hanging it on the peg near the door where Johanna had put her muffler. Bending down, he untied his snowshoes and stepped out of them. He shrugged out of his coat, draping it over the top of the nearest stall and looking around until he located his horse. "I appreciate what your brother did for Sarge last night. He looks none the worse this morning."

His words didn't inspire any comment from Johanna, so he tried another tack. "Can I do something to help? It looks like I borrowed the only other pair of snowshoes, so Fritz won't be joining us."

Without looking up from her task, Johanna shook her head, so used to speaking her disgruntled thoughts out loud to the stock that she forgot a man might overhear every muttered word. "Dang sissified fool. Need him out here like I need two heads."

"Is that so?"

Johanna jumped, so startled by receiving an answer to her unconsciously audible musing that she nearly overturned the bucket of milk. Lifting her head, she found him standing in the next stall, leaning over the wooden side, his arms resting upon the top slat. His gray eyes were fixed on her astonished face, as she recalled what she'd just said. Since she couldn't think of any words to make up for her unthinking remarks, she brazened it out, pointing over his shoulder toward his horse. "Any man who would take a valuable horse like that out in weather like this don't know nothin' 'bout animals. Why don't you go back to the house and send back my brother. I can't waste time teaching some Eastern dandy how to care for our stock."

Her barbs seemed to roll off his back with no effect. Straightening up, he walked around the wood post that separated the two stalls, leaning back against it as he looked down at her. "Eastern dandy." He seemed to mull the insulting label over in his mind before asking, "How did you reach that debatable conclusion?"

"Those fancy store-bought clothes you're wearing," she retorted unhesitatingly. "And the way you talk. All refined and educated-like. Country folks don't use them fancy big words to confuse people neither."

"So my accent and vocabulary confuse you, Johanna? Is that why you barely answer me when I talk to you? You don't understand what I'm saying?"

Both of them were aware that she'd understood every word he'd ever said to her and some things he wanted her to know without having spoken a word. His gray eyes were speaking to her now, telling her she amused him, interested him, telling her he was much more intrigued by the provocative shape of her mouth than the words that came out of it. He wanted their conversation placed on a personal level just to bait her. A test to see how far she'd go, how much teasing she'd take before completely losing her temper. Why, she worried, did he want to make her angry? Did he suspect something? Was he wondering if she was part of the gang that had robbed him? She was almost certain he was considering that possibility when he went on, "Or is it that I frighten you? Do you have some reason to be afraid of me, Blue Eyes?"

"Why should I be scared of the likes of you?" Johanna blustered indignantly, deliberately dismissing him and turning back to her milking. It was time to draw his attention away from her and off in another direction. "If you really want to help, you can stop talking and start throwing hay down from the loft. These animals don't care how we feel 'bout each other. They need new bedding and feed."

She knew the exact second when he gave up on furthering their conversation. Like the sudden loss of a warm glow from an extinguished flame, his heated gaze upon her downcast face died out. All of her senses were tuned to him, but it appeared that her total concentration was centered on milking the cow. She heard him stalk away and locate a pitchfork propped near the door, caught a glimpse as he strode past her to the ladder, then felt his presence over her head as he climbed up into the loft. A few moments later, a small forkful of sweet hay was pitched down to the farthest stall. Johanna stifled a laugh, shaking her head at his ineptitude. At the rate he was going, he'd be pitching all day.

After that, the only sounds in the barn came from the animals. When Johanna had finished milking, she slopped the pigs, fed the sheep, poured grain for the horses and oxen, then picked up a pitchfork and climbed to the loft. Trying not to look at Tyler, who upon her appearance stopped work, Johanna began forking straw over the edge. A few moments later, he went back to pitching hay, but she couldn't help noticing that he timed the swing of his fork so he'd always finish his motion a few seconds before she did.

When she stopped to catch her breath, leaning her chin on the handle of the fork, he did the same, but by some uncanny sixth sense went back to work a few seconds before she had completed her rest.

Suspecting his actions were deliberate, she ignored the implied challenge but was soon afflicted by a growing sense of irritation. She could outdo him every day until Christmas if she set her mind to it and couldn't withstand the urge to prove it. The man was far too sure of himself and needed to be taken down a peg or two. If he wanted a race, he would get one.

The heat rising from the animals warmed the loft and she had begun to perspire beneath her heavy coat. If she wanted to beat him at his own game, she knew she'd best remove the confining garment, so she propped her pitchfork against the back wall and shrugged out of it. Glancing surreptitiously across the small expanse that separated them, her irritation increased when she spied him unbuttoning his wool tunic and turning up the sleeves.

She intensely disliked the sensations she felt each time she looked at him, and that only added fuel to her determination. He might be a big man, strong enough to lift her over his head without effort, but he was unfamiliar with this kind of work, while she had done it every day since she had been a child. She couldn't wait to see his face when he admitted she had won, and she didn't feel any guilt in knowing it wouldn't be a fair test. Not only was she using a much lighter fork but straw was significantly lighter than hay. In order to keep up with her, he'd have to lift double the weight and since he must still be weak from the effects of being caught out in a blizzard, she doubted he would last very long.

They began with a vengeance, almost as if some unseen starter had pulled a gun and triggered the beginning of their race. Effortlessly, Johanna pitched one forkful of straw after another over the edge, watching out of the corner of her eye as Tyler attempted to keep pace. Although he did last much longer than she had expected, he finally had to give in when his agonized breathing gave out.

Sweat poured from his forehead, trickled into his eyes and, when a loud, profane curse signaled his defeat, Johanna couldn't quell her triumphant laugh. "Quittin', Mr. Kendall?" she inquired sweetly. "Like I said before, you'd best leave farming to folks like us and go back East where servants do all the work for you. Pitching hay ain't nothin' compared to what else you'll be doing if you stay on out here."

Although he hadn't recovered enough to speak without sounding like an exhausted weakling, Johanna was aware that he watched every move she made as she leaned her fork against the wall and reached down for her coat. "I've got to spread that straw in each stall, then start shoveling my way back to the house. Once you've rested up some, you can go fetch Fritz. The two of us will finish doing what needs to be done."

With a dismissive toss of her head, she went to the ladder and started to climb down. She was far from the last rung when both of her hands were forcibly removed from a higher position by a painful hold on each of her wrists. Fear and astonishment parted her lips for a frantic scream as she was swung off the ladder and dangled in midair like a swaying noose over the trapdoor of a gallows.

"Here's something else that needs doing," Tyler decreed angrily from somewhere over her head, dropping one of her wrists so the only thing that kept her from plummeting to the ground was his tentative hold on the other. "You'd better pray my meager strength holds out, Johanna, while you and I get a few things straight."

"P-pull me up!" Johanna begged, terrified he'd lose his grip. Her arm felt as if it were being pulled from its socket as she glanced down, her feet hanging scant inches above the dangerous horns of the oxen who occupied the stable beneath her. "You trying to kill me?"

Flailing with her free arm, she frantically reached for his, her fingers digging into hard muscle as she grabbed hold. "Don't let me fall!" she cried, hysteria drying her mouth, replacing any sense of triumph she'd gained from humiliating the man who could let go of her whenever he chose. "I'm s-sorry. It . . . it was only a trick, I tricked you." Surely if he realized he hadn't lost out to a woman because she was stronger than he was, he would pull her up to safety.

"What was a trick, Johanna?" Tyler made no move to swing her quivering form back toward the ladder, seemingly oblivious to the mounting agitation of the deadly horned animals in the stall below her feet.

She was almost too frightened to answer him, both eyes squeezed shut to stop the dizzying swirl of fog that invaded her vision. She had never fainted before in her life, but knew she was going to soon if she didn't convince him to save her. "I . . . I'm scared, Tyler. Please!"

"I believe you are," Tyler announced as if that possibility gave him a great deal of satisfaction. "Hold tight, Blue Eyes. We'll finish this talk face to face."

He swung her back to the ladder, but her limbs were useless and her feet couldn't find a rung. Unwilling to open her eyes, she felt the rough wood of the ladder bump against her shoulder but couldn't seem to do anything but hold on to his wrist, hanging like a dead branch from a fallen tree. "Easy does it, honey," Tyler assured almost tenderly, using both hands to drag her limp body up the ladder and over the edge of the loft.

Panting with relief, Johanna was totally unaware that her body lay sprawled over his. All she knew was that she was safe. She was no longer dangling in space. There was something with substance beneath her. She held on for all she was worth as the shudders of panic drained out of her, not knowing what warm, solid form had aided her recovery until she opened her eyes and found her head was resting on Tyler's chest, her torso on his stomach, her legs between his. She rolled off him quickly, oblivious to his grunt of pain as she staggered to her feet. "You . . . you . . ."

With athletic grace, Tyler got back to his feet and began brushing straw off his pants. "Eastern dandy? Sissified fool? Overgrown weakling?" He supplied several labels for her to choose from, his mustache twitching with amusement as he watched her struggle to contain her returning temper. He was sure that she had recovered from her fright when her incensed blue eyes watched every move he made. "Are you sure you want to call me any of those nasty names you've got in mind?" He glanced meaningfully over the edge of the loft.

His mocking came like a bucket of cold water poured over her head, and she backed away from him. "You wouldn't?"

"That depends. I'd like to hear about this trick you say you played on me."

He took a step toward her, then another and another until her shoulders were pressed up against the back wall. He trapped her by placing one hand against the wall on either side of her heaving chest. Very much aware of the controlled violence she sensed in him and even more aware of the danger involved if she risked challenging him again, Johanna began the explanation he wanted, telling him the difference between hay and straw and the unfair advantage she had taken by using a lighter implement. Hating herself for flinching when his hand reached out to cup her chin, she still made no attempt to swat it away as his eyes delved deeply into hers.

"Not in the least neighborly, are you? Where's all that friendly hospitality Mrs. Meeker told me I could expect from the Heinsmans? So far, I could swear you and your family wish I'd never found your place last night." He let go of her chin and gently brushed her cheek with the back of his hand, a tantalizing stroke from her temple to the corner of her full bottom lip.

"Especially you, Blue Eyes. You can't wait to see the last of me. I wonder why. Could it be you're aware that I like what I see and might steal a small sample?"

The word "steal" sent a cold blast of fear down her back but she faced him bravely, needing to prove he couldn't totally intimidate her now that she had both feet planted firmly on the ground. "My name is Johanna and it won't matter if you like me or not. Men like you don't last long out here. You'll soon give up on being a farmer and go back where you belong. All I have to do to be rid of you is be patient and wait."

"Maybe." He didn't allow her fervent speech to sidetrack him from his intense study of her lips. "In the meantime, I'll satisfy something else we've both been waiting for."

Her body was shaded by his tall, dark form as he stepped closer. Sliding his fingers under her long hair, he held her in place by clasping his hand around the back of her neck, lowering his head until his lips were a breath away from hers. "No!" she intoned, more frightened by the thought of his kissing her than if he had decided to suspend her again over the edge of the loft.

"Don't want to tax your patience, Blue Eyes," he quipped almost tenderly, preventing any response by covering her trembling lips with his warm mouth. The sensation was different, more compelling yet less demanding than she expected. He seemed satisfied with tasting her as if her mouth was a piece of rock candy, some new flavor he'd not experienced before. It was only when she struggled in his grasp, desperate-

114

ly trying to escape the feel of his lips sipping hers, that he stopped coaxing and took what she refused to give.

"You're different, Johanna. Not like any other woman I've known." It was almost as if he were speaking to himself, providing himself with the reason that encouraged further exploration. Knowing she couldn't back away, he fitted himself to her softness, moving his hand from the back of her neck to her throat so he could tilt up her head.

At the feel of intimate contact with his boldly rising desire, Johanna gasped in shock. Instantly, his tongue invaded her mouth, delving for secrets she'd never shared with anyone, discovering new facets of her with each instinctive whimper of response she couldn't manage to suppress. He drank her soft protests like rich brandy, thirstily seeking more for himself by slipping his hand between the buttons of her coat and shirt, then cupping her breast. Expertly he thumbed her nipple until it jutted through the lighter material of her underwaist into his waiting palm as she moaned in reluctant pleasure.

Johanna's legs were refusing to hold her upright. She was overwhelmed by sensations more powerful than anything she'd ever felt before in her life. All the turbulent feelings she'd experienced the night before, when she'd seen his nearly naked body in the candlelight, washed over her, doubled and redoubled as he went on kissing her. The only thing that kept her from sinking to the floor was his body pressed tightly against hers, his hard thighs pinning her softer ones, his hips providing a cradle for her soft flesh. When her knees did give way, he slid down the rough wall with her, his arms around her waist guiding the velocity of their descent to the thick mattress of soft hay.

Without knowing how or why, her inexperienced body accommodated itself to his, as if somehow sensing where each part of her could fit against him to attain the most pleasure. Forgetting who he was, who she was, everything, her instinctively inquisitive tongue sought the wondrous taste she knew was waiting for her inside his mouth.

It was Tyler's turn to be overwhelmed by new sensations. Every part of him ached to feel more of her, his devouring hunger so strong it almost frightened him. Her initial response ordained her an innocent, yet there was a passion in her that exploded through that barrier like the potent force from a gale. When he felt her small tongue slipping between his lips, he groaned like a starving man offered manna. Trembling like an innocent himself, he prayed she'd dare more, yet doubted he could control himself if she did. He was already dying for the feel of her naked breasts against his bare skin, but their heavy clothes made that impossible. He shouldn't take her, yet he wouldn't be satisfied with anything less.

It was almost a blessed relief when a loud adolescent voice, accompanied by Shep's excited yelping, announced Fritz's upcoming entrance into the barn. "You 'bout done in there, Jo? Another foot or two and I'll have shoveled the whole way by myself. Thought you'd meet me halfway."

Forcing himself away from her, Tyler rose unsteadily to his feet, moving to the ladder in order to give her some time to collect herself before her brother came in. "Someday, Blue Eyes, you'll meet *me* halfway," he promised thickly, his breathing ragged. "And when that happens, neither one of us will ever forget it."

He was down the ladder and walking toward the barn door before Johanna had recovered enough to whisper a harsh "Never!"—but he didn't hear her, and she was desperately afraid it wouldn't have mattered if he had.

Chapter Seven

TYLER SCRAPED THE RAZOR DOWN HIS JAWLINE AND rinsed the lather off in a basin of water that Berdine had poured for him. Though he had insisted that he could do for himself, the cheerful young woman managed to rise before him each morning and had the fire lit and a kettle of water boiling before he opened his eyes. As the days went on, the entire family became more comfortable in his presence, went out of their way to make him feel welcome—that is, all but Johanna.

By the end of the first afternoon, Berdine, Cordelia and little Amy had gotten over their initial uneasiness around him and Fritz eventually warmed after another day had passed. Except for an occasional nervous glance that still puzzled Tyler somewhat, the Heinsmans had done everything in their power to see to his comfort and well-being. He came to the decision that the Heinsmans just weren't used to having an adult male living amongst them, and especially not a stranger.

As he continued his morning ritual, he contemplated Johanna, a frown creasing his brow. What was there about her that made him want her so badly? She was not the most beautiful woman he had ever seen. Certainly she was different from the refined young women he was used to, but there had never been anyone else who filled his arms so perfectly, who made him want her so much that he ached every night. Yet during the day he either wanted to throttle her or do something to make her life easier. He was astounded by the amount of work she and her family completed each day, with none of them offering one word of complaint. They were certainly a different breed of people from those he'd associated with in Boston.

He hadn't wanted to care about Johanna or her family, indeed not anyone, but every day he spent with them made sentiments surface that he had thought were long gone—sentiments he had buried in order to survive. He had to get away from here and soon! Hadn't he left his family and friends behind in Boston not only because he could not stand the physical confines of the city, but because he was so emotionally drained from the years of war and months in a Confederate prison that he wanted no responsibilities? He needed to live only for himself—that was all he had the strength to handle.

Beyond the reflection of his own face in the small

mirror over the washstand, he could see Berdine busily preparing the morning's simple fare. With an uncomfortable twinge, he acknowledged, not for the first time, that the family meals were all basically the same. Salt pork, milk and corn. Even the beverage they referred to as coffee was brewed from parched corn.

Though they achieved a variety of dishes with the coarsely ground golden meal—sometimes bits of dried fruits adding flavor and texture or strong sorghum molasses to disguise the blandness—the carefully prepared meals were in sharp contrast to the sumptuous fare that his family in Boston simply took for granted. Eggs were a luxury to be enjoyed only when enough had been accumulated from their scanty flock of hens. It was better food than he had subsisted on in prison, but it made him realize just how meager were the Heinsman supplies and he felt more and more guilty with each mouthful he consumed.

While he had offered them the foodstuffs he had purchased in Hemmington, they accepted only the coffee—telling him he would need the rest more than they did, once he got to his own place. Despite his protest that it was the least he could do in payment for saving his life and providing him with shelter and food during the time he was staying with them, the family seemed insulted that he would think they expected any reward. Another emotion joined his guilt and he recognized it as anger that these proud people who worked so hard saw so little reward for their efforts.

He rinsed his razor in the basin and stood with his head bowed in concentration, unconsciously slicing the sharp metal blade back and forth in the soapy water. Johanna resented his presence. She made that obvious every time she returned his gaze with a cold contemptuous glare. Perhaps part of what lay behind her attitude was concern that the food he consumed was cutting into the family's supplies, but she had also made a number of cutting comments about his "city background" and thinly veiled insults, resenting his wealthy status. It was almost as if she blamed him for her family's meager existence.

He tried to dismiss that disturbing thought, annoyed with himself that Johanna's opinion mattered so to him. He frowned at his reflection as he wiped away the remnants of shaving lather. He had come out here needing to prove something to himself, but here he was planning ways to prove his worthiness to a flaxen-haired vixen who seemed to disapprove of his very existence.

Though Berdine was the eldest, it was obvious that in many ways Johanna was the head of the household. She was the strongest, not physically like Fritz— though she certainly shouldered her share of the heavy chores—but she exhibited a depth of character he had rarely seen in a woman. No simpering miss was Johanna Heinsman, not in the least resembling the corseted debutantes he'd left behind in the city. He found himself chuckling aloud at the ridiculous image of her crumpling helplessly with "the vapors," as he had seen many a refined society matron do.

Johanna could no longer put off making an appearance, for she could hear the rest of the family moving about the main room, Tyler's deep voice conversing with Berdine. Each sharply enunciated syllable he pronounced assaulted her nerves. She hesitated with her hand on the leather thong of the bedroom door and prayed that he was finished shaving.

Because he insisted on sleeping upon a pallet in the main room after that first night, her first sight as she emerged from the bedroom each morning was of Tyler, naked to the waist, his face lathered as he removed his night's growth of manly beard. His muscles rippling beneath the smooth skin of his broad back as he raised and lowered his arms to perform the masculine task did odd things to her equilibrium, made her fingers tingle with wanting to touch him. The scent of his shaving soap overpowered that of the sizzling salt pork and mush Berdine fried every morning at the stove, and worst of all the masculine scent overpowered her until she felt she was gasping for air.

On the first morning when she found him half-dressed and bending before the washstand, she had stood frozen with her mouth agape. He had paused, glanced toward her and smiled a greeting that she had refused to return. If the truth were known, it would have been impossible for her to form words. The view of his broad back had been one thing, his naked chest quite another. Her breasts had tingled and memories had flooded through her body of being crushed against that dark clouded expanse, her flesh separated from his by only the thin barrier of her muslin underwaist.

She braved her entrance, saw that Tyler had just finished shaving, set her mouth in a grim line and strode briskly toward the door. Thrusting her arms into her father's worn hide coat and rapidly pushing the wooden buttons through their loops, she cut off Berdine's protests with a sharp announcement. "Since breakfast isn't ready yet, I'll go milk Mazie." She grabbed her cap and mittens and was out the door before anyone could stop her.

Once outside, she leaned back against the rough wood and took a deep breath, hoping to dispel the scent of shaving soap that had filled her nostrils the minute she walked into the main room. She felt as if her body were alternately freezing and about to erupt in a heated frenzy. Her insides seemed suddenly too much for her skin to contain and as if at any moment she might burst or fly about the room.

It was days since Tyler had held her, made her aware that kissing was more than a mere pressing of lips, that her body fit so perfectly against his. Those memories made her yearn for more, something she did not understand but instinctively knew she would have found out in his arms if Fritz had not arrived at the barn so soon.

Her increasingly frequent black moods were all Tyler Kendall's fault, and the sooner they were able to get him out of their home, the better! No matter how hard she tried to convince herself that she wanted to be rid of him because he might recognize her as the ringleader in the robbery, she knew there was much more to it than that. The tension she experienced constantly arose not from the threat he represented to her and her family, but from the challenge he had issued that morning in the hayloft. She did not want to meet a man like Tyler Kendall, and all he represented, halfway in anything!

No matter how much she tried to avoid speaking to him or even looking at him, he was always there, but maybe today would bring an end to the torture. Feeling a warmer breeze against her cheeks, she thrust her cap and mittens into her pocket and started trudging toward the barn. There was peace inside its murky interior, familiar scents and sounds—no probing gray eyes, no challenging comments, not a single presence to alternately threaten and entice her.

In the short time it took her to relieve the lowing cow and fill the wooden bucket with milk, the warm morning sun had risen above the horizon indicating a thaw in the weather. The wind was gentle and the snow along the path between the barn and house was beginning to melt. Johanna breathed deeply of the air, recognizing a promise in the warmer breezes. The blizzard was over and spring would return soon. She welcomed the change in the weather with more than mere relief that the end of winter was near—it also meant that she would soon be rid of the disturbing presence of Tyler Kendall!

"Any more of that apple cake, Berdie?" Fritz inquired with a hopeful expression at the end of the noonday meal.

"'Fraid not, Fritz," his sister answered, embarrassed that anyone should leave the dinner table wanting.

"You've already had more than your share," Cordelia's soft voice inserted as she started clearing the table.

Tyler leaned back against the wall behind the bench and, with a satisfied smile he was far from feeling, directed his comments to Berdine. "That was a fine meal, Berdine." Guilt that the portion allotted to him might have been Fritz's lay like a heavy weight across his chest. These good people were willing to share their last morsel of food with him, a total stranger, while he pitied himself for having been robbed of funds that he had only to swallow his pride in order to replace. They had no such resources to fall back on, and it was painfully obvious that, compared to the Heinsmans, he was rich even without the money he had lost.

"Somebody's coming," Fritz announced from the window. "It's Doc. Don't remember anybody ailing here for a spell. Wonder why Doc Lloyd is payin' us a call. Couldn't be 'cause he wants to see anybody special here, could it?" His jesting comments were directed at a blushing Berdine, who quickly dried her hands on her apron and with uncharacteristic haste rushed to the door. Smoothing an imaginary wisp of hair into the braided golden coronet atop her head, she threw a warning glare at her brother and drew a woolen shawl around her shoulders.

A burst of giggles from Cordelia and Amy followed their sister's hasty exit, and Johanna sharply ordered Fritz away from the window. "Give Berdie and David a little privacy, Fritz!" She shook a finger at the two youngest Heinsmans. "Don't you two start geegawing the minute Dr. Lloyd gets in here, neither. Be pleasant and friendly but go about your business. He didn't come all the way out here just to listen to you two chattering magpies."

Her warnings were barely delivered when the door opened. Berdine's cheeks were flushed and her lips a bit rosier than normal as she entered the cabin. Tyler ran his hand down his mouth as if smoothing his mustache but it was a gesture to hide his grin. Berdine had the look of a woman who had just been soundly kissed, and from the appearance of the quiet man following behind her, Dr. David Lloyd had thoroughly enjoyed delivering those kisses.

Taking immediate measure of Lloyd, Tyler noted that he was a few inches shorter than himself, of medium build and in his early thirties. His clean-shaven face held a friendly look of anticipation as his clear-eyed gaze swept the cabin, nodding a greeting to each of the Heinsmans, then coming to rest on Tyler. Tyler felt a moment of unease as he realized the dark-haired visitor was silently sizing him up in return. That feeling fled quickly as Lloyd extended his hand in a gesture of greeting. "You must be the Mr. Kendall Barney Holcomb was so worried about."

"The same," Tyler replied as he rose from the bench to greet the man, offering a firm handshake. Surmising correctly that he had passed muster in the newcomer's eyes, Tyler grinned at the other man and said, "I'll have to let Holcomb know I won't be needing a tombstone."

His comments brought a look of confusion to the Heinsmans' faces but David Lloyd immediately grasped his meaning, and the two men shared a comradely grin before David turned to remove his heavy coat and hung it up on a peg. Going to the fire, he rubbed his hands before the blaze, then took a seat on the heavy carved settle nearby. Stretching his booted legs out in front of him, he leaned back and closed his eyes.

"You look tired, David," Berdine assessed with a worried look.

"I am," he sighed, then opened his eyes and smiled at Berdine, accepting the steaming cup of coffee she held out to him. "But for the best of reasons. Sam and Caroline Berkman have a beautiful new daughter who chose to make her debut last night."

The announcement was met with excitement by the Heinsmans and was followed by inquiries about the health of the mother and babe, who resided on a neighboring farm. Throughout Lloyd's explanations, his eyes rarely left Berdine, and it was apparent to all that his visit had been prompted by more than the need for a cup of coffee before he made his way back to town.

Tyler sat back against the twin settle on the other side of the fireplace, enjoying a quiet observation of Johanna in an unguarded moment. The tension was gone from her face, a radiant glow emanated from her smooth, rose-cheeked features, and he felt a resurgence of the desire for her that always lay just below the surface. If only he could make her smile like that at him, he mused, then chastised himself. What did he care if she was happy? Why should he? He would be away from her and her family soon, and other than sharing a common border at the edge of their properties, he would have little contact with them. Wasn't that what he wanted? Little contact with anyone and therefore no ties of any kind?

He was brought immediately out of his thoughts when Lloyd addressed him directly. "You must be the same Kendall who took part in the big statehood celebration in Omaha last week. Read about it in the newspaper. Said you were representing the Kendall Bank of Boston but that you planned to start a farm out here? That true?"

Tyler was slow to answer, though Lloyd's remarks were innocent enough and deserved confirmation. Once again he cursed Oliver Barthold for having forced him up on that podium. An uneasy silence descended upon the Heinsmans as they waited for Tyler's response. Glancing from one pale face to another, Tyler wished that he could deny the connection but knew it was impossible. "Ah . . . er . . . yes, the Kendall Bank is owned by my father, but I was not cut out to be a banker." He hoped his short admission would indicate that he had severed all ties with his wealthy family.

His respect and estimation of David Lloyd grew when the other man seemed to immediately understand and commented quietly, "We can't all do what our families expect." Lloyd stared into the fire for a moment as if wrestling with some painful memory from his own past. Then, turning his attention back to Tyler, he said, "I understand you had a bit of bad luck just before you arrived in our community. Not a very warm welcome, being robbed your first day out here, was it?"

"The thieves made off with my mustering-out money," Tyler growled, his anger at the ruffians who had overpowered him clouding his good judgment.

"Mustering-out money?" Fritz queried, his adolescent voice cracking as his question exploded.

"Yes." Tyler damned himself for having revealed the source of the money he had lost. He didn't want any hero worship from Fritz. He looked up and was startled by Fritz's stunned look. The youth's words had been delivered more as a statement than as a question, and Tyler wondered why confirmation of the source of his money seemed to make Fritz so uncomfortable. When he glanced around he was even more confused by the behavior of the rest of the family who seemed to stiffen, holding their breaths.

He was about to ask them why they were so distressed when David Lloyd broke through the tension that had so suddenly descended by quietly announcing, "I served as a field surgeon in the Illinois Sixth Infantry. What outfit were you in?"

Tyler supplied the information with no embellishment. In the silence that ensued, the two men exchanged a tacit understanding that no more would be said about the war. Each had instantly known what campaigns the other had been involved in and that they both had memories that were better forgotten.

Abruptly, Lloyd changed the subject. "Berdine tells me you had a close call the day of the blizzard. Get my bag, Fritz, and with your permission, Kendall,

I'll check you over since I'm here. It looks like the Heinsmans did a good job warming you up but I'd feel better about it if you would allow me to listen to your chest. Lung fever can always set in after a body's been out too long in that kind of weather."

Johanna quickly scurried across the room. Pouncing on the excuse that neither David nor Tyler needed the whole family gawking during the examination, she bundled into a coat and fled the stifling confines of the cabin. Needing time to sort out the information that Tyler had disclosed, she wandered aimlessly through the snow until she found herself in the small orchard. Leaning her back against the gnarled trunk of an apple tree, she tried to shake off the heavy weight of guilt that had descended upon her the minute Tyler identified the source of the money he had lost.

"Mustering-out money!" They had taken money he had earned risking his life for his country! She hadn't dared look at Berdine, knowing full well the mental recriminations her righteous sister was heaping on her head.

The only saving grace in the whole affair was the confirmation that he was a Kendall, a Boston-banking Kendall. No wonder he could afford that whole half section of land! Her poor father had killed himself working to provide for his family, fighting the railroad's high fees to eke out an existence and scrape together the payments on his land, while the wealthy banker's son had only to purchase the land outright. There'd be no mortgage for him to contend with! If he'd lost his mustering-out money, he could replace it easily! She doubted a Kendall had ever known hardship. So what if he served in the army during the war? His rich father had probably made sure his beloved son was safely behind some desk in Washington!

She thrust herself away from the tree and headed toward the barn. With each step she tried to shake the uncomfortable feeling that Tyler's army service had not been done in complete safety. There had been that silent exchange between the two men, a glance that spoke volumes. Something in each man's eyes had indicated that the war had been anything but glorious.

She pushed open the barn door with firm resignation: I'm not going to feel sorry for a man like Tyler Kendall. He hadn't been wounded! There were no ugly scars on his body! A vivid image of his bronzed flesh flashed in her mind and every inch of her tingled in heated reaction. Damnation, she cursed beneath her breath and, with a Herculean burst of energy, threw herself into shoveling out Mazie's stall.

While submitting to the doctor's brief examination, Tyler acknowledged to himself that it was time to leave the Heinsmans. His continued residence with them was causing a hardship. "Would you care for company back to town?" he asked. "I need to make arrangements for some wagons and supplies I'm expecting from Omaha. Since the ground is still covered, there's no use going out to my land for a few more days."

"Glad for the company," Lloyd answered as he snapped his worn black bag closed. "You're sound, Kendall. I'd say none the worse for your brush with death, but I wouldn't chance another bout with a Nebraska blizzard for a while if I were you."

Tyler noticed that the Heinsmans had busied themselves with various chores during the doctor's examination. Berdine and the two youngest girls were working in the kitchen area, while Fritz and Johanna had disappeared outside. Knowing Lloyd would be leaving soon, Tyler offered his farewells and thanks to the girls, gathered up his saddlebags and headed for the barn to saddle his horse for the trip to town.

He waved to Fritz as he passed the wood pile where the youth was busy swinging an ax and splitting wood for the cook stove. Noting that Johanna was nowhere in sight, he experienced a moment of anticipation as he entered the barn. With any amount of luck, Johanna would be in there and they would have a few moments alone.

Pausing a moment in the doorway to give his eyes time to adjust from the brightness of the outside to the dim interior of the barn, Tyler heard the sound of rustling hay coming from the loft. He looked up to the source of the sound and located Johanna's tall slender form. She was rhythmically pushing her wooden fork into the haystack, lifting and swinging each load over the edge. A narrow shaft of light, coming through the small greased-paper-covered window in the peak of the barn, silhouetted her head and shoulders, and her hair glowed almost silver in the dim light as she continued her task, seemingly oblivious of his observation.

Knowing she would never willingly come down to

see him off, Tyler climbed the wood-slatted ladder, keeping his eyes on the tantalizing movements of her body. She had removed her coat and was turned slightly away from him so that he couldn't see her face. Her silky hair swung softly against her cheeks as she bent to her task. All he could make out of her figure was the enticing roundness of her hips and the outline of her breasts falling against her shirt as she worked, the full, lush breasts that he ached to hold in his hands. The ladder creaked under his weight. Immediately, Johanna stopped work and turned toward him.

The light was behind her and he could not see her expression, but with a stab of disappointment he sensed she was frowning as she leaned against the handle of her pitchfork. "I don't need any help today, Mr. Kendall."

"My name is Tyler and I didn't come up here to help. I'll be leaving with Dr. Lloyd and I wanted to say goodbye."

"Well, you've said it." She returned to her task as if she couldn't be bothered. "I've got work to do."

Tyler swung his legs up onto the loft and advanced on Johanna. Angrily, he jerked the pitchfork out of her hands and tossed it away. She stood speechless for a moment glaring up at him, then defiantly met his gaze with an icy blue stare, as if daring him to do more. For a moment, Tyler returned her glare with a cutting one of his own, then a strong feeling of *déjà vu* swept over him. He had been the recipient of that kind of look somewhere before, but where? Even though he had seen her eyes turn to ice, her expression defiant innumerable times, this look was somehow different.

"Just what do you want?" Her challenging low voice captured his complete attention, his thoughts swiftly focusing on the enticing shape of her mouth.

"This." Without giving her a chance to move, he grabbed her by both shoulders and hauled her against him, lowering his mouth to hers, effectively smothering the protests he expected.

She struggled against him but he let go of her shoulders and slid his arms around her, trapping her arms against her sides. Her breasts softened the contact with his chest where his unfastened coat fell away and her thighs were pressed tightly against his own until he shifted his legs, sliding his hands down to cup her buttocks. He could feel the sharp point of her hipbone against his groin and the answering leap of his arousal as she squirmed in his grasp.

Stubbornly, she locked her lips against his intrusion and moved her head from side to side to escape his possession. Keeping his mouth firmly planted over hers and her squirming body under his control, Tyler opened one eye and peered beyond, spying a beckoning pile of soft hay. With a quick push, he tumbled her backward and followed her body down, never breaking contact.

Pinning her snugly beneath him, he framed her face with his hands, stilling her head. Lifting his lips from hers, he looked down into her haunting blue eyes and with his fingertips caressed the throbbing pulse point at her temples. One thumb slid along her lower lip coaxing it to a pout. "You hellion, you will open to me," he growled and lowered his mouth to hers again.

This time his lips were not hard against hers, they softly glided across her tender flesh, moistened by the tip of his tongue. His thumb continued to tug at her chin and she gasped when his teeth nibbled at her pouting lower lip. Instead of taking instant advantage of her gasp, he continued to torment her with his lips, tongue and teeth.

His mustache brushed softly against her skin, evoking such pleasurable sensations that Johanna lifted her face closer, seeking the deeper penetration he was withholding, but still he held back. Growing impatient, she raised her hands to his head and brought it down to hers, the action causing a deep moan to rumble from his throat.

As if she had unlocked a hidden storm, Tyler's tongue plunged inside her mouth, seeking and finding the virgin areas of sensitivity, urging her own to join in the discovery. His hands no longer needed to imprison her head and swept restlessly over her body, one coming to rest over her breast. His fingertips pushed aside her shirt and sought the tender flesh beneath. His voice was husky as he murmured her name against her lips, then pressed the sound into the silken column of her throat.

Johanna strained her body against him, seeking relief from the intolerably heated tension that broke across her. Somewhere in the most distant recesses of her mind was a dark reminder that this man was a threat to her well-being, that she shouldn't be allowing this to happen, but she ignored the warning. His strong compelling body was a haven of warmth amid the storm of sensations pounding her body.

In spite of Johanna's tempestuous response, Tyler found the strength to control his primitive urge to make her his. He recognized that she was new to the passions he had aroused in her, that she had no idea where they were leading. He could hear his own ragged breathing as he tore his trembling hands away from the softness of her body. Spreading them on either side of her, he carefully levered himself away to lie on his back beside her.

Neither of them spoke or moved until their breathing had returned to normal. Sitting up slowly and swiping at the wisps of hay that clung to his coat, Tyler ran a shaking hand down his face. "You're one hell of a woman, Johanna, and I'd better get out of here before I find out any more."

Rising to his feet, he offered his hand to help her up but she swatted it away. Gazing down at her, he cursed the noble impulse that had prevented him from losing himself between her still-parted thighs. Her breath was coming in halting pants from between her lips, swollen red from his kisses, and her eyes were still glazed with the remnants of passion.

Going to the ladder, he looked back at her when he heard her stirring. "I didn't mean for that to happen, Jo," he apologized, but the gleam in his dark silvered eyes and the slight twitch of his mustache belied sincere contrition.

Casting about for something to throw at him, she found an old bucket that had been discarded in the loft, but her clumsily aimed missile hit nothing. He had quickly anticipated her intent and disappeared down the ladder. The bucket clattered against a support pole, then landed with a thud on the ground floor of the barn. A loud, very male guffaw answered her howl of frustration.

Chapter Eight

WITH A JAUNDICED EYE, TYLER VIEWED THE NARROW line of plowed black earth that ribboned across the ocean of grass. He had worked since sunup, strapped to a leather harness that cut into his flesh, and all he had to show for it was one long turned-over strip of sod barely thirty inches wide. It was now midafternoon and the sun was a gigantic yellow disk burning in the sky, casting a torrent of dry heat over the endless prairie. Sweat ran in hot rivulets down the inside of Tyler's shirt until the damp cotton clung to him like a second layer of skin.

Easing out of the harness, he winced at the pull of his muscles, their soreness the result of hours of torturous strain. "Whoa!" he yelled, scowling at the team of oxen, who unlike him didn't appear in need of a rest. "You may be used to pulling a plow all day but

I'm not used to pushing one," he growled, irritated that he felt a need to justify his fatigue to a pair of dumb animals.

Apathetically swishing their tails over their broad backs to brush away persistent flies, the patient oxen stood quietly beneath the heavy wooden yoke, as if to say they were quite disinterested in the frailties of mankind. Scowling, Tyler pushed the tight strap off his shoulder and dropped the thick leather reins. Glaring up at the hot sun, he stepped out of the deep furrow of black soil beneath his boots. He removed his sweat-stained felt hat, wiped an arm over his heated brow, then lifted the strap of his canteen over his head. After unscrewing the lid, he brought the canteen to his parched lips and took a long swallow of the cool water. "Don't you bloody beasts ever require liquid refreshment?" he bellowed at the oxen, his lips twisting wryly as the animals passively lowered their heads in order to resume munching some sweet grass still untouched by the plow.

Grumbling under his breath, he raised the canteen with one arm and poured its remaining contents over his head. "Never complain, do you?" he jibed sarcastically, replacing his hat. "Well, I bet you'd love a nice cold bath in the river right now as much as I. Even a stupid ox must know it's hotter than blue blazes out here." Not expecting an answer but irrationally annoyed at the benign disinterest displayed by the two oxen, he angrily unbuttoned his sticky shirt and peeled it off. He tossed the shirt on the ground. "Don't you two wish you could peel out of that thick hide you've got?"

"They ever answer you, Tyler?" An amused feminine voice inquired from somewhere over his shoulder.

Whirling around, Tyler found a grinning Johanna seated on the bare back of a huge plow horse. Dressed in a ragged flour-sack shirt and patched overalls, her long hair tucked beneath an old dusty cap, she looked more like a ragtag farmhand that a voluptuous young woman, but Tyler felt an instant surge of pleasure at seeing her. However, when he saw the dancing glints of humor sparkling in her eyes, he was uncomfortably reminded of the time he'd caught her in a similar situation and aware that she was relishing the moment of her revenge. Embarrassment combined irrationally with irritation and his pleasure at seeing her was swiftly camouflaged. "What are you doing here?" he grunted, a surly curl to his upper lip.

Johanna's smile grew larger, knowing exactly what had inspired his inhospitable tone and perversely enjoying her tiny triumph. "Fritz had to go into Hemmington today, but since he promised to show you how deep to plant the seed once you got your plowing done, he sent me to do it for him. We Heinsmans take our family obligations seriously."

Tyler knew she'd added that last statement to make it clear that if it hadn't been a matter of familial duty she never would have come. He also knew she was having difficulty keeping her eyes from straying to his bare chest. She might act as if she didn't like him very much, but there was no mistaking her feminine response to him as a man. Punishing her a little for having overheard his disgruntled conversation with the oxen and for her attitude concerning the errand that had prompted her to come, he dropped his canteen and began walking purposefully toward her.

Johanna watched warily as he approached. Although she sensed some indefinable danger, she couldn't stop her traitorous eyes from seeking out the bare expanse of male skin exposed to her gaze. Tanned to a burnished gold, the powerful muscles of his shoulders rippled in the glaring sun. Tawny dark hair, glistening with sweat, sparkled across the hard male chest, curled damply to an alluring fork beneath gleaming pectorals, then creased downward to his waist and disappeared beneath his trousers. Her throat went dry, but before he got too close, a strong dart of self-preservation pierced her desire-dulled senses and she nimbly slid off the horse's back.

A bit unsteadily, she walked to Tyler's plow. "Fritz tell you to keep these shares clean?" she asked, kicking clumps of dirt off the heavy iron blades. Getting no answer, she determinedly focused her attention on his animals, inspecting them as if they were up for auction and she were a perspective buyer. Showing no sign of fear, she moved behind the two beasts and shouldered herself between them. With a pensive look on her face, she ran her gloved hands down their legs. "What are their names?"

Still out of sorts, Tyler wasn't ready for questions, and certainly not one that would demonstrate even more clearly how fanciful he'd become lately. Pulling his hat down low over his forehead, he hid his sheepish expression from her shrewd glance. After a long pause, her expectant stare prompted him to finally admit under his breath, "Hamlet and Macbeth."

It appeared she had no trouble hearing him, for she nodded as if she saw nothing laughable in the erudite names he had chosen. Stepping out from between the beasts, Johanna cast a critical eye over one of them. "This one Hamlet?"

Wondering if she'd ever heard of Shakespeare, Tyler replied speculatively. "Indeed. A most melancholy ox, don't you think?"

He was astounded when without hesitation she smoothly came back, "But no nephew of a reigning Danish king."

Still unsure of the extent of her education, he pointed to the other animal. "Now that fellow, Macbeth, has a more regal nature."

"But not that of a guilt-ridden murderer," she retorted. "There's not a spot of shame in his gentle brown eyes."

She lifted one brow, challenging him with her eyes, but all she read in his expression was a faint curiosity, nothing to indicate he felt he was dealing with an intellectual inferior. Certain that he was curious about how a simple farm girl had gained a knowledge of Shakespeare, but was unsure how to find out without offending her, she volunteered the explanation. "Ma was a schoolmarm before she married Pa. She brought out most of her books when we left Ohio. We've been reading Shakespeare's plays since we were knee-high," she stated proudly.

"When we were kids, we even acted them out," she went on. Surprised at this sudden urge to impress him, she declared dramatically in a voice strong with theatrical conviction. " 'I must make fair weather yet a while/ Till Henry be more weak and I more strong!' "

Instead of proving to him how well she could recite a phrase from one of Shakespeare's plays, her words seemed to infuriate him. His jaw went tense, his eyes narrowing angrily on her face. "Is that why you're really here? Making pleasant conversation with me while you smugly inspect how little I've accomplished out here? Well, if you're waiting for me to give up on being a farmer you'll have a long wait. No matter what you think, between the two of us, you'll never be the stronger."

Taken aback by the wealth of bitterness in his tone, Johanna's mind instantly formed an indignant retort but just as quickly swallowed it. She recognized instinctively that his bitterness lay not in reaction to her but had its roots in a far deeper source. Not flaring up defensively as she normally did to his jibes, she said firmly, " 'pears to me you've done a lick of work today. You should be planting by tomorrow."

Once again he totally misinterpreted her statement. His harsh laugh was without humor. "I may have done only a 'lick' of work as you call it, but once I get the hang of using this plow, I'll do it better than you. And you don't need to tell me when to start planting. It may take me longer than most this first time, but I swear, I'll make a good crop this year if only to show you I'm not the lily-livered pantywaist you seem to think I am."

"But Tyler, I didn't mean . . ."

"The hell you didn't!" he shouted. "You think I

can't see what's plainly written all over your face? I've lived with that kind of attitude all of my life, but this is one time I'm not going to fail. Wait as long as you want. I'm getting stronger and better every day."

"I can see that," Johanna assured honestly, anxious to placate him. Perhaps it was the pain she detected behind his words or the stark savagery she saw in his gray eyes that made her want to soothe him. Although his anger was directed at her, she sensed with greater and greater certainty that it was meant for someone else, someone who had expected Tyler to fail throughout his life. His parents? A woman? Was that why he drove himself so hard to get his farm started? "To someone unfamiliar with this tough ground," she declared calmly, "what you've plowed so far might not look like very much but I know better. One man can't hardly do more'n this in a day's time, Tyler."

The sincerity in her tone captured his attention, although his gaze was still angry and his expression extremely skeptical. Aware that he was warily scrutinizing every move she made, she placed both hands on her hips and surveyed the surrounding area. "There are some tricks we've learned to make the work easier. You should carry a small stick with you to clear the mud off the plowshare and the mullboard. Otherwise you'll spend half your time sharpening your blades."

A quick glance told her that he had spent a great deal of his day doing exactly that. Spying a sturdy branch half hidden in the grass, she stepped across the harness, took a few more steps, then went down on her haunches. "Like this one." She picked up a stick from the ground, wiped off the dirt that clung to it, then held it out to him.

When he made no move in her direction but stood staring at her as if she were some pesky fly come to annoy him, she gave an awkward shrug and tossed the stick away into the long grass. "'Spect you're too proud to accept advice from a woman. Specially one like me." Johanna mumbled the last remark more to herself than to Tyler. Her confidence was shattered, for she interpreted his rigid stance and glaring expression as disdain that a simple farm girl should have the audacity to advise him on anything.

Feeling the sting of tears behind her eyes, she bent her head, then reached inside the leather satchel she carried over her hip. Pulling out a hatchet, she walked to the end of the furrow Tyler had plowed. "This is what Fritz would've showed you if he'd come today." Bending down, she used the hatchet to chop into the root-clogged soil. "You make a hole 'bout this deep and drop in the seed. Then you stamp the seed in with your heel, like this." Feeling more uncomfortable with every passing moment, she clumsily showed him the motion used to cover the seed.

Afterward, she strode swiftly back to her horse, wanting to be gone now that she'd completed the task undertaken for her brother. Curiosity had been plaguing her and she was glad when Fritz provided her with an excuse to visit Tyler. She'd heard for weeks that Tyler was driving himself unrelentingly, earning the admiration of not only her brother but most of the county. Though she had hoped to discover that the praise being heaped on Tyler was unwarranted, she had been impressed the minute she had arrived on his land by all that he had accomplished in such a short time. Her greatest discovery was his disgruntled view of what he had achieved. She could only suppose that since he was unfamiliar with farming, he had expected to make far more progress, and she found herself wondering, not for the first time, what had made him leave behind a life of wealth and leisure for the uncertainties and meager rewards of farming.

"Planting that strip won't take long," she counseled as she kept her face averted, unwilling to see more contempt in eyes that always seemed to be appraising her. "While you're plowing the next furrow, these seeds will be starting. That way, if the ground squirrels don't get 'em, you can harvest a little at a time, picking each row as the corn gets ripe. Some of the last seeds might not take if you can't get the plowing done early, but most folks just starting out would be mightily satisfied with the size field you've already made."

With an agile leap, she was up and balancing across her horse's back, swinging one long leg over his rump as she moved to a seated position. "Fritz'll be by tomorrow."

"Johanna!" Tyler's shout stopped her before she'd taken complete charge of the horse's reins.

"I'm sorry I took your head off," he exclaimed hastily. Then more slowly, "You weren't casting aspersions on me or my abilities, were you?"

Not completely understanding the question, Johanna recalled the last time she'd tried to impress him with her limited supply of knowledge and decided to go with the truth. "I don't rightly know what aspersions are, Tyler, but I surely didn't intend to belittle you. Anybody'd be proud to have done this much in one day."

The apologetic expression on his face, along with his boyishly pleased smile, was her reward for being so forthcoming. Knowing there was nothing to detain her, but for some reason wishing she didn't have to leave, she stammered, "I . . . I think you'll make a good farmer, Tyler. Most of it's just being more blamed ornery than the elements."

The booming sound of his laughter brought a rush of embarrassed color to her cheeks. "I'd best be going."

"Had you?" he asked, striding toward her. Reaching out, he grabbed hold of her reins, but unlike the last time he'd approached her horse, she didn't feel threatened. "I'd rather you stayed on a while longer," her told her with a softer tone. "I'll admit that I've misjudged you but I'd like a chance to prove that you've misjudged me too."

"How?" The question was soft, her voice oddly affected by the pleading expression on his face, an expression that totally contradicted the masculine challenge in his words.

"You don't think I'll take advice from a woman but I will, especially when that woman is you. I've never met a woman quite like you before. As much as I might like it to be otherwise, you know much more about farming than I. I'd be a fool not to learn all you can teach me."

His eyes invited her down from the horse, and she

didn't realize hers had accepted the invitgation until he raised his arms and took hold of her around the waist. Before she could utter a protest, she was standing on the ground in front of him, his hands still circling her middle, dangerously close to the undersides of her breasts. "I know how to get down off a horse, Tyler," she muttered, brushing his hands away and quickly stepping to one side to escape the discomfiting sensations that came from his touch, from standing so close to his bare chest that her breath could dry the sheen of sweat glistening across the hard bronzed muscles.

"Do you think you can lift me off the ground, Johanna?" he asked, grinning as her flushed features knitted in confusion.

"No, but I don't see what that has to do with anything."

Taking her hand, he gave a low satisfied chuckle. "I have a colossal ego, and so far in my dealings with you I've come off a decided second best. I may be able to accept your advice but not without knowing there's one thing I can still do that you can't. If I'm ever feeling put upon by your superiority in other areas, I'll just pick you up and carry you around, knowing you can never do the same to me."

Immediately, Johanna thought of the first dealing they'd had and what would happen if he ever found out how greatly she'd once bested him. Even though it went against her nature, she gave him what she thought was a look of feminine supplication. Gazing up at him with admiring eyes, she said meekly, "You don't have to prove anything to me, Tyler. I might have thought you a citified dandy at first but I don't anymore. You've worked very hard ever since you came. I respect that in a man. God made men physically stronger than women but he didn't make 'em stronger on the inside. You're showing a lot of courage and fortitude, and in my book that's far more important and admirable than a strong back."

"Yes, ma'am." Tyler meekly nodded his head, but his grin showed how much she'd soothed his wounded pride. "I'll try to remember that."

When Tyler dropped her hand, she glanced up and their gazes locked. Mesmerized by the softened color of his eyes, Johanna couldn't look away and several moments passed as they stared at one another. Verbal communication was replaced by the visual sort, which was even more unsettling, so primitive in nature it cut through to her very soul. Johanna felt as if he were physically caressing her with his probing gaze, caressing her soul as if he could see it through the melting blue depths of her eyes. "You're so beautiful," he murmured. "Both inside and out."

She gave a negative shake of her head, dismissing the compliment she knew she didn't deserve but unable to break visual contact with him. It was as if he had a kind of magical power over her, a power that robbed her of speech, of mobility. Moving his gaze from her eyes to her cap, he frowned slightly. "I wish you didn't always hide your hair like that. I like to see it flowing freely down your back."

With a swift motion of his arm, he whisked the cap off her head, smiling in pleasure as the wild flaxen curls tumbled over her shoulders. "A woman's crown-

ing glory, but yours is far more glorious than most."
His fingers combed through the flowing golden mass,
catching one strand and bringing it to his nose and
then his lips. "It's like rays of sunshine."

She knew she should get angry over the liberties he
was taking, but she was so entranced by his devastating smile she couldn't muster a single word.

Taking advantage of what he was certain would be
only a temporary loss of composure, Tyler drew one
finger down the soft satiny skin of her cheek. "Kissed
by the sun yet soft as a peach. I wish a few women in
Boston could see you, Johanna. They seem to think
that a woman will lose her beauty if her complexion is
ever exposed to the sun. Compared to you, they look
like lifeless dolls."

"Do they?" she whispered, helplessly responding to
the unaccustomed compliments, pleasure sparkling in
her eyes.

"They certainly do," he reaffirmed softly as his gaze
traveled over her features, focusing on her soft trembling mouth. "Once I kissed a woman who told me
never to do it again because it would make lines in her
face," he said slowly and quietly. "You'd never worry
about such a thing, would you?"

"No-no."

"I didn't think so," he murmured huskily.

She knew he was going to kiss her, even knew that
she had somehow given him permission to do so, but
had no idea what the feel of him would do to her until
he drew her body against his. With one powerful arm,
he crushed her to his naked chest. Searing flames of
sensation shot through her breasts and her nipples

immediately hardened to probing points beneath her shirt. The skin of her thighs felt burned by his rock-hardness pressing against her, and a heated warmth spread from her belly and through her loins. Her breath caught in her throat, her long lashes sweeping down to cover the unexpected surge of longing shimmering in her eyes.

Hating the inexplicable weakness inside her that made it impossible to push him away, Johanna's soft moan was totally muffled by Tyler's devouring mouth. It was as if he were trying to absorb her essence into himself, molding her body so closely against his that she could no longer tell where her flesh ended and his began. His broad palms moved restlessly over her back, down over her hips and back up again, fitting her tighter and tighter to the hard planes of his lithe body.

The kiss was different from any he'd delivered before. There was desperation in his marauding tongue, and he plundered the inside of her mouth as though he couldn't get enough of the taste of her, an insatiable hunger in every bone and muscle that pressed into her softness. Clinging to him, she felt his body offered the only safety from a whirlwind of sensations that rose up inside her, and she responded to his hunger with such intense fervor that he shuddered.

Lifting his mouth from her burning lips, he pressed his face into her throat. "God, Johanna, you're so alive. I've seen so much death . . . so much waste . . . but you make me forget it all." The words came in disjointed phrases, muttered harshly between fiery kisses that were branded up and down her slender neck, and Johanna was sure he was unaware of saying them. "Kiss me Johanna . . . I need to feel your lips moving over my mouth."

She could no more have denied him than stopped breathing. His hat tumbled to the ground as her fingers clutched in his hair. She pulled his face back to hers, covering his lips with her soft mouth. Like women through the ages, she exulted in the tremors of response that shook him when her eager tongue delved between his lips and her fingers stroked his naked back, nails digging into the warm skin.

Oblivious to the passage of time, to anything but satisfying her growing need, Johanna arched against him, rubbing her breasts against his chest to soothe the mounting ache that threatened to explode inside her. When she felt the shudder that coursed through him, she wrapped her arms about him as if she'd never let him go. She was completely unprepared when he forced them back down to her sides, then flung himself away from her.

He turned his back on her but that didn't hide the way his shoulders heaved as he inhaled huge gasps of air into his lungs. His labored breathing was as rapid as her own, slowly calming as he stood, hands on his hips, staring up at the endless blue sky. She watched him fight for control, infected by a strange curiosity that numbed her body and delayed the advent of shame she would feel when she remembered her wanton behavior.

Shaking his head as though to clear the daunting effects of a powerful blow, he finally spoke, his voice thick with the residue of passion. "Get out of here, Johanna. Go home."

There was something much stronger than dismissal in his tone, a vulnerability that called out to every female nerve in her body, and Johanna responded to it instead of to his words. She took a step forward and placed her hand on his shoulder, but he jerked away from her touch as if she'd lashed him with a bullwhip. He turned to face her and she backed away, frightened by the savage look on his face.

"Don't touch me again," he ordered harshly, something wild surging in his eyes, chilling the warmth that had just been there to a cold steely-gray color. "I don't want to hurt you, but I will if you don't clear out of here. It's been a long time since I had a woman and everything about you reminds me of that, but you're not what I need right now. Run away while you still can, little virgin, or you'll always wish you had."

Needing no other impetus, Johanna fled, humiliated tears streaming down her cheeks. In seconds, she was on the back of her horse, frantically kicking his flanks with her boots. She didn't know that Tyler had followed her, seeing the self-degradation that ravaged her pale features, but she heard his strangled shout and it only compounded her desperate need to escape. Forcing the horse into a gallop, she rode away from him, never once looking back.

Tyler watched the fleeing figure, clinging to the bare back of the large horse as it galloped across the fields, until she disappeared out of his sight. Lost in a fog of self-condemnation, he had no way of knowing that if she'd seen the agonized look in his eyes, it would have swiftly erased the shame he'd glimpsed on her features before she managed to turn her horse away from him. Eventually, his shoulders slumped in defeat and he turned away from the empty horizon, calling softly to the pair of oxen who patiently waited for him at the end of the narrow furrow of tilled earth.

Hours later, as the sun became an orange globe dipping behind the low hills, he was still pushing the heavy plow through sticky sod. Trying to work himself into an unfeeling stupor so he'd no longer be tormented by the memory of tears falling from a beautiful pair of large blue eyes, he stoically trudged on until he had doubled the width of freshly turned earth. In time, as darkness made it impossible to continue, he unbuckled himself from the harness.

Guiding the ponderous oxen back to their rope-enclosed paddock, he finally had to admit something to himself. He would find no solace in his empty surroundings, no peace in the vast landscape he could now proudly proclaim as his own. There was only one way to relieve the growing ache inside him, relieve the restlessness that ruined his sleep. He needed Johanna, needed her naked body writhing beneath his.

The force of his desire for her terrified him. Tyler Phillips Kendall, the man who had disavowed any need for human ties, had disowned everyone and everything who might interfere with the course he'd set for himself, had been reclaimed by a blue-eyed farm girl who was completely unaware of the power she had over him.

Gazing into his small cook fire, he vowed to keep it that way. He didn't want her or anyone else depending on him for anything. Emotional ties brought pain, pain that cut into the soul, infected the spirit with so much hurt it had taken him over two years to become functional again. No, he wouldn't let Johanna Heinsman get to him. He didn't need a woman that badly and, if he ever reached the point where he did, he'd travel to Omaha and buy the services of the kind of woman who'd make no other demands on him.

Chapter Nine

"SURE YOU DON'T WANTA COME ALONG?" FRITZ LOOKED down at Johanna from the wagon seat, a hopeful expression on his sun-burned face. "We 'spect to be finished raising Tyler's barn today and there's going to be a dance afterwards."

Seated beside him on the wagon, Berdine advised, "Leave her alone, Fritz." A look of understanding passed between her and Johanna, then she continued, "Jo's right, you know. We can't all go traipsing off for the whole day." Tightening her grip on the handles of the reed basket she balanced on her lap, she added, "Besides you'll come back this evening after the work's done and find out if Johanna wants to join us at the celebration."

Satisfied by Johanna's nod of agreement, Fritz slapped the reins over the team's withers and set the two lumbering horses into plodding motion. Cordie and Amy waved gaily from their places in the back of the wagon, and Johanna waved back before turning away to the house. Shep started to run after the disappearing wagon but Johanna's sharp whistle brought him racing back to her side.

"C'mon boy, we've got work to do," she said to the obedient animal as she kicked a pebble with the toe of her dusty boot. "I'd only be in the way today, anyway," she remarked, trying to talk herself into believing she had several good reasons to stay behind. After all, Fritz's youthful strength was necessary for the actual building of the barn, Berdine and the girls would be kept busy providing nourishment for the workers, and she . . . ? She would have had to pull on a dress and remain with the women all day, gossiping and laughing, pretending she was enjoying herself, all the while trying to avoid any contact with Tyler.

While it was true that there were always chores to be done on the farm, a barn raising and the promised dance and feast that followed were reasons enough for almost everyone to leave their own farms for the day. All essential chores had been completed that morning and, with the exception of milking Mazie again, a job that could easily have been done by riding home for a short while that evening, there was no task that could not be put off until the next day.

For farmers, occasions for any kind of celebration were few and far between, so there was no way of knowing when the next get-together would be. Most farmers had their fields sown by now and it was a relatively slack time, perfect to help a new neighbor raise a barn, a welcome opportunity to visit with friends. There was some exchange each Sunday after church, but it was get-togethers like this that gave them the chance to catch up on the news of the community, obtain detailed accounts of all that had occurred since the last time they'd seen one another.

Johanna looked out over the low hills. The rolling untilled prairies were covered with wild flowers. Black-eyed susans waved in the gentle breeze at the edges of the fields, and tiny star-shaped blue blossoms peeked out from behind the stems of blue-eyed grass in the pastures. Tiger lilies and spiderwort added color to the creek banks. The beauty of the fully awakened countryside was all around her, but Johanna ignored it as she concentrated on her work—anything to take her mind off the activities going on at the neighboring farm and especially the man who owned it.

She had not seen Tyler since that horrible day in his cornfield but had been continually apprised of his activities by her family or the townsfolk of Hemmington on the rare occasions she had made a trip into town. It had been all Johanna could do to keep from screaming when, at the mercantile, Mrs. Meeker rambled on and on about the community's newest resident while she filled the Heinsmans' basket with supplies. "He's an able-bodied man and mighty handsome to boot, Johanna. You'd be wise to catch his eye before somebody else snatches him up."

Her guilt was becoming an increasingly heavy burden as she constantly recalled the day she and Fritz had gone to pay off the second mortgage on the farm.

Realizing that posting the large sum of money they'd inexplicably acquired would arouse questions that might be hard to answer, she and her brother had made the long trip to Omaha to send off the draft to the Kendall Bank. It was a wry twist of fate, Johanna had thought as she handed the bundle of paper dollars to the teller. Money stolen from a Kendall was being used to pay a Kendall.

Her conscience repeatedly reminded her that the Kendall Bank itself had had nothing to do with the misfortunes of her family, that Tyler had earned that money fighting for his country, and it was increasingly difficult to shake off her guilt. Nor was it any easier to cling to the image of Tyler as a rich man's son, who would soon tire of playing at being farmer. He was working too hard. His coming to Nebraska was no temporary whim. From his reference to visions of death and the delirious rantings she'd overheard the night of the blizzard, she knew that his reasons for coming to the new state had something to do with his experiences in the war, experiences so horrible that he didn't want to talk about them.

She searched continually for a means of undoing what was done but could not. Giving the money back and begging for Tyler's mercy and understanding might have erased the crime, but their farm would have been lost and she couldn't have allowed that to happen. She would just have to learn to live with her remorse.

After toiling most of the day mucking out the barn, Johanna cleaned the resulting grime off her body by taking an invigorating bath and washing her hair in the slow-moving waters of the Elkhorn River. It was dusk when she dried herself off and slipped into her faded wrapper to make her way back to the cabin. Hearing Shep's excited bark off in the distance, she assumed that Fritz must be returning home to see if she had changed her mind. She stepped inside the cabin and started toward the bedroom, intending to slip into a nightgown in order to convince her brother that she was too tired to attend a dance and was making an early night of it.

Her fingers had just grasped the leather-thonged latch of the bedroom door when there was a loud banging on the outside door and she heard what was unmistakably Tyler's deep voice calling her name. She had not bothered to light a lamp and frantically prayed he would think she was not at home. Holding her breath, she stood perfectly still, willing him to go away.

"Johanna?" Tyler called as he pushed the door open, a lump of fear settling in the pit of his stomach as he peered into the darkened cabin. He had already checked the barn, after noticing there was no light shining from the windows of the cabin, and when he did not find her there, he had raced to the house. "Johanna?" he called again as he stepped inside, searching for any sign of her.

His gaze flew around the main room, then stopped as he spied her standing silently in the shadows by the bedroom door. The fear that something disastrous might have happened to her fled and was instantly replaced by anger. He stalked across the cabin floor, his heavy tread echoing loudly in the silence. "Why didn't you answer me?" he demanded.

Refusing to be intimidated by the angry man facing her, Johanna stubbornly lifted her chin, placed her hands on her hips and confronted him. "Why are you here? Isn't there a barn dance going on at your place?"

There was just enough light in the cabin for Tyler to glimpse the outline of her feminine curves beneath the thin wrapper. It was the first time he had seen her in anything other than male clothing and he halted his advance. His gaze ran hungrily from the top of her damp shining hair, over the soft creamy roundness of her breasts exposed by the open vee of the wrapper, appreciating the tiny waist where she had belted her garment and the gentle flare of her hips, down to the bare feet that shifted nervously on the rough floor. The temptation to sweep her into his arms and finally make her his on the soft feather-filled mattress of the bed beyond the door was almost irresistible. The only reason he didn't do exactly that was because almost half of the county knew he had come to fetch her.

"There is," he answered, a slow smile spreading to reveal even white teeth beneath the shadow of his mustache. "But the prettiest girl in the county isn't there so I came to personally escort her to the party."

Johanna could feel a heated blush covering her body, a blush caused more by the way he was looking at her than his flowery words. "I . . . I'm not the prettiest girl in the county," she stammered, embarrassed. "And I'm not going."

"Yes, you are to both denials, Johanna."

"No," she insisted.

"Yes," he countered just as firmly.

"Why?"

"Because I'd like to see you in a dress and have some excuse to hold you in my arms."

"You never needed an excuse before!" No sooner were the words out than Johanna wanted to call them back. She cringed against the door as he closed the little space between them.

"No, I didn't," Tyler mocked, "And I don't need one now." He reached for her and caught her around the waist before she could scramble beyond his grasp. She swung her arm but her wrist was caught in midair, and as she brought up the other one it was just as quickly grasped and locked behind her. Having only her feet for weapons, she brought her leg back to deliver a healthy kick at his shin, but he anticipated her action and stepped aside. Before she could launch another assault, she was forcibly hoisted over his shoulder and carried into the bedroom where he dumped her on the bed.

"Who do you think you are?" Johanna railed, scrambling to her knees. "You have no right to barge into my home and manhandle me like this."

Tyler seemed as surprised as she by his actions, raking one hand through his hair while he looked down on her furious face. Releasing a frustrated breath, he took a step backward, then gestured for calm. "Johanna," he began apologetically, "I didn't plan it this way. I intended to politely invite you over to see my new barn, but you're so damned stubborn!"

"I am not! I just don't want to go."

"Not even if I tell you the occasion means nothing to me if you're not there to share it?"

"What?" Johanna was astonished, confused by the affectionate look in his gray eyes. "We hardly know one another. The last time we saw each other you made it very clear that you wanted nothing more to do with me. What difference can it make to you whether I'm there or not?"

"But we do know each other, Johanna. Know each other very well," Tyler disagreed, a tender smile curving his lips. "We also know we each have something the other one needs, have known it since the night we first met; no matter how hard we try to fight against it. I've tried to stay away from you but I've discovered I have very little willpower where you are concerned. I need to be with you."

"Well, I don't need anything from you, Tyler!" Johanna moved into a seated position, refusing to let his honeyed words affect her. What was to prevent him from using her again as he'd done the last time they'd been together? She was still suffering from that humiliation and wasn't prepared to risk another such encounter. Pulling the wrapper more securely around her, she lifted her head to stare into his eyes. "And I don't know you, not at all."

She jumped when he expounded, "There you go again, being stubborn! You can sit there and deny that you don't want my kisses, don't want me to touch you? Don't you know how easily I can prove you wrong?" He gazed meaningfully at the bed. "We're all alone, Johanna. What's to stop me from joining you on that bed, kissing you until you admit that you want me as badly as I want you?"

Ignoring the threat, Johanna sneered sarcastically, "Lust! You don't want me—Johanna Heinsman. No, you want a woman to satisfy your carnal cravings. Well, I'm not like that!"

"I'm well aware of that," Tyler retorted gruffly, as if the knowledge had plagued him for a good length of time. As she watched, his features relaxed and a teasing light began dancing in his eyes. "I've found a beautiful woman I desire like no other, but because I can't help kissing her a few times, she pretends I don't exist, lets me pine away to practically nothing. Is that what you want, Johanna Heinsman? Do you want me down on my knees, begging for another chance to get close to you?"

Still skeptical, Johanna frowned. "You don't strike me as the begging kind."

"Why not?"

Unaware of the trap she was walking into, Johanna decreed, "Because you've got too much pride. You're an arrogant, short-tempered man and . . . and as stubborn as I am."

"How well you know me, Johanna," Tyler pronounced. "Very well indeed, just as I know you. For instance, I know that you dearly want to go to that dance with me but your pride won't let you admit it. So I'm going to make it easy for you. You can either get ready for the dance or I'll come back in here and make love to you."

"What?"

"You heard me." He walked to the door. "Since you know how arrogant I am, you also know I mean it. I don't see why you should have everything your own way. I've told you that I think you're beautiful, that I want to get close to you, but you haven't been honest about how you feel about me. I'm willing to court you properly, and if you agree to go to the dance I'll know you're willing to accept my noble intentions. However, if you want to eliminate the preliminaries and get right to the heart of the matter, you can take off that flimsy wrapper and wait for me to come back in the room so we can make love. I'm leaving it all up to you."

He closed the door on her outraged scream, chuckling when he heard the sound of something hard bounce against the wood. Crossing the room, he lit one of the lamps, then leaned his elbow on the mantle over the fireplace, waiting for the storm in the next room to subside. He had no doubt that he'd convinced her to go with him to the dance, for she would hardly consider the alternative, even though he felt she knew as well as he did that inevitably someday it would happen. He'd had plenty of time to reach that conclusion and, recalling her response to him the last time she'd been in his arms, she had to know it too.

With nothing left to throw, Johanna sat curled up on her knees in the middle of the bed, impotently fuming at the closed door. He had tricked her! She had no choice but to go with him. He'd long since made it plain that he wanted her and she'd foolishly done the same, but he didn't love her and she certainly didn't love him! Whatever had happened those times before had been lust. Pure, unadulterated, sinful lust!

She crossed her arms over her heaving breasts and leaned back against the high headboard her father had carefully and lovingly carved for her mother during one long winter, years ago. She remembered the rustling and the murmurs coming from her parents' bed when she had slept above them in the loft, before Pa built on the extra room. Pa and Ma had loved each other very much. Had those muffled sounds had something to do with what Tyler termed "making love"?

She and Berdine had never discussed what kind of intimacy occurred between a man and a woman after they were married. The knowledge they had obtained had come through their religious training and it had been purposefully vague. Of course, they both knew about the animals and that mating was necessary between the male and the female in order to produce young.

She supposed it was much the same between a man and a woman but, knowing what it felt like to be kissed by Tyler, she wondered if mating could possibly be as cerebral a matter as church teachings indicated. According to Pastor Braun, children were the blessed result of the highest form of spiritual love resulting from the sanctity of marriage. The spirit had nothing to do with her feelings for Tyler, and the divine state of marriage was not what he wanted from her.

"Johanna, are you getting ready or do you want me

to come in there?" Tyler's deep voice rumbled into her musings.

Scrambling off the bed, she quickly made her decision, or more aptly bowed to his threat. "No! I'm getting ready!" She hastily lit the lamp and reached for the best of her two dresses, a pretty blue calico that Berdine had made up from the lengths of material Johanna and Fritz had splurged on during their trip to Omaha. It had not been her desire to have a new dress, but Berdine had insisted a new one was long overdue. Pulling open one drawer of the old scarred bureau that occupied one corner of the small room, she extracted a clean muslin camisole, drawers and the only petticoat she owned. Tossing them on the bed, she searched the room and found her moccasins. They would have to do for dancing slippers, her only other choice of foot covering being a pair of heavy boots.

Satisfied that the sounds coming from behind the door indicated that they'd soon be starting back to the dance, Tyler relaxed. God, she was stubborn! He had guessed long before they arrived at his place that the Heinsmans would be minus one family member. As the day had worn on and the sides and roof of his barn had taken form, he became increasingly aware of his disappointment over Johanna's absence.

Although he resented it, he'd been forced to alter his stance on a few matters since their last meeting. Ever since that day in the field, he'd had no peace. Knowing what was at stake, he'd still fallen victim to the memory of a pair of cornflower blue eyes that haunted him wherever he went. Wanting nothing more than to be left alone to work his land by himself, he'd found himself anxiously searching the horizon for the sight of her or any member of her family.

He railed against it, but yet he missed her more with each passing day. She was always pointedly absent during a family visit, and it had been weeks since he'd last had one glimpse of her. She was behaving as if she wanted nothing more to do with him, but before the night was over he planned to rectify that.

After his barn had been raised and the dancing got underway, he'd experienced a sharp twinge of envy when he saw the longing gazes exchanged between Berdine and David. He found himself yearning for Johanna to look at him in that special way, promising that he would make it happen, and not long in the future. When Fritz had announced he was going home for his sister, he quickly volunteered his services, surprised that he was enjoying the speculative looks his offer had prompted in his new neighbors, confidently shrugging off their doubts that he'd have a rough time convincing Johanna Heinsman to attend a dance.

As he stood silently contemplating the simple furnishings of the cabin, remembering the few days he had spent with her and her family, he recalled how kind they'd been to him, a total stranger. He'd seen how even the smallest of them, little Amy, was familiar with hard work, and that had given him strength to face the countless tasks he'd been required to do in order to begin farming. He had crawled out of the bedroll in his tent each morning at dawn, spent part of the day felling trees and notching them for the barn and another part behind the slow moving team of oxen, guiding the heavy plow as it cut a deep furrow in the black soil beneath the tight layer of grass.

In exchange for the use of Tyler's team of horses, while Tyler cut and stripped logs for the barn, Sam Berkman, but more, often Fritz, had helped him complete his plowing and planting. On those days either Berdine or Caroline Berkman had sent over a basket of food. Sometimes the Berkmans invited him to supper, but most of the time Tyler had to make do with his own cooking. It was during the long evenings, sitting on the ground beside a small fire, that Tyler found himself envying Sam Berkman for his wife and growing family. Too often, an image of Johanna floated in the smoke of the small fire and he found himself musing at what it might be like to be greeted by a wife at the end of a long day in the fields. At night, as he tried to find comfort on the hard unyielding ground, he constantly thought about Johanna's soft body and how she would feel welcoming him into her softness as they lay together on a bed.

He leaned back against the mantle, stretched his arm along the smooth surface and spread out his hand. His fingers began drumming impatiently on the wood as he pushed the domestic daydreams aside. Berdine was definitely much better wife material, so why didn't he think of her like that? Even before he knew there was something between her and David

Lloyd, he hadn't felt the faintest stirrings toward her. She was pretty and soft-looking, very warm and feminine, whereas—her sister?

Johanna was all unyielding stubbornness! Well, not always, he reminded himself. Underneath that stubborn facade were fire and passion ready to erupt each time he took her in his arms. Except for that day in his field, he'd had to fight her whenever he'd taken her into his arms, had to kiss her senseless. He wondered if he'd ever get through the new barriers she'd erected against him since their last meeting. He had no one to blame but himself if she wanted nothing more to do with him because of that day, when he'd known his hasty words would hurt Johanna but he hadn't been able to stop them. He'd wanted to call them back, apologize for them—anything to erase the pain he had caused her, but it had been too late and she'd ridden away, frightened and humiliated.

Even before that, it had sometimes seemed as if she thought he was dangerous, his presence posing an invisible threat to both her and her family. He couldn't think of anything he'd done that would foster that kind of fear. Recalling the episode in the hayloft, he knew that Johanna might have had reasons to avoid him but there was nothing that should make her feel he would bring harm to her family. Dismissing all that had happened between them, he wanted to start afresh. "I'll make her forget everything but how good it feels to be in my arms."

Glancing down at the clock, he noted with a frown that almost an hour had gone by since he'd arrived. He would give her another five minutes and then go in after her. He watched the shining brass pendulum swinging back and forth behind the glass door of the exquisitely carved clock. His gaze wandering over the details and admiring the craftsmanship of the timepiece. Something white caught his attention at the base of the clock. Curiosity prompted him to probe with his long fingers, until to his complete amazement he extracted his own ivory-handled service revolver!

"How in the . . . ?" he exclaimed, dumbfounded, as he fitted the smooth grip in his palm and ran his free hand over the gleaming barrel. A pair of glittering blue eyes leaped out of his memory to challenge him. Defiant blue eyes beneath a crudely fashioned fur cap just like the one . . . He stalked across the room to stare openmouthed at an array of heavy winter clothing hanging on the pegs. Still holding his revolver in one hand, he reached out the other to finger the coats, recognition sweeping over him.

Fury at his own stupidity exploded inside him, then as he recalled Johanna's daring, its velocity doubled. While he had been standing here like some lovesick swain waiting for a glimpse of his lady love, imagining all sorts of tender domestic scenes with her, she had reason for far different thoughts about him. No wonder she acted afraid of him. The damnable woman was a conniving thief! Had robbed him of his entire stake! He didn't doubt for a moment that she'd been the brains behind the whole scheme, the gang's blue-eyed leader! Clearly remembering his other assailants and the conductor's comments about a boy and his cow holding up the train, his fury boiled to new heights as he estimated the dangers shy little

Amy, timid Cordie and the flustered Fritz had faced under Johanna's orders. What on earth had driven mere children to go along with her foolhardy scheme!

Another recollection gained his attention. That humiliating wire he'd sent to his father, requesting funds from the trust his grandfather had left for him, the same money he had previously refused. Because of Johanna, he'd been forced to his knees, to swallow the pride she well knew was a major part of his makeup. Because she had robbed him, he had gone begging to his father, admitted all that had happened to him before ever stepping foot on his own land. Although he'd burned the return wire, he could recall each word of the scathing message.

SENDING GOOD MONEY AFTER BAD. SUGGEST USE IT FOR RETURN TICKET. FORGET FOOL'S ERRAND. ED-WARD KENDALL.

Hearing a noise from the bedroom, Tyler swiftly recrossed the room and shoved the revolver back behind the clock. He would make damned certain Johanna paid for her crime against him, but not yet. First he meant to find out exactly what she'd done with all his money. He shook his head. Children! He'd been played for a fool by three children and one blue-eyed hellion of a girl!

The door opened and Johanna stepped soundlessly into the main room, her hands clutching nervously at the stiff folds of her dress, feeling terribly uncomfortable wearing the scooped neckline edged by old lace that dipped toward the rounded fullness of her breasts. The décolletage was cut well within the bounds of propriety, but she was used to wearing loose shirts buttoned to her neck and baggy overalls. She felt exposed and vulnerable in the snug-fitting bodice that faithfully outlined her curves. "I . . . I'm ready."

Not at all immune to her loveliness, Tyler wouldn't allow his appreciation of her feminine appearance to show on his face. He didn't move from his place by the mantle. Instead he left his fingers resting inches away from the base of the clock, watching her for any reaction. He was not disappointed when he saw her eyes widen at the sight of his hand so close to the ivory peeping from behind the clock.

"Ah . . . er . . . Why are you staring at me like that?" She let out her pent-up breath in an almost audible sigh when Tyler slowly pulled his hand away from the clock and turned his back to the mantle.

Johanna had never felt such relief. Why had she not gotten rid of that revolver? She would bury it behind the barn, first chance she got!

"I'm sorry if I make you uncomfortable, *Jo,*" he gritted between his teeth. "I'm absolutely at a loss for words to describe my reaction to you. You are a woman of many roles and I am just beginning to understand how contrasting they are." The smile that turned up the corners of his mouth did not quite reach his eyes and Johanna shivered from the piercing gaze that cut through her.

He was behaving so differently. A short time ago, he had laughingly thrown her on the bed and threatened her to get dressed for the dance, his eyes full of amusement. She had prepared herself for more of his mocking male taunts but couldn't understand what had brought about the implacable set of his jaw, the cold storm in his eyes and the hard tension in his tall body. She felt cornered, as if at any minute he might spring at her.

He seemed to be wrestling with some violent emotion as he continued to stare at her. Finally, he stepped toward her and held out his arm. "To the dance, Cinderella. I haven't a couch-and-four so I'm afraid you'll have to make do riding double on Sarge. Of course, I'm sure an enterprising woman like yourself is prepared for any occasion."

Unable to make any sense out of his words or the stiff manner in which they were pronounced, Johanna allowed him to propel her outside, pausing only long enough to grab a knitted shawl along the way. Without ceremony, he tossed her up on his horse and mounted behind her, immediately kicking the horse into a jolting trot. Though he had placed her sideways in front of him and her seat on the horse's back was precarious, she was in no danger of falling, for Tyler's arm was clamped around her waist.

She tried to pull away from him but he tightened his grasp at her every movement. "You don't have to hold me so close!" she protested.

"Oh, but I enjoy holding you like this. Helps me remember what a soft feminine creature you are." As if to punctuate the mocking words that seemed to be spat from between his teeth, he moved his hand from her rib cage and covered her breast. She tried to move his hand away but he persisted in keeping it where he wanted it, his palm covering her hardening peak and his fingers rhythmically kneading her burgeoning fullness.

Using all her strength to pry his hand from her breast, she twisted slightly in order to see his face. "I demand that you stop mauling me! Just what kind of woman do you think I am?"

Her question was answered by a humorless chortle. "I don't think I know, but I'm certainly going to find out." Looking down into the pinched features of her face, he realized she was both furious and frightened. Not yet ready to confront her with his knowledge of her crime, he relaxed his grasp and let her slide his offending hand to her waist, his initial fury subsiding as cold reason took over. A time was coming when he wouldn't allow her to escape him as easily, a time that would occur very soon. To think he'd agonized for weeks over compromising her high moral standards, telling himself she deserved much more than he was prepared to give her. Ha! She deserved anything she got.

They rode the rest of the distance in silence, each lost in private jumbled thoughts. For Johanna, it was a journey of torture. Each time she took a breath, she could detect the scent of Tyler's soap and surmised that he had washed up and changed clothes just before coming to fetch her. His crisp white shirt strained across the breadth of his chest, its color in sharp contrast with his deep tan. Snug-fitting dark breeches, tucked into shiny brown boots, reached to his knees. Berdine's estimation of him as a fine figure of a man couldn't have been more apt.

The side of her breast brushed against the unyielding hardness of his chest with every stride of the horse, while the strength of his arms held her secure. She had been wrong about him. He was not a lazy dandy from the East. According to what she'd seen the day in his field, Tyler had thrown himself into farming, working just as hard as anyone. He was strong and willing to learn. Fritz's worshiping reports since that day had revealed that Tyler was maintaining the relentless pace she had witnessed. He was as committed to the land as she was.

Tyler's thoughts were far from the fields he had labored over during the past weeks; rather, he was replaying the day of the robbery. He could not have completely misjudged the Heinsmans, could he? Berdine had not taken part in the robbery, he was sure of that. He could not match her height or demeanor with any of the assailants he had mistaken for youths that fateful morning on the train. He figured it had to have been Fritz who did most of the talking, and Cordie must have been the one cowering by the doorway. He remembered her dropping the gun and her frightened whisper: "Sorry, Jo." The lushly curved young woman he held in his arms this minute had once held a gun on him, laughed at his helpless state and stolen his own revolver. No wonder she couldn't wait to get rid of him after the blizzard! He was probably damned lucky she had not recognized him as he lay nearly frozen on their doorstep. If she had, he doubted she would ever have taken him in.

The sound of fiddles and merry laughter could be heard long before Tyler and Johanna arrived at the new barn. Johanna grew even more uneasy, if that was possible, as they rode into the barnyard. Without a word, Tyler dismounted, tied his horse to the new hitching rail and reached his arms up to lift her down from Sarge's back. She shrank back for a moment but he clasped her waist firmly and set her on the ground. "What's the matter, now?" he inquired, lifting a sardonic brow.

"I . . . I don't know how to dance." Johanna admitted her failure in a low whisper, her face bent as she concentrated on making patterns in the dust with the toe of her moccasin.

Tyler hooted in self-satisfaction. "Then there's one more thing I just might know more about than you."

"It's never been important that I know how to dance." She brought her head up sharply and glared at him, showing the stubborn spirit he had come to expect from her.

"No?" He lifted one brow, then continued, "That's right. There are other things you're far more eager to learn." When his gray eyes dropped to the fitted bodice of her flowered calico dress, she pulled her shawl defensively over her breasts. "We both know you have yet to receive all of your lessons and I'm greatly looking forward to being your teacher."

Johanna would have liked nothing better than to smash a fist into his mocking mouth, but Berdine and David emerged from the lighted barn and joined them. "Johanna, how lovely you look," David complimented, his arm securely fastened around Berdine's waist as the couple advanced. "Is that a new dress?"

"Yes . . . I didn't want it but Berdine made it anyway." Her reply was sullen as she guiltily contemplated the source of the money that had paid for the pretty material.

Covering her sister's rudeness, Berdine said, "Oh, Tyler, I am glad you were able to persuade Johanna to join in the fun." Taking both Johanna's hands in her own, she pulled her into the light spilling from the opened barn doors. "Jo, you look so pretty, don't you think so, Tyler?"

"I'm almost speechless with awe, never having seen your sister in this sort of guise."

Johanna was getting used to Tyler's enigmatic statements, but Berdine's smile froze for a moment before David grabbed her hand and led her back to the frolicking.

Following suit, Tyler firmly encased Johanna's hand in his and started with long strides toward the barn, pausing only a moment at the entrance to lean down toward her. "You do look beautiful tonight, *Jo*. As do all the Heinsman women. It must have been a good year, for I see that all of you are attired in what appears to be new finery. Have you some special secret you'd care to divulge to a beginner on how to turn a fast profit?"

Chapter Ten

LIGHT FROM MORE THAN A DOZEN LANTERNS ILLUMINAT-
ed every corner of the new barn as brightly as if it
were midafternoon. Only the small black squares cut
into the walls for windows, which would someday be
covered with greased paper, indicated that the hour
was late. The lack of skill of the two fiddlers was more
than made up for by their enthusiasm in providing the
music for the prancing couples. Young and old alike
joined in the merriment as the dancing continued
throughout the evening hours and on into the night.
The weariness that the men and women felt by the
time the last roof shingle had been hammered into
place was all but forgotten as they celebrated the
completion of the barn and the official welcoming of
their new neighbor, Tyler Kendall, to the community.

Despite her wish to remain on the sidelines, Johanna had been whirled across and around the dirt floor again and again. Tyler had swiftly pulled her into the center of activity the moment they entered the barn. "Tonight, you're my lady, *Jo,*" he vowed, but within minutes she had been claimed by one new partner, then another, as the dancing progressed through endless do-si-do's, bows and curtsies. Glad for the respite from the challenging remarks Tyler had been issuing, she eventually relaxed and let herself get caught up in the festivities, finding that she needed no instruction in dancing. It was easy enough just to skip beside her partners and enjoy the fun, except for the end of each dance, when as if to remind her of his pledge, Tyler claimed her for the final swing of partners.

Johanna had never felt more relieved than when the two fiddlers finally laid down their instruments, announcing they were finished for the night. It was well past midnight and most of the food and drink spread out on sawhorse tables at the back of the barn was gone. Edging her way past the crowd collecting baskets and sleepy children, Johanna started for the open doors, hoping to find Fritz and the rest of her family, so they could be on their way home before she had to spend any more time in Tyler's company.

Glancing over her shoulder, she saw that Tyler was surrounded by well-wishers, his attention fully occupied by Pastor and Mrs. Braun, who were no doubt extending an invitation for him to join the congregation. She frowned. It seemed the entire population of Hemmington and the adjacent countryside had turned out for his barn raising and dance. There was no doubt about it—Tyler had been fully accepted into the community.

Johanna herself was no longer totally sure she wanted him to go away. She had never met anyone like him, never known a man who could start her pulses leaping by a single look from his dark gray eyes. She was frightened of the feelings that inundated her whenever she was near him, and she now wanted only to escape before he found her again. Looking about for any of her siblings, she spotted Berdine standing just beyond the doorway with David. Just as she started toward them, she was stopped by Mrs. Meeker.

"Johanna, I'm so glad you came. You look so nice in that dress. Blue is just the color for you." Clasping both of Johanna's hands, the woman successfully blocked her escape.

"Thank you, Mrs. Meeker," Johanna replied, nervously scanning the room for Tyler's tall form. He was no longer with the Pastor but she couldn't spot him elsewhere.

"Why, I was just telling John that I didn't know you when you first whirled by me," Mrs. Meeker declared enthusiastically. "Land's sakes, you been hiding all that beauty too long under those men's clothes you insist upon wearing most of the time. Time you started acting like a woman." The plump matronly woman pulled Johanna closer and whispered in her ear. "Looks like our new Mr. Kendall thinks you're mighty pretty, too. That man couldn't take his eyes off you all night. I hear you all rescued him from that last blizzard we had. Why, I just knew the minute I laid eyes on him that he'd be real glad to meet you Heinsman girls. Course, looks like our handsome young doctor may have staked a claim on your sister already. There ain't really nobody else round here who hasn't been taken. I'd say that Tyler Kendall'd make a mighty fine husband for a gal like you."

Johanna pulled away in embarrassment, "I . . . don't think he wants a wife, Miz Meeker. He . . ."

"Hush now, men never know what they want," Mrs. Meeker interrupted sagely. "We women just have to put the idea in their heads for 'em. I know you've had a hard time of it since your Pa died. Berdine told me you scraped together enough to pay off that second mortgage that was hanging over your head. Most folks thought you'd surely lose the farm, since there weren't a man to shoulder some of the work. I ain't told you this before, Johanna, but folks in Hemmington really admire how well you've managed without your Pa or Karl to look after you. A lot of us doubted it was possible but you and Berdine have made a go of the farm and kept your family together without asking help from anyone. You should be right proud."

She looked beyond Johanna's shoulder, then smiled broadly. "Why, Mr. Kendall, I was just telling Johanna here how glad we all are that you managed to persuade her to come to the dance. Every young girl deserves a good time once in a while and she's one of the prettiest girls in the county. Don't you think so?"

Johanna would have liked nothing better than to

dash out the door into the cover of darkness, but Jenny Meeker wouldn't loosen her hold until Tyler dropped a possessive hand over one of Johanna's shoulders. "Mrs. Meeker, I believe Johanna is possibly the most remarkable young woman I've ever met." Somehow anticipating her desire to take flight, his strong fingers tightened on her shoulder and she was forced to remain standing by his side. She kept her gaze downcast as if the trodden grass beneath her feet were the most interesting thing in the world, but a nudge from Jenny Meeker's elbow brought her head up just in time to catch the older woman's encouraging wink before she left to locate her husband and lead him away.

"I brought you some cider," Tyler explained as he placed a cup of amber liquid in one of her hands. "I thought you might be thirsty."

"Thank you," she murmured, wondering how much of Mrs. Meeker's speech he had overheard or if he'd read the matchmaking light in the woman's eyes. Swiftly returning her gaze to the ground, she turned slightly away from Tyler as she brought the cup to her lips. The sharp tang of the cider satisfied some of her thirst but completely failed to deaden her awareness of the large heavy hand on her shoulder or the warmth of Tyler's chest just inches away from her.

She drained the cup and Tyler instantly relieved her of it, placing it on one of the cross supports along the wall. "Let's get out of here. I've discovered some interesting things this evening and I want to talk to you." His command was delivered in a deep forceful tone, while he propelled Johanna through the open door and out into the darkness of the night.

"I don't see that we've got anything to talk about," she protested, as they passed several families wearily making their way toward their waiting wagons. Wrenching away from him, she whirled, but managed only one step back to the barn before Tyler grabbed her hand and started pulling her along behind him.

She might not think so but he had plenty to discuss with her. He'd discovered many things about her tonight and intended to confront her with them all. Finding out that she had led the gang who robbed him had made him violently angry but now he was suffering from conflicting responses. Part of him wanted to throttle her and the other to find a way to keep her safe and secure. She was far too impetuous and headstrong, and he feared that she might take desperate measures again but with disastrous results. She had stolen once and had gotten away without a scratch but he vowed it would be her last crime.

She tried to plant her feet solidly, but the smooth soles of her moccasins slipped in the damp grass and the unrelenting pull on her arm continued until she was forced to follow Tyler. "Shouldn't you be thanking these good people for coming to help you?" she asked breathlessly.

"I've already done that," was his curt response as he continued with long strides to lead her beyond the people and wagons, nodding and acknowledging the greetings of several as they passed.

"I need to find my family," she insisted. "They'll be looking for me."

"No, they won't. Fritz has already left with your little sisters."

"Without me?"

He stopped so suddenly that she ran into his back and he whirled around to steady her, keeping his hands firmly on her shoulders. "Amy fell asleep and Cordie could barely keep her eyes open. I told Fritz I'd take you home and David is taking Berdine."

"I'll just get a ride with them, then." Searching around in the darkness, Johanna frantically tried to locate her sister.

"I don't think so, look over there." He turned her slightly, sliding an arm around her waist, and pointed to a couple locked in each other's arms not far away. "I think one Heinsman woman is all David wants tonight. I know one is more than enough for me."

"I . . . I'll . . ."

"You'll go home with me," he announced firmly.

She shrank away from contact and again started toward her sister when she saw the couple break apart. "Let me go!" She managed to free herself from Tyler's grasp, but stopped in her tracks when she heard the agonized tone in Berdine's voice.

"I can't, David. I can't leave the family."

"Darling, I love you," David beseeched. "I want you to be my wife."

"Oh, David, I want that too, but unless we live at the farm, it's just not possible."

Johanna took a step backward, realizing the conversation she was overhearing was intensely personal. How embarrassed Berdine and David would be if they knew she could hear them. Her retreat, however, didn't come soon enough, for at that instant David's usually calm voice grew louder as he continued to plead with her sister.

"We've been over this before. I have to live in Hemmington—it's centrally located and I'm more accessible there. I'm a doctor, Berdine, not a farmer."

"I know that, but you know why I can't stay in town," Berdine insisted. "I can't leave Cordie and Amy. They need a woman to look after them."

"They have Johanna."

"Johanna has enough on her shoulders working the land. She can care for the animals and the fields but knows nothing about running a household. If I leave, there will be no one to see to the children's welfare— their school lessons and clothes, not even the cooking. Johanna can barely boil water. Mama often said she should have been born a boy for all the interest she shows in womanly things. She and Fritz handle the outdoor work and I'm in charge of the house. Don't you see, David? I can't leave my family. They need a grown woman to care for them. Johanna behaves more like a man than a woman. She just couldn't handle everything if I got married and moved away from home."

Johanna's cheeks burned with humiliation. Tyler had overheard Berdine's disparaging estimation of her as clearly as she. Unable to face him, she hiked up her skirts and started running. Berdine was right, but why did it suddenly hurt so much to hear the truth about herself? Hadn't she always wished she'd been born a boy? Didn't she pride herself on being able to work as hard as Fritz?

Ever since Karl's death, she'd tried to fill the void, prove to her father that she was as great an asset as another son would have been. Instead of bringing the joy she had hoped for into her father's eyes, he had died still mourning Karl and now, even though she'd taken Pa's place in the fields, she was nothing but an albatross hanging around her sister's neck. Because of her, Berdine felt she couldn't marry the man she loved.

Hot tears blurred her vision as she ran, oblivious to direction, to the sound of heavy boots following her. Stumbling as her racing feet slipped in the dew-moistened grass, she would have fallen if two strong arms hadn't caught her around the waist. Struggling, she cried, "Let me go!"

Tyler locked his arms around her, holding her tight against his chest. Held securely in the circle of his arms, she lost the last of her control and gave in to the sobs that tightened her throat. Tyler started swaying gently as if he were comforting a child. No one had held her like this in so long, maybe not since Ma had died. Tears she hadn't been able to shed when Karl had been killed, grief for her father who had died a broken man—all of it struck her now, like a dam bursting over her head.

She responded to the soft crooning in her ear and turned toward the strength that held her, burying her face into Tyler's shoulder, weeping bitterly as she clung to him. "I . . . I had to . . . had to save the land . . . There wasn't anybody else."

"I know. I know," Tyler murmured into her hair, stroking her back.

"I can do it. I can take proper care of Cordie and Amy. I'm a woman, too," she moaned in anguish.

Overcome by a fierce surge of protectiveness, Tyler shuddered and wrapped her closer in his arms. "Oh God, Johanna, don't you think I know that?" He pressed his lips in her hair, breathing deeply of the fresh scent that clung to the silken strands.

His words brought her head up and she looked into his face. "What?" she asked as if realizing for the first time who had been comforting her. "How?" she breathed in wonder at the softened warmth of his gaze.

Smoothing the damp tendrils away from her face, Tyler cradled her chin in his palm. "I told you before that you are a lot of woman, Johanna Heinsman." He bent his head toward hers and brushed his lips gently across her mouth. He'd intended to do no more until a soft sigh escaped her lips and she tightened her arms around his waist.

"Show me I'm a woman, Tyler," she entreated, distraught shivers wracking her slender figure.

He'd lost most of his anger with her after hearing Jenny Meeker's remarks about her family's financial situation after the death of their father, and he was rapidly losing the rest as she clung to him till his senses were attuned to nothing but her womanly body pressed against his. His certainty of her innocence still prevented him from pushing her down on the ground and fulfilling her tremulous request. "Johanna, you don't mean that. You don't know what you're asking."

"Don't you want me?" she cried. "I know I'm not

like the women you're used to. I'm not feminine, I'm not . . ." Her voice broke and she turned away, her shoulders shaking.

Her crestfallen expression and the sight of her usually proud shoulders slumped in defeat were his undoing. He pulled her back into his arms. His mouth covered hers and his tongue sought and received entrance. Johanna strained toward him, needing the feel of his masculine body against her, assured by the crushing strength of his arms around her.

She returned his kiss without restraint, her tongue following his lead and finding all the secrets of his mouth until he lifted his head slightly away from hers, then buried his face in the hollow between her neck and shoulder. "I want you, Johanna. God, how I want you." His words were muffled against her skin and he placed one hand over her skirt-covered bottom, pulling her against the stiffened evidence of his need for her. She arched into him, raising her arms to entwine around his neck, tugging gently at his hair to draw his lips back to hers.

Tyler hungrily took all she was offering, running his hands over her body until the need to possess her completely was so overwhelming he lifted her into his arms and started walking steadily back to the now dimly lit barn. Only his own lantern shed a faint guiding light through the cut-out windows as he strode across the grass, all the other lamps having long since been extinguished and taken home by their departed owners.

Johanna nestled her head against his shoulder, pressing her lips into the warmth of his throat just as his lips occasionally brushed against her hair, forehead and eyes, pausing repeatedly to capture her lips. Her soft sighs joined the chirping of the crickets in the fields beyond and were accompanied by the swishing sound of Tyler's boots striding through the tall bluestem grass. "Do you really want me?" she asked dreamily between kisses.

Tyler stopped in the now deserted barnyard, even David Lloyd's buggy having left. Carefully easing his arm from beneath Johanna's thighs, he lowered her feet to the ground. "I want you, Johanna. I want to show you that you're more woman than any man could need. Are you sure that's what you want?" His query cost him every ounce of restraint he possessed, but he knew he'd damn himself forever if he didn't offer her one final chance to say no.

"Yes, Tyler," Johanna breathed, "Oh yes."

Her heartfelt words swept away the last of his restraint. Scooping her back up in his arms, he strode into the barn. Moments later, he had settled her on a bed of thick blankets he'd rolled onto the floor in one corner. He left her for a few seconds to fetch the lantern, which he placed a few yards from the bed roll. He turned down the flame till it cast only a pale glow over the blankets, then came back to her, going down on his knees in front of her. "Let me make love to you, Johanna," he murmured, capturing her eyes with his. "Let me erase the tears in those beautiful blue eyes."

Tenderly, he reached out with one hand, gently stroking her cheek and leaning forward until his mouth hovered above hers. He gazed deeply into her eyes as if seeking the answer to some question, and only when it seemed he had found the answer he sought, did he claim her softly parted lips. He kissed her thoroughly, deeply, drinking in the sweet taste of her.

The world began swimming around her as Johanna felt her body responding to the warm probing of his tongue. Her tongue met his and she satisfied her own thirst for him. Tyler emitted a deep-throated groan and gathered her close, running his hands gently down her spine, then splayed his hands across her back, pressing her soft body into his.

Johanna trembled, a tide of urgency rising from the deepest recesses of her body. She wrapped her arms around him, threaded her fingertips through the springy waves at the nape of his strong neck, mindless of anything but the aching need for fulfillment in Tyler's arms. When she felt the warmth of his breath against her neck and the press of his lips against her tender flesh above the neckline of her dress, she arched her hips into his, excited further by the hardness she found there.

Tyler's hands shook as he set her slightly away from him, impatiently slipped the row of buttons down the front of her dress from the fragile crocheted loops and pulled the garment over her head. "Look at me, Johanna," he coaxed in a gentle tone. When her lashes lifted, he caught his breath in reaction to the depth of passion he saw in her darkened indigo eyes. He lifted her hands to his shirt and silently instructed her to undress him, then tugged at the ribbon of her camisole.

Their concurrent disrobing was synchronized between kisses and caresses until they lay facing each other on the blanket, the flickering lamplight throwing a golden glow across their naked bodies. Tyler ran a hand from her shoulder to her thigh, skimmed across her stomach and up to cradle one breast in his palm. "You're exquisite," he declared in a deep-throated rasp, then lowered his head to her breast, taking one rose-tipped peak into his mouth.

Johanna writhed beneath the assault of his tongue curling around her nipple, his lips gently tugging at the throbbing tip while his fingertips duplicated the action at the swollen bud of her other breast. Her hands closed over his shoulders, kneading the hardened muscles beneath her fingers. "Tyler," she urged unwittingly with her husky pronouncement of his name and the rhythmic clenching of her hands at his shoulders.

His mouth continued to feast on her silken curves, sliding moistly between her breasts and down to her stomach while his hands swept to her inner thighs. Mindful of her innocence, he stroked her gently but ever closer to the golden triangle between her thighs. When at last his fingertips delved into the very core of her, she was moist and ready for the preliminary invasion. Gently, he prepared her for his possession, sending exquisite torrents of pleasure through her body until Johanna thrust her pelvis upward, stiffened, then shuddered at the pinnacle where his expertise had led her.

She collapsed in his arms, his name a breathless sigh on her lips as she gazed up into his face. Seeing the tension revealed by the taut lines of his features, she curved her palms to his cheeks, lightly caressing his temples with her fingertips. He turned his head, pressing his mouth into her palm, "That was only lesson number one," he explained. "You haven't met me halfway, yet."

A frown of confusion was her response but it was met by Tyler's tender smile, accompanied by light kisses across her forehead. He shifted his position until she felt his turgid virility push against the softness of her stomach. At first she was startled, her limited knowledge not preparing her for the dramatic change in his body or the reason for it. Involuntarily, she cringed away but Tyler covered her mouth with his, thrusting his tongue in and out as he caught her hand and brought it to his manhood. He closed Johanna's fingers around the hot, throbbing hardness before she could shy away and guided her until she understood how to pleasure him. His hands skimmed over her body, paused to knead her breasts and then swept down to part her thighs.

The satisfaction Johanna had enjoyed had eased the overwhelming urgency controlling her earlier reactions, and she eagerly explored the new terrain he offered. Her confidence soared when he tore his mouth from hers and buried his face between her breasts. "Good . . . so good," he complimented as his fingers slid inside her again, stroking until she was wild with the pleasure of it. Rising above her, he knelt between her thighs, "Come with me, Johanna. Come with me."

"Yes . . . oh yes," she cried huskily as he pressed

his velvet-tipped shaft to her burning entrance. Her hands swept restlessly over the bunched muscles of his back, digging for purchase as little mewing cries burst from her mouth. His hands lifted her to complete their union and slowly entered her tight virgin territory, pausing at the threshold of the final barrier.

"Trust me," he crooned and would have waited for her body to accommodate itself to his, but it was Johanna who rose against him, driving him through the barrier and deeply into the rich cavern beyond. Catching her sharp cry with his kiss, he was ablaze with need for her, unable to stop the rapidly escalating pace she had unconsciously inspired. Again and again he plunged and she met his every thrust, their mating melding them into one being, a mutual possession that carried them to an explosive climax.

Their damp bodies lay intertwined as harsh breathing slowed to normal rhythm, and they drifted languidly down from the summit they had reached, replete in each other's arms.

"You met me more than halfway," Tyler whispered intimately as he brushed wisps of flaxen silk away from her face. He felt humbled at the experience they had just shared. He had been lost within her, more aroused than ever before and finding more satisfaction than he'd ever known, but still there was more. The first feeling of complete peace he had known for years. "Don't ever doubt yourself. You are a woman, more than even I dreamed."

Johanna was unable to identify her awe with words. For possibly the first time in her life, she was glad to be a woman. She glowed with the aftermath of their lovemaking, but beyond that was the innate knowledge that what she saw in Tyler's velvety gray eyes was approval and admiration. She felt an acute sense of loss when he eased himself from her but when he nestled her securely in his arms, she cuddled like a contented kitten in the warmth of his body.

Tyler forced himself out of the drowsy contentment that threatened to lead to sleep. "We have to get you home." He pressed a kiss on her forehead and tightened his arms around her for only a moment before setting her away from him and rising shakily to his knees. The responsibility for their actions swept over him as he interpreted the beginnings of regret in Johanna's expression. "Don't," he commanded softly as she rolled away from his gaze. "Don't be ashamed of what you are and never for what just happened."

Johanna couldn't meet his eyes. She fumbled for her scattered garments and with shaking fingers pulled on her undergarments. Her own honesty kept her from denying that she had enjoyed every moment, but the years of righteous training overshadowed the pleasure of it and brought home with chilling clarity the enormity of what had just happened. The rightness of giving herself totally to Tyler warred with the sermons she had heard expounding upon the sinful weakness of the flesh.

She jumped when Tyler touched her shoulder and stiffened when he wrapped his arms around her. "You're not a wicked woman, Johanna."

"How . . . how did you . . . ?" She turned up her face, raising wondering eyes.

"I said we knew each other very well. It was easy to

surmise what was going through your head just now. I know you and your family well enough to guess that you've been warned of the sins of the flesh." He gathered her closer, stroking her back with a gentling touch as he tried to comfort her for the second time in the course of a few hours.

"I said I wanted to court you and I still do. I won't apologize for taking advantage of you tonight. It was inevitable that we make love. It only happened sooner than propriety might dictate." He was surprised by the extent of the gratification he experienced when he felt her relax against him.

Johanna would have stayed secure in his arms for much longer, but Tyler's fingers replacing the little buttons of her dress into their fragile loops brought her back to reality. How considerate and tender he could be—in such contrast to the harsh taunting mood that had dominated his attitude during the early part of their evening.

She stepped away from him. "Why were you so angry with me earlier tonight?"

"It doesn't matter, now."

"But . . ."

He placed a silencing finger over her lips. "We'll talk about it some other time. You've had enough to deal with for now." He looked around the darkened barn as if searching for something, then strode away in the darkness, returning scant moments later with her shawl. With a lopsided grin, he draped it around her shoulders, then scooped up the lantern and guided her out of the barn. "As I said before, we need to get you home."

For Johanna, the ride home was far too short. This time there was no coldness in the strong arms that held her secure, only a warm firm possession. Her misgivings were eased somewhat by the soothing words he offered and the tenderness in his eyes when he dismounted and lifted her down from the horse. He kept his arms around her and pulled her close, lowering his head to bestow one last kiss on her waiting lips.

"Sleep well, my Johanna," he breathed against her mouth, then turned reluctantly back to his waiting horse.

Johanna didn't enter the quiet darkened cabin until long after she had returned his wave and watched him disappear into the darkness of the night. Wrapping her arms around herself, she stared up into the star-studded sky, listening to the fading sound of hooves prancing on the hard-packed earth as the big bay stallion carried Tyler away. "My Johanna." How good that sounded! With the feel of his kisses still fresh on her bruised lips and the solace of his reassurances calming her racing pulses, she crept quietly to her bed, wanting to spend what little remained of the night in dreaming of Tyler.

Sleep did not come readily as her body felt a renewal of tension with every thought of the discoveries she had found in Tyler's arms. Every inch of her longed to be back in his arms and she hugged the pillow to her breast, its softness a poor substitute for the hard male body that, not long before, had been pressed to hers.

Chapter Eleven

A BRIGHT SHAFT OF SUNLIGHT FILTERED THROUGH
open window of the church, streaming across
dusty floor and highlighting the small wooden cr
that stood in the center of a white linen-covered tab
Beside the cross lay a worn leather Bible opened
the sixty-fifth Psalm, though Pastor Braun could re
the verse from memory and never once looked do
as he stood before the simple altar. When he
finished reciting, he offered a prayer for a bount
harvest, the same prayer he uttered for his r
parishioners every week as the summer progresse
Johanna bowed her head, adding her own ferv
plea to the Pastor's, knowing a good harvest was
only thing that would enable her family to keep
with the rising costs of farming their land. Finger

the thin faded material of her brown gingham dress, she prayed that the harvest would yield enough surplus to show a profit.

When eventually the long prayer was over, Johanna peeped around the side of her frayed yellow bonnet and smiled across at Berdine, who occupied the other end of the long wooden bench, but her sister didn't return the smile. Instead, Berdine glanced sightlessly away, obviously preoccupied with other thoughts, her expression sad. Having overheard Berdine's conversation with David the night before, Johanna had a good idea what was troubling her sister, and she was determined to do something about it. There had to be some way Berdine could marry David, despite her misgivings over leaving the family in Johanna's hands.

"Today we welcome a new member to our congregation," Pastor Braun announced from the crudely fashioned oak pulpit. "Will you stand for a moment, Tyler Kendall?"

Like everyone else in the congregation, Johanna swiveled in her seat until she sighted Tyler. She had completely forgotten that he'd been invited to the service! There in the back of the room, he rose to his feet, acknowledging the Pastor's proclamation with a discomfited smile. Wearing a clean pair of denim breeches and a dark cotton shirt, he looked as much a farmer as any of the other sun-browned men in the room, but Johanna knew he was not like any of them.

Holding his hat over his chest with one large hand, he nodded at the friendly faces seated around him, then seemingly uncomfortable with the attention he was receiving, sat back down. His eyes searched the congregation, coming to rest on Johanna, but before registering any recognition, she quickly faced the front of the church.

Immediately thereafter, Pastor Braun called for a hymn and everyone stood, joining their voices in song. Knowing she was probably imagining it, Johanna thought she could discern Tyler's deep tones from amongst the voices, and the sound of it caused her to lose her place several times as she attempted to follow the words. Receiving a sharp jab in the side from Fritz when she mistakingly sang the wrong phrase at the close of the hymn, she swiftly sat down on the bench, her cheeks burning with embarrassment as her family bestowed their visual chastisement on her for the lapse.

All during Pastor Braun's sermon, Johanna thought of nothing else but Tyler, wondering what she should say to him the next time they met, which would probably be right after the service. How could she face him? How could she act as if nothing had happened? What if anyone who saw them together was able to tell what they had done the night before? How could she live with the shame? Would the righteous members of the congregation have welcomed Tyler so readily into their fold if they knew that he'd deflowered a virgin outside the bonds of matrimony? She barely heard the closing prayers as she recalled the tumultuous pleasure she had discovered in Tyler's arms the night before, finally losing her battle with the guilt that had grown steadily larger in the bright morning sun. Shame over the magnitude of the sin she'd willingly committed with him overwhelmed her as the Sunday service came to a close.

Wanting nothing more than to quickly get back to their wagon and begin the trip home, Johanna mechanically offered the usual casual greetings to friends and neighbors as she followed her family out of the church. She lost sight of the others when she was stopped by the schoolmarm, who politely inquired how the family was progressing with their lessons. Johanna couldn't see a single member of her family by the time she made it to the door. She could barely mumble a few words as she shook hands with Pastor Braun, then hurried down the steps, certain he had read the sinful knowledge she feared was revealed in her eyes.

"Berdine has invited me for dinner, Johanna." Tyler joined her at the bottom. Adjusting his stride to hers as she walked briskly toward her wagon, he offered, "If you wait up a minute, I can tie Sarge to the back of your wagon and drive your family home."

Refusing to look at him, Johanna stammered, breathlessly, "It . . . it's best you ride over later. Berdine likes a few minutes to get prepared when company's coming. We've left a few things undone. She won't want to make a bad impression."

Not waiting for his response, she quickly climbed up on the wagon, grabbing for the reins. "Hurry on now, Amy, Fritz. Get in the wagon, Cordie," she called to her brother and sisters who were clustered with their friends near the church.

"It doesn't appear as if Berdine is unduly concerned about my visit," Tyler said, pointing to where David had parked his buggy. "It looks like she and David will be riding out to the farm together, so why shouldn't we?"

Momentarily taken aback by the sight of her sister's smiling face and the sound of her laughter as David handed her up into his buggy, Johanna spoke without thinking. "I thought they were fighting? Is David coming for dinner too?"

"He is," Tyler replied, answering her unspoken question. "Lovers often fight, Johanna, but it doesn't prevent them from wanting to be together."

"Lovers!" Johanna gasped, immediately clasping her hands over her mouth for fear someone nearby might have heard her. Turning horrified eyes on Tyler, she lowered her voice. "My sister and David are not lovers. They . . . they'd never do what . . ."

"What we did?" he inquired, a steely light invading his eyes. "Don't be too sure about that, Johanna. Your devout older sister is quite human and so is the good doctor."

At her doubting expression, Tyler laughed cynically. "When a man finds a woman he wants, the forces of nature take over. Last night you found how that can happen. I think Berdine and David may have discovered the same thing."

"Oh, no!" Johanna exclaimed, fearing that Tyler might very well be right and terrified by the possibility. "This is even worse than I thought. I'll have to do something and soon."

"Johanna?" Tyler warned, distrusting the pensive look on her face, recognizing the glint of determination in her piercing blue eyes. "What goes on between your sister and David is none of your business. Is that clear? When left alone, most problems resolve themselves."

"If I believed that, we wouldn't even have a roof over our heads! When something goes wrong in our family, it's my duty to fix it. I've handled worse problems than this. And you have no right to tell me what I can and cannot do," Johanna snapped irritably, as she searched her mind for some way to erase Berdine's reasons for not getting married, fearing her sister might suffer the humiliation of conceiving a child out of wedlock, if she delayed marrying David much longer.

Her features were set in the resolute expression that Tyler knew he would have seen if she hadn't been wearing a scarf over her face the day of the robbery. He knew if she had made up her mind to involve herself in Berdine's problems, he would be hard put to convince her that her meddling could cause a permanent break between Berdine and David.

As Cordie and Amy scrambled into the back of the wagon and Fritz climbed up on the wagon seat, taking the reins away from her, Johanna's attention was diverted and she didn't see the brooding look on Tyler's face. "Let's go," Fritz decreed enthusiastically. "I can almost smell that fried chicken from here. Follow us, Tyler. You ain't tasted heaven till you've swallowed a hunk of Berdie's green apple pie."

Camouflaging much darker thoughts, Tyler grinned, his caressing dark eyes lingering on Johanna. "When you're older, son, you'll find you can taste heaven in places that have nothing to do with food."

He turned away, striding toward his horse, but after taking a few steps seemed to make up his mind about something and quickly turned back. "Johanna! You talk to me before you start 'fixing' anything. I'm not so sure I approve of your methods. You tend to plunge in head first without thinking of the consequences."

Johanna's eyes went wide. The color drained from her face but Tyler swiftly restored her equilibrium. "Remember our little skirmish in the loft? Push someone too far and it's you who'll pay the price."

"I don't recall," Johanna insisted half-heartedly, so thankful he was referring to something other than the robbery that she didn't sound a bit convincing.

He obviously didn't think so either as he decreed mockingly, "Then it will be my pleasure to refresh your memory. May I suggest this afternoon after dinner?"

"That won't be necessary," Johanna retorted tartly. For the moment she was more disturbed by Tyler's outrageous suggestion than the problematic situation between Berdine and David. Her fiery blush prompted a loud chorus of giggles from the two girls seated in the back of the wagon, so she didn't see the triumphant expression on Tyler's face. "Start up the horses, Fritz," she ordered sharply. "Berdine and David have already left for home."

During the ensuing wagon ride, which seemed to take much longer than usual, Johanna discovered how it felt to be the subject of her siblings' outrageous teasing. While Amy and Cordie made faces, mimicking Johanna's supposedly lovesick expressions whenever she viewed Tyler, Fritz taunted her about mooning after him, making the same remarks she'd often heard him say to Berdine about David. When he laughingly pronounced that the roses in her cheeks were most likely caused by spooning in the moonlight after Tyler's barn raising, she had had enough and soundly boxed his ears. "Don't you dare say such things in front of another soul, Frederick Drexel Heinsman, or I'll beat you from here to Sunday."

Berdine had never resorted to physical retaliation, but Johanna was not so patient or forgiving as her gentle older sister. Satisfied with the chastened silence that descended over the wagon following her punishing attack on Fritz, she intoned, "And that goes for you girls, too."

Left in peace, she gave a dismissing shrug of her shoulders and refocused her thoughts on solving the problem of Berdine. Even after recalling Tyler's words about the natural way of things between men and women, she couldn't quite reconcile herself to the possibility of Berdine giving in to any weakness of the flesh. I'm the one who did that, she admitted in self-disgust, and with a man who could have me put in jail if he ever finds out what I've done to him.

No, it wasn't Berdine who had to worry about the possibility of conceiving a child out of wedlock, but herself. The thought that she might be carrying Tyler's baby prompted another one that was almost too frightening to consider. The blood drained from her cheeks but she forced herself to think calmly, rationally. Everyone would expect Tyler to marry her if she were pregnant. Would her family think so too? What of his? What would the Kendalls of Boston think of their son marrying a farm girl?

She couldn't waste time contemplating the opinion of people she knew nothing about, and besides they were far away. It was only those people around her that she must consider right now. Her family truly liked Tyler, and Berdine had pointed out to her that he needed a wife. Everyone in the family, excepting herself, seemed to have forgotten what they'd done to him.

Recalling a newspaper article she'd read, she came up with the best possible motive yet for marrying Tyler. The article had recounted a trial of a man accused of murder. The only witness to the crime had been the man's wife and the courts didn't allow a wife to testify against her husband. Since that was true, wouldn't it follow that a man couldn't testify against his wife? If she married Tyler, he couldn't testify against her and since he was the only witness to the crime, nothing could be done about it. Marrying him would solve everyone's problems.

The longer she thought about it, the more the idea made sense. Tyler was a strong man and his hard work so far indicated that he was determined to make a success of his farm. He owned a prime section of land and needed someone to help work it, someone to care for his needs. Why not a wife who came complete with a family of farm hands?

She could learn to cook, to sew and look after his home properly. She already knew quite a lot about such things but hadn't devoted much time to them because there were far more interesting and challenging tasks to be undertaken out of doors on the land and with the animals. Forcing herself into the role of a conventional wife wouldn't be easy, but the sacrifice would be worth it if she could secure a happy future for her family. Besides, she would no longer suffer from guilt. She would be an asset to Tyler and make up to him for what she had stolen.

She made her decision, then thought of another problem standing in the way. Would Tyler want to marry her? Johanna Heinsman? He had said he planned to court her and last night she had learned he was an expert at lovemaking. Back East, he must have had his choice of several beautiful, refined women. She was certainly nothing like the society women he had left behind in Boston. She wasn't small and feminine, didn't have elegant manners. Rather than the soft white hands of a lady she had the strong, capable, workworn fingers of a farmer. Yet that day in the field his words had told her that she represented something he felt was missing in his life.

He had enjoyed making love to her, had even said she was beautiful. He wouldn't find many marriageable women in Nebraska and a man needed a wife. She was just as good a choice as any, perhaps better. She could teach him several things about farming that he'd need to know in order to make a success of it.

I'll make him a business proposition he'd be a fool to refuse. Of course, if her scheme was going to work she would have to make sure her family believed she had fallen in love with him and he with her. That way, no one would guess that it was a marriage of convenience, that is, no one but herself and Tyler.

She refused to contemplate the exciting prospect of sharing Tyler's bed on an ongoing basis, telling herself that she'd only submit out of wifely duty and for no other reason. Anyone who had grown up on a farm knew that producing sturdy children was the only way to ensure the future of the land. A primitive gush of awareness flooded her loins as she remembered the power in Tyler's body. His hard muscles and inherent virility gave her every reason to believe that he would sire strong sons.

Deciding the first step in her plan was to convince Berdine that she could make herself useful in the kitchen, Johanna joined her in the lean-to as soon as they had all arrived home. While David and Tyler stayed outside to enjoy a pipe of smoking tobacco, Johanna helped Berdine and Cordie prepare the meal which would be served outdoors, laid out on a long table set up between two cottonwood trees in the yard. Much to her surprise, she discovered there was a rewarding sense of pride in serving up food to an appreciative, though small, gathering of anxiously hungry males. Both Tyler and David appreciatively eyed the fresh brown bread, huge platter of crisply fried chicken, buttered potatoes, greens, rice pudding, and Berdine's green apple pie as if they'd been offered treasures fit for a king.

Not quite knowing how it was arranged, Johanna found herself seated between Tyler and Fritz as Berdine asked David to say grace over their meal. After the food was passed, conversation turned to mundane things, but Johanna didn't offer more than a few words. Just as in church that morning, she was aware of little else but Tyler. She could feel the warmth of his thigh pressing against hers beneath the table, their shoulders brushing as he reached for a second helping of some dish. After last night she was more aware of him than ever, noticing every detail as if all of her senses were tuned with expert precision to his presence.

With every breath she took, she smelled the sun-kissed tang of his skin, the rich smell of his tobacco, and the clean aroma of soap. She noted the dark golden hairs on the back of his hands as he lifted his fork, the tensed muscle of his forearm whenever he turned his wrist. The sound of his low voice as he responded to a question seemed to set off a sensual reverberation deep in her stomach, a thrilling sensation that effectively destroyed her appetite. "I'll start clearing," she stated, standing up from the bench.

"Some of us haven't finished yet, Johanna." Berdine gestured to David, who was just sliding another large piece of pie onto his plate.

"I've finished," Tyler inserted, reaching out and taking Johanna's hand before she could step over the bench and leave the table. "Why don't Johanna and I take a walk and leave the rest of you to finish what's left of this wonderful feast? I've wolfed down more than my share already." He patted his middle to illustrate his words, though his belly was as flat as always.

"Do that, Tyler." David pounced on the suggestion much too quickly for Johanna's piece of mind. Evidently, David was hoping for an alliance between her and Tyler. "And don't worry about cleaning up, Johanna," he assured. "We can take care of things— once I'm absolutely certain there's no more pie."

"Cordie and I don't have beaus calling on us," Amy supplied, adding to Johanna's suspicion that everyone hoped she was falling in love with Tyler. Jumping to her feet, the child began scraping the plates in front of her. "We'll do the clearing so's you two can properly entertain."

"Much obliged, Amy," David said politely, suppressing an amused grin. "See, Tyler? Even our young Nebraska women know how to properly entertain gentleman callers."

"And it's greatly appreciated," Tyler pronounced, his voice taking on the stiff accent of an Eastern gentleman. "So if you ladies and gentlemen will kindly excuse us, we shall commence with our promenade of the grounds."

As Johanna was politely led away, she could hear Amy's puzzled question. "What's a promenade, Berdie? And what's commencing?"

Berdine's answer was muffled by David's loud laughter, but Johanna didn't find Tyler's words that amusing. His ability to use cultured speech only made her more aware of the vast differences between them. He was a city man, a worldly man with experience in things she'd probably never have reason to learn all of her life. Even for the sake of securing her family's well-being, could she consider spending the rest of her days as Tyler's wife? Not realizing that Tyler was placing an entirely different interpretation on her brooding silence, Johanna continued her private musings, trying to rationalize away her fear of marriage to the man.

They were alone and she knew that she had been given the perfect opportunity to present her proposal to him but she couldn't seem to find the right words to broach the subject. After all, what did she really know about him? He'd come to Nebraska for reasons he had not seen fit to divulge to anyone. There was a family she knew nothing about back in Boston. She didn't even know if he had any brothers and sisters or if both his parents were still living. What had he left behind? Had there been a sweetheart? Was that why he was working so hard? Was it to hasten the time when he could send for her? No, that couldn't be it. Surely, Tyler wouldn't be toying with her if there was someone else.

It was a hot summer day, the sky as bright and clear as blue glass. As they walked along, covering a good distance of grassy terrain, Johanna was unaware that they were approaching the riverbank until she felt the softened ground under her feet. Still preoccupied with her own thoughts, she sat down on the ground, intending to remove her shoes so she could wade in the cool water.

"What are you doing?" Tyler sat down next to her, surprise and curiosity evident in his expression.

"I'm taking off my shoes," Johanna replied, unreasonably annoyed with him for snapping her out of her reverie. "What does it look like?"

One slashing brown brow rose in question. "Do you plan to remove anything else or shouldn't I hope for that much good fortune?"

Johanna emitted a deep sigh. Ever since they'd met he'd made such outrageous remarks to her. Did he do it to make her lose her temper or to continually remind her that she was a woman and he a man who desired her body. Did he behave this way with all women or only with her? "Why do you say things like that to me, Tyler?" she asked quietly. "Is it because I wasn't raised in a fancy home so you don't consider me a lady?" Her blue eyes fixed on his face, for she needed an answer to this question and many others before she risked posing the proposition that might tie her to him for life. She could never live with a man who considered her a woman of loose morals. Was that the result of their lovemaking? Did he now feel he could make ribald comments without offending her? No. He had made suggestive remarks to her from the beginning. Did her sinful nature show in her features?

Tyler was taken aback by the heartwrenching sincerity in her tone. Being forced to think about his reasons for continually baiting her, he could come up with very few that made much sense, even to him. Unfamiliar with how to respond to a woman who demanded an honest explanation of his motives, he didn't quite know what to say. Finally, unable to help himself, he replied in a way he hoped would erase the frightened look in her beautiful eyes. "You are very much a lady, Johanna. And that isn't something a woman can learn to be, it's bred into her. It's there on the inside, no matter where she lives or how she's been raised. I guess I enjoy teasing you because I love the color of your blush and because you provoked my temper."

"I haven't said one word," Johanna cried, not showing how pleased she was with his estimation of her. "How can I have made you angry?"

"Last night we experienced something wonderful together, did we not?"

Her long hesitation ended as soon as Johanna noted the gathering storm in his gray eyes. "Yes."

"Then tell me why you wouldn't look at me this morning in church? Why you reacted to my coming here for dinner as if someone had told you the devil himself had been invited into your home? Why you barely said two words during the meal?"

Johanna felt he deserved an honest answer, even when she knew that she might eventually have to attack him with her feelings in order to gain his acceptance of her proposal. "I . . . I guess I was afraid that people could look at us and know our sin."

"Dammit, Johanna!" Tyler came up on his knees and pulled off one of her shoes, then the other. "I thought we got through all this nonsense last night. We both wanted it and there was nothing sordid or sinful about it." Quelling any interruption from her with a threatening glare, he went on, "It's probably going to happen again so you'd better resign yourself to accepting it. There is something between us that doesn't consider the conventions and until we get it out of our systems or make some sense of it, nothing will change that fact. Believe me, I don't like it any better than you."

With tense angry movements he pulled off his own boots, rolled up his pant legs, then jumped to his feet, pulling her up with one hand. Half-dragging her behind him, he strode toward the river. "Let's cool off. It may not seem like it, Johanna, but I'm trying my level best to do things your way, when what I'd like to do is strip off your clothes and take you right here on the riverbank. Furthermore, I know you'd enjoy that just as much as I would."

Certain it would be wise to keep her mouth shut until he'd calmed down somewhat, Johanna barely had enough time to hike up her skirts before stumbling into the water. Without saying a word, she waited for his anger to subside. After a few moments, his long strides shortened so she was able to keep up with him, but neither one was enjoying the cooling frolic in the slow-moving water. The silence that had been there during the beginning of their walk was back again, neither of them speaking, as hand in hand they waded along the meandering banks of the muddy river.

Although Tyler's terse speech had certainly not been a declaration of love, Johanna couldn't doubt the male frustration that lay behind the words. He still wanted her and wanted her badly. This might be her only chance to take advantage of that need. Now, before he got her out of his system. She wondered how he would react when she boldly asked for his hand in marriage.

They had wandered far away from the house and she'd be hard put to find a better time to confront him with her idea, yet something prevented her from doing it. Perhaps it was the granite tightness to his jaw, the hard line of his mouth, or the flinty coldness in eyes that hadn't once looked her way since he'd angrily pulled off her shoes. Whatever, she couldn't allow her own fears to delay her plan much longer. She had to get Tyler to marry her as quickly as possible, for if he found out about her involvement in the train robbery before they were married, not only would the resulting scandal destroy Berdine's chances with David but there was a very good possibility they'd lose the farm, forever.

She had always known Tyler had a volatile temper and could be cruel, but today she sensed something else. He could be merciless if he chose, and somehow she sensed he would be if he found out she, a woman, was the culprit who had robbed him. She might not be able to prevent him from punishing her but she could stop his penalizing the rest of her family for something that had been entirely her own idea.

Thrusting aside her discomfort with Tyler's brooding expression, she searched for something to say that would lighten the tension between them, something to put him in a receptive frame of mind. "You've done a fine job getting your fields ready and planted, Tyler."

"Thank you." His answer was brief and he kept his gaze directed straight ahead.

They walked on through the shallow waters of the river for several moments until Johanna again broke the silence with, "Don't you miss your family and the kind of life you must have had back East? Don't you think you'd ever want to go back there?"

"No."

His negative response was spoken in an emphatic tone. Johanna was so shocked by the bitterness the single syllable conveyed that she gave up trying to get him to divulge any further information. They continued their walk. Tyler maintained his silence. There was no sign that his black mood would soon dissipate and Johanna discarded one notion after another of a means to break through the thick wall he had built up around himself.

Chapter Twelve

"WHAT WOULD YOU SAY TO MARRYING ME, TYLER?" Johanna blurted, keeping her head down so he couldn't read the terrified expression in her eyes.

"What!" Tyler expounded, coming to a dead halt in the water, jerking her around by the arm until they stood face to face. "Did I hear you correctly? Are you proposing to me?"

Now that she'd so bluntly broken the tense silence between them, she had no choice but to brazen it out. Keeping her eyes focused anywhere but on his face, she stammered, "Well . . . well . . . yes, I am. You need a wife. Someone to help you on your farm. You admitted that I know a lot more about farming than you do and . . . and . . ."

"Hold it, hold it, hold it," Tyler interrupted gruffly,

a look of total astonishment on his face. Surveying her, he noted the determined tilt to her chin and continued in a much softer tone, "I think this conversation would be better held on dry land." He tugged on her hand, pulling her toward the bank.

Pausing on the muddy shore, he searched the surrounding area, and spying an ancient willow standing alone atop a small knoll beside the river, he led Johanna toward it. "Since you're the one who is going down on one knee, let me get comfortable while I hear the rest of this . . . this proposal." Raking a hand through his hair, he groaned aloud. "You'll have to forgive me, Johanna, but I never envisioned a woman asking for my hand. I need to sit down."

Johanna was mortified by the amused twinkle she saw in his gray eyes and his unsuccessful attempts to stop a telltale twitching of his mustache as he lowered himself to the grass, then gazed up at her expectantly. "Ah . . . ah," she stammered, her cheeks already beet red, "I'm not trying to amuse you, Tyler. I'm dead serious about this."

"Well, I would hope so." He nodded in agreement, lifting one dark brow, but the slashing dimples in his cheeks were deeper and he was obviously having difficulty keeping a sober expression. "Marriage is a serious matter. Nothing to take lightly."

Angry sparks shot from her blue eyes, but since she had finally found the courage to address the subject, she refused to back down until she had said it all. "This isn't an ordinary proposal," she insisted grimly. "It's a business proposition. I'm proposing to provide you with good strong labor and a knowledge of farming that comes with experience. I'll cook your meals, wash your clothes and . . . and . . . make a home for you." Her voice trailed off. Twisting her hands in the folds of her dress, she waited for his answer, her heart pounding.

Trying not to laugh in the face of her determined, though faltering, businesslike tone, Tyler drawled, "That sounds like a reasonable offer, but what's in it for you?"

"Well . . ." She paused to consider. "You're strong and in good health . . ."

Tyler could no longer suppress the deep rumbles of laughter. Between bursts of hilarity, he queried, "Do you intend to check my teeth? You sound like you're acquiring a new horse, not a husband."

Johanna fixed him with a quelling gaze, her mouth set in a furious line, until Tyler's boisterous guffaws subsided. Forcing her voice to remain steady, she agreed with his assessment, astounding him even further. "The same qualities are important in both. I have to consider a man's strength and sound body. A farm depends on a man's being able to work it."

Having gained some control of himself, Tyler leaned back against the trunk of the tree. "I see, but there are other men in the area with strong backs. I'm sure any one of them would meet your requirements. Why have you chosen me? May I assume you feel some affection for me?"

With her shaky limbs no longer able to hold her, Johanna sank to the ground. Folding her legs beneath her skirt, she began plucking nervously at the stems of grass on the ground beside her. "I think we're a suitable match. I'm sure this is the most practical solution for all concerned."

Enjoying her confusion but irritated that she was avoiding his question, Tyler asked, "Is sharing my bed going to be part of this proposition?"

Lifting her chin, Johanna cleared her throat and strove for a matter-of-fact tone. "Well, of course. A good wife must submit in order to have sons, children who will preserve the land for the future. But there are other reasons for us marrying. You are a man with a strong constitution. What's more, you are a wealthy man. We'd never have to worry about losing the land, and when we're gone, our sons will still be farming here."

Tyler swallowed his growing irritation. She was making it sound as if his prime land, strong body and wealth were her only reasons for marrying him. Her proposal had definitely caught him off guard. To his chagrin, he acknowledged that if she had waited until he worked out his own feelings about her, she would probably have received a similar offer from him quite soon. With grudging self-honesty, he admitted that he might have used the same reasons to convince her that she was presenting to him, but somehow, coming from her mouth, those reasons insulted him. He wanted more, some balm for his dented ego, and was determined to extract his pound of flesh.

"Is that all you want out of sharing my bed?" he probed. "Strong sons?" His gaze raked her full breasts that were straining against the thin fabric of her dress. "Is that why you lay with me in the barn?"

If he meant to hurt her, he had been successful, but

there was too much pride in Johanna to show it. Without changing her expression, she stated quietly, "Since we have already lain together, it's possible I am now carrying your child. Perhaps you had best consider that, as well." She fixed him with a pointed stare, her clear azure gaze revealing none of the tumult she was experiencing. He had backed her into a corner and she shot out defensively, "How do you think this community would feel if they knew you had sullied one of their young women? Do you think you'd still be welcome here?"

Tyler's gray eyes glittered dangerously. She was blackmailing him! First robbery, now blackmail. She had to be feeling desperate but why now, why today? What had brought her to the state of mind that she would dare make such an outrageous proposal? Perhaps, he'd come on too strong in the churchyard. Remembering how she had blanched when he'd reprimanded her about her headstrong inclination to plunge into things without considering the consequences, he wondered if she feared he had discovered the truth about her. That possibility must scare her to death. "What would you do if I turned down your proposal, Johanna? Inform the church elders I've stolen your virginity?"

"If I must," Johanna admitted, wishing she hadn't had to resort to such a threat, but it was fast becoming clear that Tyler didn't have any affection for her. He hadn't considered her offer at all seriously until she'd mentioned the possibility of her carrying his child.

He was unable to keep the cold fury from his gaze, but his voice was deceptively congenial. "Why don't you move a little closer? Come sit next to me." When she made no move to come near him, he went to her. Sitting down beside her, he draped a possessive arm over her shoulder and felt her stiffen in reaction to his touch. "Am I to conclude that you feel no pleasure in my arms?"

"Pleasure isn't important." Johanna avoided a direct answer. "The main purpose of marriage is procreation."

The weight of his arm across her shoulders increased and Johanna tried to shrink away. "I'm not sure I like being considered nothing more than a prime stud. There's also the possibility that you aren't making a good bargain. As far as I know there is no proof that I can beget children." Her continued refusal to acknowledge that her emotions were involved incensed him.

Deliberately crude, he jibed, "I've been brought to stand before many women but as yet have no issue from my loins. In breeding, a stud must usually service twice in order to ensure the success of the mating. Are you going to delay the marriage ceremony until your belly begins growing with my child?"

A fiery blush spread across Johanna's face and she had heard enough. "You've said such coarse things to me for the last time!" She wrenched away from under his arm and jumped to her feet. "I withdraw my proposal, sir! You were right. There are other men around here who will satisfy my needs even better than you!"

Lifting her skirts well above her knees, she began running up the slope, intending to put distance be-

tween them as quickly as possible. Indeed, she hoped
never to see him again. Bitter tears streaked down her
face and she flung them away with the back of her
hand. She was so intent on getting away from him that
she didn't hear the sound of Tyler's bare feet crushing
the deep grass with each long stride as he steadily
gained on her.

Like a wolf bearing down on a fleeing deer, he
veered closer until he was able to grab her about the
waist. The abrupt break in their momentum caused
them both to lose balance and tumble to the ground.
Tyler broke Johanna's fall and she landed on his chest.
In a tangle of arms and legs they rolled together back
down the sharp incline.

With the breath knocked out of her, Johanna lay
gasping beneath Tyler's weight as their bodies came to
a rest beneath the same willow tree she had just run
away from. Taking advantage of her loss of breath,
Tyler made sure she was securely pinned under him.
Using one hand, he grasped hold of both of her wrists
and forced her arms over her head. His thighs trapped
her lower body, pressing her against the damp
ground. Looking up, Johanna was terrified by the
ruthless glow in his gray eyes.

"You were made to receive a man, my Johanna, but
today I'll prove there's only one man who can satisfy
you."

"Not you!" she cried frantically, twisting her head
from side to side as the breath came rampaging back
into her burning lungs. She saw the muscles along his
jaw harden and knew that the words had provoked
him even more than her struggles to free herself.

"Forever me," he rasped. "Until you're unable to deny it, even to yourself."

Exhibiting an iron determination, he caught hold of her hair, coiling several long golden strands around his fist until he was able to force her head still. His mouth came down to smother her lips. Knowing he was much stronger than she, Johanna went limp. Immediately, his punishing kiss softened, and became sensually persuasive. The feel of his body pressing into hers almost overwhelmed her, but she knew that she couldn't succumb to him without losing every ounce of her pride. She allowed herself a tentative response to his kiss and could sense the triumph in him, but she knew it would be short-lived. Confident of his impending victory, he was only half-aware that he had released the restraining grip on her wrists. This was the moment she had been waiting for.

Using both hands, she roughly grabbed hold of his hair, pulling with all of her strength. The instant she felt the involuntary movement of his legs, as he tried to relieve the pain she was inflicting with her hands, she brought up her knee. Although not reaching the vulnerable male target she sought, her action served the purpose, for he grunted with pain as her knee grazed his groin. Concerned with countering her unexpected and savage attack, he wasn't prepared when she released his hair and thrust against his shoulders with both hands. In seconds, she was out from under him and scrambling to her feet.

"Hellion!" he snarled. "You'll never fight me again!"

Only a step away from freedom, Johanna screamed

as his hand closed around her ankle. He bent his arm sharply and she was pulled off her feet. Dragging her struggling body back down the slope, he used the natural weapons of the uneven landscape to pull at her dress, drawing her skirts up above her waist. She fought like a wild animal but he was unrelenting and easily overpowered her. As she kicked and clawed ineffectually, he yanked her dress over her head, but didn't pull it off completely until he'd used it as a restraint to keep her arms trapped while he stripped off her underclothes. A few moments later, he'd removed his own clothes and she felt the naked, rippling muscles of his shoulders and chest when he subdued her twisting body beneath his own.

"Oh, we shall marry, Johanna Heinsman," he bit out between clenched teeth. "But it won't be for any of those practical reasons you've proposed. It will be for this!"

The warmth of his mouth found the sensitive cord along her neck, nibbling at the soft skin while she unsuccessfully tried to inch away. She dug her fingers into his skin, raking his shoulders, but despite his muffled curse of pain he did not relent, gave her no chance to escape. He adjusted her beneath him, swiftly, easily, as if she weren't a strong, tall, supple woman but one of the delicate creatures he'd bedded in the past. Lifting her waist, he forced her hands under her, then trapped them there with the weight of his body over hers. One thigh firmly held down her squirming legs, clamped over her upper thighs. "What are you waiting for?" she cried, when she felt the surging male hardness against her thigh and realized she couldn't fight him much longer. "You want to rape me. Then get it over with!"

His voice was husky and smooth like velvet. "No, I only want what you want, Blue Eyes. When you tell me how much, then I'll give it to you."

Softly, he ran one finger down her bare skin from neck to flank. "There are so many things I can teach you and you shall love them all."

"No!" she screamed, but his mouth swallowed the force behind it, taking her sweet breath between his warm lips. Johanna moaned in torment, finally admitting that he would not be denied, knowing that he would soon strip away the last of her pride. At the very first touch of his naked flesh upon her bare skin, she had felt pleasure gather like a coiled spring inside her belly and with each touch of his hands it tightened further. He abandoned her mouth only after her lips had melted with response, her tongue willingly entering into the competition his had begun.

His finger trailed down between her breasts and his mouth followed, languidly kissing the sensitive skin as he slowly progressed toward the throbbing pink nipple at the peak of one curve. Aware of her desperation for him to complete the journey, he delayed, circling the taut point with his warm tongue but not touching it until her small gasps told him of her need. When he finally took the aching nipple into his mouth, his hand simultaneously captured the other, rolling it gently between two fingers.

Desire for him rose and overtook her, obliterating everything but the onslaught of pleasure he gave her,

her need for more. Her head was spinning helplessly in the torrent of pleasure that was wracking her body. "Tell me you want me inside you," he advised seductively, lifting his head to gaze into the passion-laden pools of her eyes.

Without the words, she would have shown him, but upon hearing them she could not, shaking her head in weak defiance. He gave her a brief, sideways smile before lowering his head to her breast. He doubled the erotic onslaught, his lips, tongue and teeth tantalizing her swollen breasts as his fingers slid down to her belly. At the juncture of her thighs, he paused, then began making agonizingly slow tactile forays along the delicate flesh at the inside of both legs.

She thought she would die of the exquisite torment, trembling like one of the willow leaves in the tree above her that twisted wildly in the hot summer wind. "Please, Tyler . . . please," she begged, mindless that her pleading sounded exactly like a woman demanding release from the one man who could satisfy her, the only man she wanted.

"Please stop?" he demanded thickly, his gray eyes devouring the naked, writhing female curves beneath his hands. "Or please do this." His fingers delved repeatedly, tenderly stroking the moist flesh of her womanhood. "And this." Gently, he probed inside her again and again, relentlessly coaxing her convulsive response. His own torture rasped in his tone. "Tell me, Johanna, before I die from wanting you."

He withdrew his hand, then parted her thighs and knelt between them. His broad, muscular torso blotted out the sun, shading the shame that darkened her cheeks as she whimpered, "Please, Tyler. I want you."

"Not a son?" He lowered himself between her legs, releasing her arms so she could touch him. As her eager hands instinctively closed on the tight skin over his lean hips, frantically trying to pull him into her, he held back. "Not a strong back, prime land, not security. This," he growled thickly, touching her with the hard male satisfaction only he could provide. "This is what you want from me."

He plunged inside her, filling her completely, the instant she gasped, "Yes, Tyler . . . oh, yes."

His pulse was racing as wildly and hotly as hers. She could feel his blood pounding through his veins as he crushed her softness to his taut flesh. Each heated thrust of his loins compounded the fiery hot tension in his skin, burning against hers like an all-consuming brand. The combustive heat seemed to fuse them together and in the glaring blaze of the summer sun, he proved his ownership of her willing body.

The primitive tremors shook them both, built in intensity, then exploded as fulfillment quivered through them. In the long aftermath that followed, Johanna lay weak and spent, unsure if the tears that dampened her cheeks were caused by ecstasy or shame. She had never experienced such overpowering sensations, yet by enjoying them she had lost every shred of her self-respect.

Tyler moved, his bronzed shoulder brushing across her breasts as he rolled off her and flung himself on the ground beside her. Lying face up on his back, he stared into the sky, but his hand sought hers, pulling it across his chest, laying her palm over his heart. "I accept your proposal, Miss Heinsman," he stated quietly, his breathing still more rapid than normal, his staccato heartbeat throbbing in the center of her palm. "We will be married within the week."

Still unable to move, barely able to think, Johanna said nothing. What was there to say? He had only to touch her and she became a wild wanton creature, so filled with desire he could do anything he chose. Like him unmindful of her nakedness, she stared upward into the silver-green cascade of weeping-willow branches. Since meeting Tyler, her life had become as complicated as the twisted tangle of long leaves hanging over her head. She had no more chance against him than the leaves had against the wind, buffeted this way and that until it was difficult to tell which delicate green shaft belonged to which branch.

Propping himself up on one elbow, Tyler leaned over her. His breath fanned her cheek as his hand shifted to her jawline. Tracing the outline of her lips with his thumb, he asked, "Did you hear me, Johanna? I said I'll marry you."

Johanna's nerves tingled at his closeness, lying next to her naked, so virilely masculine and vitally strong. With her hand, she could feel the slightest change in his heartbeat and it had barely slowed. She nodded, fighting back more tears, refusing to look up and see the triumphant knowledge of her defeat reflected in his gray eyes.

He accepted her nonverbal answer, lying back down beside her. A throaty male chuckle was the next sound she heard. "I wonder what my parents will say when I inform them of my marriage."

Grateful for any switch of subject away from herself, Johanna pulled her hand out from beneath his. "Considering your age, I imagine your taking a wife will come as something of a relief." Trying to appear calm, though her stomach was clenched in a tight knot, she reached for her underthings and started to dress. At that moment she was too overwhelmed to ask about his parents, information she'd wanted earlier and would no doubt need to know later. For now, it was frightening enough to know that they were alive and that for some reason Tyler thought it amusing to contemplate their reaction. "I'm surprised you haven't married before now. Most men your age already have large families."

Sighing, Tyler sat up but didn't reach for his own clothes as he watched her, his eyes memorizing each section of smooth bare skin she was slowly covering. When she picked up her dress and pulled it down over her head, he looked around for his own clothes. "Do I appear that old to you, Johanna? I am thirty. Do you consider that a great age?"

He almost sounded as if he were frightened of her answer, but she knew that wasn't possible and stated without pretense, "It means you're a full-grown man. I hear women age quicker and that must be so because Fritz is still growing and filling out. I stopped developing when I was his age."

Tyler cleared his throat, and when she glanced at him, she saw the amused twitching of his mustache. "Well, I did," she insisted, unconsciously thrusting out her full breasts as she planted both hands on her slender hips.

It was his turn to suffer a loss of words, and he simply nodded, fighting the urge to make love to her again as he stood up to pull on his pants. She had no idea how beautiful she looked to him, with her long flaxen hair blowing wildly about her face, her curvaceous figure clearly outlined as the wind whipped her skirts around her long shapely legs. Turning away to hide the returning desire she might easily read in his eyes, he bent down for his shirt.

Unable to stop herself, Johanna stared. Looking upon his body had become a source of great pleasure to her, one she could not deny herself as she watched him complete his dressing. The thought of repeating today's sensual encounter every night after they were married increased the tension in her stomach. Her eyes were enormous by the time he was tucking his shirt into the waistband of his pants, and the sight of his powerful muscles stretching the coarse material tightly across his massive chest almost choked her. She knew she was in the throes of reignited desire and miserably she recognized the cause. Somehow she had fallen in love with this man!

"I . . . We can't marry that soon, Tyler," she said, addressing the issue of a wedding date. "We'll have to wait until the family has accepted the news." She didn't want him to guess that she wanted to delay the inevitable as long as possible, strictly out of fear, fear of her newfound discovery. "We'll have to have a proper engagement."

The slashing grooves on either side of his mouth

proved how much her words amused him. "At least you're not thinking of backing out on the marriage. I think I've finally proved to you whose woman you are and will be until I determine differently."

Her eyes immediately dropped to her bare toes. There was no way she could deny his sensual power over her body, but did he have to taunt her with it? Make her admit it again and again? No matter how much he wounded her pride?

"Come on," he commanded, evidently not needing a verbal acknowledgment of their relationship. "We've been gone quite a while. On the way back to our shoes, we can discuss our upcoming wedding. You were right, you know. Today I learned just how much I need a wife."

But they didn't discuss anything as they walked back to the river, each occupied with his own thoughts as they retraced their path. Upon reaching the place where they had removed their shoes, Johanna sat down. "Tyler . . . I want my family to think we've fallen in love. Berdine won't marry David if she doesn't believe that. Can . . . will that be too difficult for you to pretend?" On her part, she knew there would be little pretense behind her behavior. Hardly able to comprehend how it could have happened, she again acknowledged that she had fallen in love with him. He must never know. Not once had he implied that he loved her, only that he needed an accommodating woman to share his bed.

At first she thought the anger in his eyes was caused by her request that he feign deep affection for her, but she soon found out otherwise. Taking a place beside her on the soft grass, he gritted darkly, "So! Now I know the real reason why you're so anxious to marry me. You're hell-bent on 'fixing' things for your sister. You amaze me, Johanna. You're so independent, yet you offer yourself to a man, body and soul, just so your sister can be happy."

"I love my sister," Johanna intoned, stung by the censure in his eyes. "My family is more important to me than anything else on earth! I would do anything for them."

"Them and your land," he affirmed coldly. "My God! How well I know that."

After pulling his boots back on, he jumped up, looming over her. "But there's one member of your family you haven't taken into consideration at all."

"Who?" she demanded, feeling her own temper ignite under the lashing contempt in his voice.

"I've had you twice," he ground out. "A perfect breeding. Our son may be growing inside you right now. If you want him to look on you kindly, you'll marry me before the week is out. That way, if you're pregnant, no one will dare call him a bastard!"

"And if I don't?" she retorted, not showing how badly the vile term he'd imposed on a possible child of theirs had disturbed her. He only saw anger shooting like poisoned darts from her large blue eyes.

"Then the marriage is off! You won't get my strong back or my land." A muscle leapt in his jaw. "More importantly, your dear sister will probably die a spinster. I know I wouldn't risk leaving you with those children. And if you are pregnant and we don't marry, you won't keep my son. You might have coveted Kendall money when you considered marrying me, but see how you'll like it if you don't. I'll take my child away from you so fast you won't even remember the color of his eyes."

The cruelty she had always suspected below the surface charm he displayed to others was readily apparent in every clipped syllable. He meant every word. If she didn't marry him within a week, as requested, and if indeed it turned out she was pregnant, she wouldn't be allowed to keep the child. The newfound love she felt for him shrank inside her, but he was giving her no other choice than to agree. By proposing marriage herself, she thought everything would be arranged to her own satisfaction but she was now swiftly discovering that Tyler was not a man she could easily manipulate. He wanted her and intended to have her on his own terms! Terms that had nothing to do with love, family or land, the three things that were all she cared about.

There was no impatience in his expression as he waited for her to make up her mind, only indifference. It was as if he didn't really care one way or the other. Swallowing the hard lump that constricted her throat, Johanna forced herself to speak. "All right. We can marry next week. Couples usually marry after Sunday meeting. We won't have to invite anyone. Everyone in town will stay on for the ceremony, once Pastor Braun announces our intention to the congregation."

"How nice," he pronounced sarcastically. "But we both know I'm not interested in who attends our wedding, only in what will take place once you're my wife."

Again, a small, humiliated nod was all she could muster. Getting to her feet, she started the return walk to the cabin. She didn't show any response when he walked up beside her, and he made no attempt to take her hand for the return journey.

Before descending the small knoll that rose behind the cabin, Tyler spoke again, an unrecognizable note in his voice. "Your family will believe I'm marrying you out of love, Johanna. I'll play my part. I only hope you can be half as convincing. You won't be if we return to the house with you looking at me as if you'd like to stick a knife in my guts."

"I'm quite good at playacting." Stopping in her tracks, she turned to face him, offering such a devastating smile that he sucked in his breath. "If you knew me better, Tyler, you'd know I can do anything once I make up my mind to it. I can even convince the others that I'm plumb crazy about you."

Linking her arm through his, she tenderly rested her head on his shoulder. "How's this, Tyler? Do you think this looks loving enough? Or should I make calf eyes at you too?" Moving her head slightly, she looked deeply into his eyes and he couldn't quite hide the effects of her limpid blue gaze.

A deep furrow creased his brow and his jaw tensed. From her viewpoint, she could see a furiously throbbing pulse point in his temple, and beneath his mustache his lips were pressed together in a tight line. Throwing caution to the winds, she jibed softly. "Surely you can do better than that, Tyler. I don't want everyone to think my attention turns your stomach."

His arm pressed hers intimately against his ribs, the pressure almost painful as he retaliated. "You know what your attention does to me, and in another week I'll have it all to myself."

"Not quite," Johanna said smoothly. "There will still be the family to consider. Since you have no house, we'll have to live in mine. Fritz, Cordie and Amy will be up in the loft every night and the bedroom walls don't provide very much privacy."

"If you're thinking the presence of your family will dampen my ardor, you're sadly mistaken, my dear." Tyler flashed her a barbed grin. "As soon as they learn how often I intend to take you, I would guess they'll get bored with our endless frolics and turn their attention elsewhere. That is, unless you give them reason for continued interest. I enjoy those little kittenish moans you make when I am inside you, but who knows how they may affect your impressionable younger sisters and brother."

Chapter Thirteen

"Johanna!" Berdine insisted sharply. "You should have told Tyler about the robbery before today."

"The time was never right," Johanna retorted heatedly. "What do you expect me to do now? I certainly can't stall the ceremony while I confess. I promise you that I'll tell him, but it will have to wait until after we're married." She purposely avoided meeting Berdine's gaze and concentrated on helping her pack up her remaining belongings. Feeling her sister's disapproval as strongly as if Berdine were holding a fiery brand to the middle of her back, Johanna straightened her shoulders in an unconscious effort to throw off the heavy guilt weighing her down. "You keep your mind on your own part of this double wedding," she ordered. "You and David have waited a long time for this day and you shouldn't be thinking about anything else."

Effectively diverted from the subject, Berdine whirled about the small bedroom. "Oh, Jo, I think I've wanted to be David Lloyd's wife since the day I first saw him. I can't believe it's finally happening. Remember when he first came to Hemmington and how good he was with Papa those last months? He's so wonderful, so thoughtful, so . . . so . . ."

"I know, Berdie," Johanna smiled, hiding her relief. "You've gone on and on since Sunday, when Tyler and I announced our intentions and David suggested that we make it a double ceremony." Remembering the events that had led up to her and Tyler's announcement and the lies she had been forced to tell ever since, she inwardly shuddered.

There had been a moment of stunned silence when Tyler jovially proclaimed to her family and David that he had finally "persuaded" her to marry him, how he had fallen in love with her when he'd first opened his eyes that fateful night of the blizzard. He'd kept his arm tightly round her waist and beamed smiles down at her throughout his fulsome description of his perilous courtship of her, smiles that to Johanna seemed more like challenging sneers than expressions of great joy.

David had been the first to congratulate the couple, crossing the grassy expanse beneath the cottonwoods and clapping Tyler on the back, then bestowing a brotherly kiss on Johanna's cheek. David's sincerely delivered wish for their happiness had almost been

Johanna's undoing and she would have ended the entire farce had she not seen the look of longing and question that passed between him and her sister. In that moment, Berdine had quietly smiled, given a slight nod of her head. It was exactly what David had been waiting for. He calmly announced that the ceremony would unite two couples. "That is, if you and Tyler don't mind," he had offered. His suggestion was met with instant acceptance from Tyler, and Fritz's excited "If that don't beat the nation!" expressed everyone's hearty approval. After that, everything had become a blur, a chaotic mixture of laughter and tears, with everyone in the family talking at the same time.

Any lack of enthusiasm that Johanna had displayed over her upcoming nuptials was completely overshadowed by that of those around her. In a daze, she listened as the plans and logistics for a double wedding were discussed to all but her satisfaction. Soon after, both Tyler and David left for Hemmington to inform Pastor Braun of their plans and request that he perform the ceremony. News about the double wedding spread through Hemmington and the surrounding countryside like a forest fire, and all week friends and neighbors had dropped by to offer their heartfelt congratulations.

The days certainly sped by far too quickly for Johanna, each hour bringing her closer to the time when she would become Tyler's wife, a role she looked on with a mixture of excitement and dread. Her body warmed every time she thought about the overpowering pleasure she had experienced in Tyler's arms and would again and again after they were married. Yet it was thoughts of that pleasure that instigated her greatest fears.

That he wanted her with a passion as great as her own she knew, but how would he feel about her once he discovered that she was the one who had duped him out of his stake? How was she going to live with a man who might never want to touch her again? Might despise her for tying him to her in marriage? What would she do if he deserted her after he found out?

"I can hardly believe it," Berdine said, breaking into Johanna's disturbing contemplation. "It's our wedding day, Jo. In a few more hours, I shall be Mrs. David Lloyd and you'll be Mrs. Tyler Kendall." Hearing Johanna's future name spoken out loud brought a dazed look to Berdine's face. "Imagine what Mama and Papa would've said if they'd known you would someday marry a Kendall. Our Jo catching the eye of a rich Boston banker's son."

"More'n likely, Pa would've taken a stick to him and chased him off our property," Johanna declared tartly, placing the last of Berdine's clothing into the large trunk. "I don't think he'd have taken to me marrying into the same family that holds our mortgage. He often said the banks were almost as bad as the railroad for taking money off'n folks."

"Tyler doesn't know that yet, either. Does he?" Berdine walked to the bed where she had laid out her best underclothing. "You haven't told him that the Kendall Bank holds our deed, have you?"

"Does it matter?" Johanna shrugged dismissively,

camouflaging her anxiety. "Once I 'fess up to robbing him, I'll have to tell him everything. I plan to get it all over with at one time. That way we'll be able to start fresh with a clean slate."

Berdine bit her lip, shaking her head as a worried frown spread over her face. "Johanna, if you love him, you should have told him everything before the wedding. There should be no secrets between a man and his wife."

"I know Tyler better than you, Berdie, believe me." Johanna forced far more conviction than she felt into her tone. "Everything will work out much better this way. I won't risk losing him over this. You can understand that, can't you?"

"Yes," Berdine acknowledged grudgingly. "I know I'd do 'most anything to keep David. Once I pushed Lucy Boggs into the river so she'd stop making up to him," she confessed with a musical giggle. "Can't wait to see her face when we stand up and make our vows."

"Why, Berdine Heinsman!" Johanna laughed, glad that once again her sister had been sidetracked from the issue of Tyler and herself. "And you such a peaceable soul. Now I wonder what Ma and Pa would've said if they'd known about you trying to drown poor Lucy."

"I think they'd have been right proud," Berdine judged, grinning.

"Me too," Johanna agreed. "Neither Ma nor Pa ever was ones for letting much stand in the way of getting something they really wanted."

Fighting tears of sentimentality that came from

remembering happy times with their parents, both girls turned to the matter of getting dressed for their wedding. Standing by the bed, Johanna looked down upon the pale blue lawn dress that had been their mother's wedding gown. "I wish she could've seen you wearing that, Berdie. It's only fitting that you be the one to wear her gown. You're so much like her. I remember how sweet she was and what a wonderful smile she had. She was beautiful, and so are you."

"No more than you," Berdine said softly, emotion breaking in her voice. "And you've got the joy of knowing your intended thought enough of you to have Jenny Meeker make up a wedding dress," she stated merrily. "You could've knocked me down with a feather when she brought it out yesterday and said Tyler'd ordered it special. Probably knew all you had was that new blue calico I made you."

"That dress would have been fine for a country wedding and you would have been beautiful in it but it's nothing near as elegant as this silk gown. Just think of all those yards of silk flowing around you when you walk up that aisle. You'll look like a queen. And that petticoat!" Berdine raised her eyebrows in mock horror.

"Some might think it unseemly that your intended presented you with a set of lace-ruffled silk underthings all the way from St. Louis, but it would have been just sinful to wear cotton under that gown! Besides, no one who'd disapprove will even know," she offered in a conspiratorial whisper. "Those slippers he bought you fit perfect. It just goes to show you what good sense he has, consulting Jenny in all this.

She knew your size, and if I know Jenny, she loved every minute of helping outfit you. You're marrying a mighty generous man, a man who loves you very much."

Johanna knew Tyler's motivation for providing her wedding attire had had nothing to do with love but she let Berdine keep on thinking that way. In her own mind, she knew better. He didn't talk about his family by what little reference there had been to them, and she sensed they were estranged. Still, though he may have chosen a life far different from his roots, she was sure that a high and mighty Kendall wouldn't want to be seen marrying a girl who wore a homemade calico dress and moccasins to the wedding.

Reaching down, she fingered the delicate silk skirt of the gown. She'd never seen anything so fine. In an uncharacteristic burst of feminine vanity, she smiled. No matter what had prompted Tyler to have the gown made, she couldn't wait to be seen in it. The people of Hemmington would talk of Johanna Heinsman's beautiful wedding gown for years to come.

"It's time we got dressed," Berdine said, then added, "Mind your hair, Jo. It took me most of an hour to plait those wild roses into it."

Both girls removed their wrappers at the same time and began putting on their undergarments. Helping each other with hooks, buttons and ribbons, they completed their toilettes, then stood back and stared at one another.

"Oh, Berdine," Johanna breathed, thinking her sister had never looked more lovely. The soft blue material brought out the color in her eyes and height-ened the gold of her hair, while the old-fashioned design was perfect on Berdine's gently rounded figure. A slender satin ribbon woven into her golden coronet made her hair look almost like a crown, and in Johanna's eyes it was her sister who looked as regal as a queen. "You're the queen, Berdie. David will be so proud."

Berdine took hold of Johanna's hand, tears glistening in her overbright eyes. "Johanna," she murmured softly. "Papa always said you were the real beauty in the family, if only you'd accept being what God made you. There's no denying he was right. Come look for yourself in Mama's mirror. I'll hold it up for you." Pulling her sister along behind her, she lifted the oval glass off the wall. Taking a few steps back, she angled it so Johanna could get a complete view.

"Gosh all hemlock! Is that really me?" Johanna asked, astonished delight lighting her eyes to shining blue crystals. "I . . . I look like an honest-to-goodness lady."

Berdine simply nodded, her face beaming.

Johanna's gaze was locked on the tall slender figure in the mirror, a beautiful young woman in an ivory silk gown. She could hardly believe that the woman was herself. An off-the-shoulder silk ruffle draped lovingly across her full breasts, then gathered around her arms into short puffed sleeves. Below the ruffle, the smooth ivory material molded her small waist, then was gathered into soft folds that fell gracefully to the floor.

Bemused, she stared at the shimmering flaxen waves of her hair that were pulled back from her face, then allowed to tumble over her shoulders. She turned to one side in order to see the delicate pink flowers woven into the single plait of blonde hair that cascaded down the center of her back. In wonderment, she went on staring, confident that the rosy flush in her cheeks, the wild pink blossoms in her hair and the sapphire glow in her eyes were the perfect accessories to enhance the richness of the elegant ivory silk.

"I wonder what Tyler will say," she whispered, letting herself believe for at least that moment that somehow, someday he would love her. Holding tightly to that hope, her lips curved into a bemused smile when Berdine offered her opinion.

"He's got eyes. He'll say you're beautiful. No man will ever be prouder of his bride."

The two young women would have spent more time admiring themselves, but Fritz's impatient voice came booming through the bedroom door. "You two 'bout ready in there? If you don't stop fiddling round, you're going to be late for your own weddings! Sunday meeting's 'bout done. If I don't get you to the church right soon, David and Tyler will have my hide."

The normally garrulous Fritz could think of nothing to say that would properly convey his awed feelings when, arm in arm, his two older sisters emerged from the bedroom. His blue eyes went wide. He blinked a few times and shook his head, obviously struggling for the right words to express himself. "Je-ru-salem!" he breathed. "I'll be plumb jiggered! All decked out, you two look fine. Right fine."

"You don't need to sound like you've just witnessed a miracle," Berdine scolded, directing an amused grin at Johanna. "Did you think we'd dress up in old flour sacks and patched overalls for our own weddings?"

"No, ma'am," Fritz replied politely, his newfound gallantry amusing his sisters even further. "But I didn't 'spect you to look so . . . so. . . ." Faltering, he shook his head once more. "Folks won't hardly know you're my sisters with you looking so beautiful an' all."

"Why, thank you, Fritz," Johanna stated solemnly in a refined voice, stepping to her brother's side. "And you look right fine yourself. Got your hair all combed and you look mighty handsome dressed up in Pa's best coat. He'd have been proud of you today, and I can't think of a man I'd rather have take my arm when we walk into the church."

"Papa would have been proud of all of us," Berdine declared with equal gravity. "We'll miss him, but we're awful proud we have you to take his place."

Fritz seemed to grown an inch taller upon hearing the adult responsibility they'd bestowed on him, but neither woman made a disparaging comment as he straightened his shoulders, then started to the bedroom to fetch Berdine's trunk. "Wait for me to help you into the buggy. It was real thoughtful of David to leave his rig and take the wagon when he picked up Amy and Cordie for church. There might have been a nail sticking out in our wagon and we wouldn't want any holes in them dresses."

Without a trace of a smile, both girls nodded, waiting patiently as he helped first one, then the other up onto the seat. All three of them were acutely aware of the momentous change that was going to occur in their lives once Berdine and Johanna were married, and the knowing affected them all in like manner. Little was said as they drove to Hemmington, each silently questioning what the future would hold for them, each contemplating the past. This time was their last together as Heinsmans. After today, the names Kendall and Lloyd would appear in the family Bible, and with those signatures would come a new line of people, part of, yet separate from, the original family of German immigrants who had settled the farm.

Nearing Hemmington, Johanna couldn't help but recall her parents. How often she had ridden into town in the back of the Heinsman wagon, feeling proud that she belonged to the tall broad-shouldered man and lovely blond woman who sat upon the seat. That pride had fostered her fierce loyalty to the land, her concern for her brother and sisters, even her marriage to Tyler Kendall.

Passing a grove of tall oaks, she thought of the many community picnics that had taken place under the trees. How many times had she and her family stood side by side beneath the lofty branches and joined hands in prayer before they began sampling the sumptuous dishes generously donated to the gathering by each family, rich or poor? How many Sundays had she spent sneaking off to the creek with childhood friends, praying no adult would catch them wading on the Sabbath? She could almost hear that joyous laughter she'd heard so often in the past as she and the other children had escaped the censorious eyes of their parents and scampered off into the tall prairie grasses. Sunday had always been a welcome break from the week's work, a day reserved for rest and relaxation, but this day there would be no opportunity to relax. Today she became a married woman, Mrs. Tyler Kendall. Today brought an end to childhood things forever.

"You've gone quite pale, Johanna." Berdine took hold of one of Johanna's hands, giving it an encouraging squeeze. "They tell me that bridal jitters are normal. I'm feeling them myself but I just keep remembering how much I love David. Think about Tyler, Jo. Remind yourself how much Tyler loves you. That'll bring some color back in your cheeks. At least we're doing this together. I don't think I'd be near as calm if I didn't have you beside me. We can take courage from one another, always remembering that when the day is over we'll be starting a better life with the men we love."

Berdine had no idea that the color flooding Johanna's cheeks wasn't brought about by her sister's sage advice. What she was feeling was far more complex than a simple case of bridal jitters. She did remind herself how much Tyler loved her, which was not at all. It was remembrances of his lovemaking and her own passionate responses that brought the rush of color to her cheeks. Their life together would be based not on love but lust, and how long would that last?

"A better life," she agreed woodenly, then forced some enthusiasm into her voice. "Just think, you'll be living with a doctor in his pretty brick house. I know you've been itching to make his place into a home. He'll buy you pretty new dresses, bonnets and shoes. I'm happy for you, Berdie. Real happy."

"And what of you?" Berdine laughed delightedly, enthralled with the picture her sister had painted for her. "You and Tyler will own one of the best farms in the county. One day he'll take you to Boston and show you off to his folks. Your gowns will be satin and lace, and I'll die of envy just looking at you."

"Any more jawin' will have to wait," Fritz decreed, pulling upon the reins. "Now's the time for saying the 'I do's.'"

"Do you see David?" Berdine cried, twisting around to survey the churchyard.

"Bad luck for the groom to look on his bride before the wedding. I was told to have you wait in the back of the church whilst I let Miz Braun know you're here." Fritz bounded from the buggy and tossed the reins to young Jeremiah Meeker before helping his sisters to the ground.

"Miz Braun's about to pop her corset. She's so plumb full of excitement 'bout playing that new reed organ for a wedding," Jeremiah explained as he fastened the reins to one of the hitching posts. The grinning red-haired boy had the double duty of watching the horses during both the morning's service and the wedding. It was a task the boys of the congregation coveted, since it allowed them to be excused from the lengthy sermons Pastor Braun had a penchant for delivering.

"You'd think, to hear her go on, that folks ain't

proper married less'n music's played for 'em. She's been playing that thing steady since the service was over." Suddenly, Jeremiah blushed as he realized to whom he was talking. He whisked off his cap, as if remembering the manners his mother had no doubt drilled into him, and stammered, "My . . . ah . . . congratulations to the brides."

"Thank you, Jeremiah," answered Berdine, while Johanna ruffled the boy's already unruly thatch of hair.

"This is it," announced Fritz as he ushered his sisters toward the church.

All three Heinsmans sobered as they mounted the wooden steps and heard the final strains of "Lo, How a Rose E'er Blooming" drifting from the open doors. Fritz bestowed a quick kiss on each sister's cheek before leaving them in the small vestibule and striding into the church. They could hear the shuffling of feet and rustling of clothing and knew the congregation had turned expectantly toward the doorway as soon as Fritz had been sighted. The organ stopped and all was silent, except for Fritz's footsteps as he made his way back up the aisle.

"There's two mighty nervous-looking men up at the front. My guess is they're waiting for a glimpse of their brides." Fritz winked and offered an arm to each of his sisters.

Johanna and Berdine exchanged one last hug just as the organ sounded the first notes of the processional. Johanna felt tears threaten behind her eyes as she took her brother's proffered arm and bit her lip to keep it from trembling. Fritz guided them to the doorway and paused for a brief second before starting up the aisle.

Johanna concentrated on placing one foot and then the other, thankful for the supporting arm of her brother, sure that without it she would have crumpled to the floor. Glancing toward the front of the church, she nearly tripped in reaction to what she saw there. Pastor Braun stood in front of the pulpit, flanked by Tyler and David. Both men were tall, handsome and smiling at the two women being escorted toward them by their brother, but it was what Tyler was wearing that startled Johanna. That same dove-gray frock coat, cream-colored doeskin trousers and black boots that he'd been wearing that morning on the train! They were cleaned and pressed, a very different state from the crumpled, whiskey-stained condition they'd been in when she'd first laid eyes on him, but they were unmistakably the same suit of clothes.

She could feel her body begin to shake and prayed fervently that she would swoon, that the earth would open and swallow her up—anything to prevent this ceremony from taking place. Berdine had been right. She should have told Tyler before the wedding. She shifted her eyes to glance at Fritz to see if he recognized Tyler's attire, but her brother was still smiling and his pace hadn't faltered. She felt a surge of unreasonable anger toward him for apparently suffering no guilt whatsoever, even though he was just as guilty as she.

Too quickly, Fritz was handing his sisters to their prospective husbands and it was Tyler's arm Johanna was now clasping for support. Her fingers clutched the smooth fabric of his sleeve while every muscle in her body seemed ready to spring into action and carry her out of the church. She kept her eyes straight ahead, unable to look at Tyler now that he was so close. She'd had a blurred image of a smiling handsome face coming toward her, but couldn't manage to even attempt an answering smile.

Her trembling increased and Tyler placed his warm hand over her chilled fingers. The gesture was no doubt meant to be reassuring, but for Johanna it only increased her discomfort and misgivings. The enormity of the step she was about to take nearly overwhelmed her. She was about to marry a man who had no idea he was marrying a thief. And she . . . she was marrying a man she really knew little about. Only the resolve to do nothing to mar this day for Berdine kept Johanna beside Tyler as the two couples stood before the beaming minister.

The music came to a stop and Pastor Braun began the ceremony. Berdine and David exchanged their vows first, and then it was Johanna and Tyler's turn. Johanna didn't know how she found the strength to utter her responses but Tyler's voice was strong and clear as he promised to love, honor and cherish her. Oh, please, God, Johanna silently prayed, someday make it so. Don't let him denounce me when he finds out the truth.

Tyler slipped a shining gold band on her finger, a symbol of the bond between them. It was final. She was Mrs. Tyler Kendall—there had been no escape. Her hand was tightly clasped in Tyler's as Pastor Braun offered a final blessing and a prayer for the happiness and prosperous future of the two couples. Tyler bestowed a soft kiss on her lips and then turned her toward the congregation.

They were down the aisle and out of the church before Johanna had summoned any courage to even look at her new husband. Tyler curled his arm around her waist and pulled her close, tipping up her chin with his fingers until she was forced to meet his gaze. "I thought you were supposed to be a good actress." He smiled down at her. "This isn't a tragedy. It's a wedding and you're the happy bride. Smile, my beautiful wife," he commanded. "Everyone will be out here in a few seconds. We're in love, remember? Make it look good." His lips covered hers and he folded her into his arms.

Johanna was still too stunned to respond and Tyler lifted his lips from hers. "You could try to muster a little enthusiasm for your new husband," he teased, humor shimmering in his eyes. He shifted his gaze to Berdine and David. "Your sister is having no trouble."

Following Tyler's gaze, Johanna saw her sister wrapped in David's arms, her own arms wound around his shoulders. The tears that had threatened to fall throughout the ceremony glistened in her eyes and moistened her long lashes. Berdine and David were unmistakably deeply in love, while she and Tyler . . .

She looked back at her husband and for the first time that day really saw him. Her eyes widened at the softness in his eyes, the warmth of the smile. She'd expected mockery, but there was none, and for a moment she let herself believe that he might actually love her. She leaned into him and he kissed her again. Her arms went around his neck and she returned his kiss. "Mmm, that's right. All you need is a little practice."

He turned to greet the first of the well-wishers but kept his arm around her waist. Johanna forced a smile on her face as she accepted the congratulations of the people she'd known most of her life. At the end of the line were Amy, Cordie and Fritz. "Are you really my big brother now, Tyler?" Amy's large eyes were dancing with pleasure as Tyler picked her up and whirled her around.

"I certainly am. Why do you think I married your sister?" he asked with a broad smile. "I've always wanted a little sister and this was the only way I could get one." He set her down and gave Cordie a greeting more dignified but just as warm, instinctively sensing that the fourteen-year-old would be embarrassed by such a display. "And I was lucky enough to get two, one who's quite a lovely young lady."

Johanna stood aside and watched the little tableau with tear-moistened eyes. Tyler was playing his part well. No one could doubt his sincerity as he greeted his newly acquired family, not even herself. It was obvious that he cared nearly as much for them as she did. Whatever he felt for her cast no shadow on his feelings toward them, and she fortified herself with that knowledge. At least, they had that much in common. That and their mutual love for the land were the things she hoped would make him understand and forgive her when she revealed the damning evidence that they were all thieves.

Tables were being assembled beneath the shade of the tall oaks behind the church, and for a time Tyler and Johanna were separated. She found it easier to relax and maintain the role she was being forced to play when Tyler was not beside her. For once, she eagerly assumed a place solely amongst the women-folk as she assisted in placing the food on the table and chattered gaily with Caroline Berkman until Jenny Meeker shooed her away. "No work today for you. There's plenty ahead of you. Go join your handsome husband."

She didn't have a chance to pretend she didn't know his whereabouts, for Tyler had magically appeared by her side and stayed there the rest of the day. Johanna found the role she was playing more difficult each time she saw Berdine and David. Their love was so evident that she felt a sharp pang of envy every time David looked adoringly at his new bride, wishing with all her heart that someday Tyler would look at her the same way.

By the time the sun was low on the horizon, spreading colorful streaks of gold, salmon and red across the summer sky, Johanna felt exhausted. The smile she had displayed all day was becoming more and more forced; her jaws were aching. It was time to leave. After the brides had made their farewells, the two couples raced to their waiting conveyances through a shower of rice. Tyler laughed up at her as he tossed her onto the wagon seat and bounded up beside her. Giving the horses a sharp crack of the reins to start them off at a brisk trot, Tyler effected their escape from the merry crowd.

They were hundreds of yards down the dusty road when Johanna turned to Tyler, a look of anxiety pinching her features. "Tyler! We forgot Fritz, Cordie and Amy. We'll have to go back."

"Relax, Johanna. Your brother and sisters are going to spend a few days with the Berkmans. It's their wedding present to us. Didn't they tell you?"

"No. I suppose they forgot in all the excitement of the day." Her reply was given in a dispirited tone, conveying all the fatigue, loneliness and trepidation she was experiencing. They were going to be alone for several days—and nights.

Chapter Fourteen

"STAY RIGHT WHERE YOU ARE UNTIL I CAN HELP YOU down," Tyler ordered, as he brought the horses to a halt in front of the Heinsman cabin. Placing one hand firmly but gently on Johanna's shoulder, he restrained her from leaping down from the wagon seat.

"I can get down from a wagon by myself," Johanna sputtered, trying to shrink away from his touch.

"I know you can, sweetheart, but humor me—just this once. A man likes to think he's needed." He slowly forced her to turn and face him. "Please." He emphasized his request, studying her mutinous expression, a teasing smile on his face and a mischievous glint in his eyes.

Johanna glared up at him, fighting a losing battle to maintain the rebellious stance she had taken. The warmth of his hand on her shoulder seemed to be spreading heat throughout her body, and though his smile was amused it was effectively leveling the walls of her resistance. The attraction he had for her was a potent force she could not withstand very long. Fearing that her feelings for him might show in her eyes, she dropped her gaze to stare at her hands clenched tightly in her lap. "All right. Since it means so much to you."

Her begrudging response was met with a low deep chuckle. "Now that wasn't so difficult, was it?" Obviously not expecting an answer, he released her shoulder, jumped lithely down from the wagon and looped the team's reins around the hitching post. Within seconds he was around to her side, his hands on her waist. Summoning up a fragile shred of independence, Johanna resisted the tug of his hands and remained on the wagon seat for a moment before relenting. With a sigh, she turned toward him, and placed her hands on his shoulders. There was no way to delay the inevitable.

"That's better," he remarked with a broad smile. "See how easy it can be to act like the weaker sex?" He didn't set her down after lifting her from the wagon but instead swept one arm beneath her thighs and slipped the other behind her back.

"I'm not so weak that I can't walk!" She struggled to gain her footing, but her actions were fruitless as he tightened his grasp and began striding to the cabin's door. "What are you doing?" she demanded, kicking her slippered feet. However, her exertions only served to raise the delicate silk fabric of her gown, exposing the rows of ruffles and lace of her petticoat and giving Tyler an expansive view of her slender ankles and graceful calves.

"I'm carrying my new bride across the threshold— or isn't that the custom out here in Nebraska?" He fumbled with the latchstring, shouldered the door open and carried her inside. Still not releasing her, his foot caught the door and he kicked it shut behind them. "Hello, Mrs. Kendall," he greeted in a deep-throated tone as his head slowly descended toward hers.

His lips brushed lightly over hers, the tip of his tongue barely grazing the outline of her mouth. Johanna caught her breath. His tantalizing kiss was more enkindling than a live ember on dry prairie grass. No matter how greatly she wished otherwise, she couldn't control her response. Her arms wound tightly around his shoulders and she yielded her mouth to his.

Tyler's tongue swept inside her mouth with hot, hungry penetration as if her yielding had shattered all his control. He released her legs and allowed her to slide down his body, but his hands caught her hips, pulling them against his taut thighs, giving her a startling awareness of his arousal even through the many layers of clothing that separated them. He rocked her against him in a lazy rhythmic motion that matched the thrusting of his tongue, an action that Johanna recognized from other times with him. The knowledge of what was to come didn't frighten her. Indeed, she trembled with it, wanting and needing to release the heated tension he was relentlessly building inside her.

"That's my Johanna," he murmured against her lips, then took them again, this time less hungrily, but the effect was just as devastating. She moved against him enjoying the feel of her breasts pressed against the strength of his chest, the total mastery of his kisses. He released her mouth and buried his face in the graceful curve where her neck joined her shoulder, breathing deeply and harshly. He held her tightly against him for several moments, then stepped away. His hands came up to rest shakily on her shoulders. "I'd better unhitch the horses and get them settled for the night." he stated, his reluctance to leave etched upon his features.

After he had gone, Johanna stood staring at the closed door. "My Johanna, my Johanna." His words rang in her head just as they had done the first night he had ever said them. "I am yours, Tyler," she whispered dazedly into the gathering darkness of the cabin. "I love you."

Outside, she could hear the jingling of the harnesses and imagined how Tyler must look striding through the dusky light as he led the team toward the barn. She could see him clearly in her mind, as though she were standing on the threshold watching him. The brisk strides of his long legs, the muscles flexing beneath the soft fabric of his doeskin trousers. She pictured his wide shoulders stretching beneath his gray frock coat. Weeks of heavy labor had hardened and broadened the muscles of his shoulders, chest and back. That same coat that had shown off his well-developed physique the first time she had seen him was now almost bursting at the seams. She grimaced. The first time she had seen him . . .

"Oh God, why did he have to wear that suit today?" Reality cut through the dreamy mists blanketed around her and she felt cold. The vows she had exchanged with Tyler mocked her. She couldn't let this deception go on any longer, but would he still want her, would he still think of her as "my Johanna" after she confessed?

Shaking herself, she looked around the cabin and realized how dark it had become. Stumbling to the closest lamp, she lit it with shaking fingers. All the doubts and fears that had plagued her during the past week replayed themselves in her mind. Her wedding day should have been the happiest day of her life, but she had never felt more miserable.

Johanna lit one more lamp and then another, as if their soft glow might erase the chilling dread mounting higher inside her with each passing moment. Nervously, she started to pace back and forth across the main room of the cabin, her eyes involuntarily returning again and again to the opened door of the bedroom. The four-poster dominated the little room, the soft bed Tyler would soon be sharing with her, had every right to share with her. The kisses he had bestowed on her when he carried her into the cabin were a clear statement of what he expected when he returned, and in self-honesty she knew that her ready response had proved she would be more than willing.

Frustrated by how easily he could arouse her, she smacked a fist into her hand. Her silk wedding dress rustling softly around her ankles proved the only sound in the room and her slippered feet crossed and recrossed the floor, as her thoughts continued. I melted in his arms the second his lips touched mine! I have to be stronger than that, much stronger! I have to tell him before he touches me again. Berdie was right. You can't start a marriage under a blanket of deception, not even a marriage that isn't based on love.

The sound of the door scraping open startled her and she whirled around. Tyler stood in the doorway, his broad shoulders filling the wood frame. "The lights were a welcoming sight when I came out of the barn," he drawled, a hint of indulgence in his tone. "But do you really think we need all of them?" He folded his arms across his chest and leaned back against the closed door. His dark gray eyes skimmed her pale face. An amused smile tugging at the corners of his mouth, he slowly lowered one hand and pulled in the latchstring.

"I . . . I thought we might need more light while we eat," Johanna stammered, offering the only feasible excuse she could think of. "I'll start supper right now." She took a few steps toward the cooking area, before his laughter caught up with her.

"Supper!" he expounded. "The ladies of the congregation made sure I was kept well fed all day. In fact, Mrs. Meeker and Mrs. Braun were so concerned about our nourishment that they sent along a basket of food. You won't have to cook tonight." As Tyler bent down, Johanna noticed for the first time the large reed basket sitting on the floor just inside the door. He crossed the room and placed it in the center of the table. Dancing gray eyes captured hers and she was unable to look away. "Food is the last thing I want right now and I think you know it. However, if you're hungry, go right ahead. I wouldn't want you to think I'd deny you a meal."

Though she had barely touched any food during the day, Johanna doubted she would be able to swallow one bite. Her throat constricted and her stomach fluttered with what felt like a thousand butterflies all flapping their wings at once. "No, I'm really not hungry," she blurted nervously. "I just thought you might be." Tearing her gaze from his, she sought the sanctuary of one of the settles that flanked the fireplace. Stubbornly, refusing to look at him, she studied the empty grate. "I didn't want to shirk my wifely duties the very first day."

She wanted to recall the words as soon as they were out. Wifely duties! She knew full well what "wifely duties" he expected her to perform. She chanced a look at him from beneath her lashes, praying that he wouldn't make anything of her remark. He hadn't moved from his relaxed stance by the table but his deep gray eyes were devouring her. She could feel his gaze as strongly as if he were actually touching her. When he blew out the lamp above the table and started across the room, she held her breath until he sat down on the opposite settle.

This was it—the perfect time to confess, and she opened her mouth but couldn't find the right words.

Instead she stuttered, "I . . . I . . . thank you for the gown, Tyler. It's very beautiful."

"Not as beautiful as the woman wearing it," was his husky reply.

"You didn't have to do it, you know. It must have cost you a lot of money. I could have worn my blue calico." She knew she was rambling but couldn't seem to stop. "I really didn't need an expensive dress that I'll probably only wear once. It was a waste of good money to try to fancy up a country girl like me."

"Johanna, look at me." His command was given in a quiet tone, but the strength behind his voice made her raise her eyes and look across the few feet that separated them. Her eyes widened when she saw the softened expression on his face, rather than the irritation she had expected. "It wasn't a waste of money," he assured. "I wanted you to wear something very special and I wanted to show you off to everyone. I told you once that you are the prettiest girl in the county and I meant it. That gown wasn't intended to 'fancy' you up. It only provides a background for your beauty."

He stood up and held out his hand, his eyes demanding that she place hers into it. When she did not, he reached down and pulled her slowly to her feet. She knew she had to stop him but was able to offer only token resistance, spreading her palms against his chest as he enfolded her into his arms.

"What happened to the passionate bride I left?" he queried seductively, sensing her reluctance. As if to bribe it away, he ran his hands soothingly up and down her back, gathering her closer as he pressed short little kisses across her forehead, down her cheek and into the curve of her throat.

Johanna felt her traitorous body respond immediately to his gentle seduction, and although she tried to push herself away from him, it was a weak attempt. "I have something to tell you, Tyler," she tried, but arousal won over the desperation in her tone. Delicious shivers were racing down her back as his lips moved moistly across her bare shoulders.

"Whatever it is, it can wait," he murmured against her skin. "I've waited a week to make love to you. Thought of little else, and knowing I will share a bed with you tonight has been driving me crazy all day." He muttered each phrase between kisses and she could feel his fingers efficiently slipping the row of tiny buttons from their loops down the back of her gown.

She gritted her teeth to fight the onslaught of sensations he was creating. "It can't wait, I . . ."

His mouth covered her and her protests were lost as his tongue swept inside her mouth. It effectively broke through her resistance by alternately teasing, then coaxing, a response from hers. When she gave it by darting her tongue across his lips and into his mouth, he groaned and picked her up in his arms. He carried her into the bedroom, never breaking the kiss until he stood her beside the bed.

Guided by his fingers, her wedding gown slid to the floor in a shimmering pool around her feet. Her petticoat, camisole and drawers quickly joined the gown and she trembled from more than the unfamiliar sensations of silk sliding across her bare skin. She stood naked before him. "You're so perfect," he whispered as he ran his hands lightly across her shoulders, over her breasts and down her ribcage to circle her waist.

His eyes were like soft gray velvet as they gazed down at her. Her heart quickened its beat. His features seemed more compellingly handsome than ever before, but she couldn't give herself over to him, not until he knew the truth about her. "Oh Tyler, I can't . . . I have to . . ." Now, tell him *now,* her reason ordered, but his warm mouth took possession of one breast, his tongue laving the nipple into a throbbing sensitive peak, and the words died in her closed throat.

"I know, I know," he groaned and released her breast. In a lightning-fast motion, he whisked the coverlet aside and lifted her onto the bed. "I'll get the lamps," he muttered, his voice rough with desire as he swiftly shrugged out of his coat and untied his neckcloth.

She lay limply back against the pillow, willing her body to stop quaking. She could hear every step he took as he blew out the lamps she had lit. He returned carrying one lighted candle, which he carefully placed upon the bureau. As she watched, his clothing was hastily thrown aside until he was as naked as she. The sight of his blatantly aroused maleness renewed her trembling and Johanna looked away, but her mind betrayed her for it had long since memorized every line and plane of his body.

Even with her eyes squeezed tightly shut she could see his broad shoulders, his powerful chest heavily clouded by dark curling hair that wedged to a narrow line leading downward to his flat belly, only to spread again above his jutting manhood. It was an image that both thrilled and terrified her, drawing forth such an intense response she was shaken to the core, helpless to resist him. She felt the sinking of the mattress as his weight joined hers on the bed.

Tyler swept one hand down her body, closing his palm over her hip and pulling her toward him. He sensed her resistance, but totally misjudged the reason behind it. The little minx was trying to deny the pleasure she always experienced in his arms, to renounce her own passionate nature. An affectionate grin curved his lips. He'd known, ever since he'd bluntly challenged her the day he agreed to her marriage proposal, that she would try to resist but also knew she couldn't hold back very long.

He chuckled softly, barely making a sound. "You *will* come alive for me, Johanna," he vowed. "You always have and you always will." His mouth swooped down to take unerring possession of hers in the darkness.

Johanna tightened the line of her closed lips against his invasion, knowing if she yielded even the slightest she would be lost. She concentrated on stoking her anger, an anger directed both at him and herself. At him for the power he had over her body, at herself for not being able to withstand it, not even long enough to make her delayed confession. Her concentration was already slipping away as his hands swept over her, his fingers tracing erotic patterns down the outside of her thighs and then to the inside, edging steadily closer to the threshold of her womanhood.

He shifted his weight and his chest covered hers, but rather than crushing her beneath him, he seemed to hover a breath above her, just close enough that the hair on his chest teased the peaks of her breasts as he moved back and forth. His tongue lightly outlined her lips but did not attempt to push past the barred entrance. The sensual ploy was more effective than if he had forced her to yield, and Johanna's lips began to soften as his moved lanquidly over hers.

Suddenly, without warning, a deafening clamor shattered the stillness of the night. "What the . . ." Tyler stiffened, then attempted to push himself away from her, but at the first frightening peal of raucous sound Johanna wrapped her arms around him, clinging to him for protection. The staccato noise seemed to surround the entire cabin, a crashing of metal against metal that grated louder than the most forceful summer thunderstorm. They stared deeply into each other's eyes, neither knowing what danger was being heralded by the ear-splitting noise. Tyler's hesitation lasted only a moment, then he firmly pulled her hands from around his waist. In one quick motion he rolled away and off the bed.

All of his senses were tuned to the sounds reverberating through the logs, every instinct telling him to grab the nearest weapon, defend his wife and new home. Crouching low to the floor, he bolted toward the main room and the rifle that hung near the outside door. He heard a rustling behind him and, glancing back, saw Johanna starting to scramble off the bed. "Stay where you are," he ordered in a low whisper, relieved that for once it appeared she would follow his orders. He carefully straightened to a standing position, then flattened himself against the wall as he edged toward the rifle. Once he had it in his hands, he started toward the door, checking to see if the weapon was loaded. Easing the hammer back, he reached for the door.

"Mr. and Mrs. Kendall!" hailed a deep voice from somewhere outside the cabin. That voice was immediately joined by others until Tyler and Johanna could hear their names being called out from every direction.

"What the hell is going on out there?" Tyler demanded angrily, looking over his shoulder to see his wife slipping on a long white nightgown. At first he thought she meant to join him at the door, then he heard her choked laughter. "This is no time for hysterics, Johanna," he commanded gruffly. "Pull yourself together."

His terse orders only increased the intensity of her giggles, while the threatening voices outside continued to call their names and the clanging sound got louder. Torn between comforting his hysterical wife and confronting the unknown danger outside, he turned around, his back against the door as he watched Johanna button up her gown. He didn't recognize the look on her face, completely nonplussed that she kept on laughing, bending over at the waist and holding her sides. Whenever she looked his way, her eyes seemed glued below his waist.

"Oh Tyler . . . you look so funny standing there wearing nothing but that gun," she managed between another fit of the giggles. "I suggest you exchange that rifle for a pair of pants before you greet our friends."

"Our friends?" he asked incredulously, fearing the horrendous noise had driven her mad. "Those are no friends of mine out there!" He started to lift the bar, but Johanna raced across the room and stopped him.

"We're being shivareed, Tyler. You'll be the talk of the county for years if you storm out there naked as a jaybird!" She grabbed his arm and started pulling him toward the bedroom. "Come on, get dressed. They'll keep that up until we go out there."

"What in the name of all that's holy does 'shivareed' mean?" He stumbled along behind her, still keeping a firm hold on the gun.

"Shivaree, you Easterner! It's a party for newlyweds."

"They already threw a party that lasted all day!" he exclaimed, disbelief written on every feature of his face.

Johanna pulled on a wrapper over her nightgown. "We sometimes party all night out here in the country after a wedding. Hurry up, Tyler, before they come in here and drag us outside." Still not completely convinced she was telling him the truth, he accepted the weak possibility and scrambled into his clothes.

Johanna slid her feet into her moccasins. "They've probably already got David and Berdie. Be sure and put on your boots, there's no telling where they'll take us."

"Take us? David and Berdie? What kind of party is this?"

"You'll soon find out. It's best to go along with

whatever the crowd wants," she advised calmly as she picked up her wedding dress, Tyler's coat, waistcoat and neckcloth. She carefully hung them up while a disgruntled Tyler finished dressing. "Just remember one thing." She made no attempt to hide her large grin. "This is all done in friendship, so try to enjoy it."

"This is definitely not what I envisioned for our wedding night," Tyler grumbled as he pulled on his boots. "I've half a mind to chase them off with that rifle, friends or no."

He'd obviously intended to say more but the crowd gathered outside their walls burst into song. The off-key lyrics implied they had little time before they'd have several unwanted guests inside their small bedroom. Muttering a string of curses that Johanna had never heard anyone say, Tyler grabbed hold of her hand and started for the door. "Wait a minute!" He stopped in mid-stride. "No one but me is going to see my wife in her nightclothes. Go change into something decent."

"I'll only have to change back," Johanna replied, her expression leaving him in little doubt that she was right.

"Stop dallying, you lovebirds!" The bass voice resounded from right outside the door.

"Want company in there?" another voice demanded.

"Hell!" Tyler grunted, then lifted the bar over the door.

As soon as they stepped outside they were pulled apart. Having been present on several similar occasions, Johanna meekly allowed herself to be dragged away, but Tyler had no such experience to draw upon. She heard him call out her name, emit several more angry curses, then looked over her captor's shoulders and saw that he stood alone in the center of a large circle of men. She had a difficult time seeing more as she was hustled toward a waiting wagon, but once she was lifted into the back she had a fine view of the proceedings. As she had suspected, Berdine was already in the wagon and immediately came to stand beside her. "At least David knew it was coming," she said, grabbing hold of Johanna's hand. "They've got him trussed up in Meeker's wagon. I hope he's fit to live with tomorrow."

"Tyler won't be. I can guarantee that and it won't be due to any corn liquor," Johanna declared, unable to keep the amusement out of her voice.

"Mind you're not too rough." Jenny Meeker's familiar voice instructed the men from a spot beneath a cottonwood tree. "Sometimes we get carried away with these hijinks," she exclaimed loudly to the group of women prancing around her who were beating their pots and pans in a savage rhythm.

In the light from several torches, Johanna could easily make out the irate expression on her husband's face. He was not entering into the festivities with any degree of enthusiasm. His stance was threatening as—like a pack of hungry wolves closing in on a lone sheep—the circle of men drew tighter.

"Cain't fight us all, Tyler," one man chided humorously, and Johanna recognized his voice—their nearest neighbor, Sam Berkman, was the leader of the men. "Only want to give you one night you'll never forget."

Tyler held up his hands, backing away, but stopped when he saw the men behind him had no intention of letting him get through. "I'll have that if you boys just get back on your horses and leave us in peace."

His gruff statement brought about a whoop of laughter that didn't die out until Sam raised his arm. "All right, men. On my signal, we charge."

The instant Sam lowered his arm, the men surged at Tyler and within minutes he was wrestled to the ground. Tied hand and foot, he was carried toward a wagon and unceremoniously dumped beside David.

"Say goodnight to your men, ladies," Sam called, waving at Johanna and Berdine as he drove his wagon past theirs.

"Goodnight, Tyler," Johanna shouted.

"I love you, David," Berdine cried, then both girls quickly sank to the floor of their wagon, searching for something to hang on to as their driver cracked his whip over the horses.

What followed was a wild ride over the rolling countryside. The parade of wagons careened down the dirt road, several turning in opposite directions at the first fork. Although she knew she was supposed to be frightened, all Johanna felt was exhilaration as the night wind lifted her hair from her shoulders and whipped it over her eyes. She had been given a reprieve!

Wedging herself in one corner, she advised Berdine to do the same, then held on for dear life as the galloping team carried them swiftly over the hills.

Their escorts on horseback were singing a familiar ditty at the top of their lungs and Johanna joined in. She laughed as loudly as the others when the song came to an end, unaware that her sister couldn't fathom her good spirits.

It was when the long ride was over and they were being returned to the cabin that Berdine questioned Johanna's exuberance. "I'd think a new bride wouldn't greet being separated from her husband with such zest."

"What's one night, Berdie? This was a lot of fun." Johanna leaned her head back on the side of the wagon and looked up at the stars. "We'll have plenty of time to be together after this."

"Hmmph." Berdine shivered in the cold air, wrapping both arms around herself. "I'd sooner we'd forgone all this 'fun.' I'm about froze and I was positive the wagon was going to turn over after every turn. Shivarees are one custom the world could do without."

Johanna made no comment. If it hadn't been for their neighbors' timely interruption, she'd have offered her body to Tyler once again, her resistance as weak as a newborn calf's. She knew that in the very near future she would be confronted with the same curcumstances again, but at least she had one more night.

"Do you think the men are all right?" Berdine inquired anxiously. "What if their wagon did tip over?"

"They're fine, Berdine," Johanna stated confidently. "We'll have them back tomorrow. Course, they may be so much the worse for drink they won't be worth nothing."

"You almost sound as if you hope that's the way it will be."

"Nope." Johanna turned away to hide her expression. "But you've got to admit it's possible."

"Guess so," Berdine admitted sadly. "I'll have to brew a pot of Mama's special tea and have it waiting just in case."

"Do that," Johanna advised, then returned to her silent contemplation of the sky, eventually feeling a strange sense of loneliness welling inside her as she viewed the dark fathomless reaches overhead.

Chapter Fifteen

TYLER AND JOHANNA STOOD ON THE THRESHOLD OF THE cabin, waving as Berdine and David's buggy disappeared over the rise. Tyler's arm about her waist felt like the cutting edge of a sword but Johanna didn't dare complain, not once she'd seen the explosive lights in his smoldering gray eyes. "Perhaps you'd like a cup of Ma's herbal tea," she suggested, breaking free of his hold and hurrying back into the house, aware of little else but how closely behind her he followed. "It seemed to help revive David."

"All I'd like is a new head," Tyler grunted sarcastically. "But by all means make me some tea. It's such a *wifely* thing to do." She could feel his eyes burning holes into her back as she made for the lean-to and hastily reached for the kettle.

Pretending total concentration with the preparations for his drink, she risked several surreptitious glances at him from beneath her long lashes. He looked terrible! His hair was rumpled, his gray eyes rimmed with red, and there was a decidedly green tinge around his mouth. The night's growth of beard that shadowed his cheeks and chin emphasized the pallor of his face. He walked with a most peculiar gait, finally holding onto the back of the settle by the fireplace and lowering his tall frame onto the seat.

"Do you know how I spent my wedding night, Johanna?" he inquired, his voice sounding as low and ominous as distant thunder.

"No," she replied vaguely, though she had a very good idea what had transpired during the long hours he'd been gone. "I'm only familiar with what goes on with the bride. The ladies don't take part in any drinking."

"Then it will be my pleasure to tell you," he sneered, rearranging his tall frame more comfortably on the hard bench. "Although I had far more interesting plans for the evening, I learned to dance something called the Nebraska jig in the middle of a deserted cornfield. My lovely dancing partner wasn't my dear wife, but that addlepated old geezer from the train station, Barney Holcomb."

Turning her back on him to hide the tiny smile that was threatening to become a huge grin, she muttered "Oh," then acted as if she were completely engrossed in her task. Her shoulders shook with suppressed laughter, but she didn't dare make a sound, not when it appeared for some reason that he blamed her for the whole of last night's festivities.

As soon as she'd controlled her inner hilarity, she stated firmly, "I had nothing to do with the shivaree, Tyler. Folks in these parts always plan the like for newlyweds. There wasn't any way I could have prevented it from happening."

"After a few drinks of that corn liquor," he continued as if he hadn't heard her, "I didn't even care that they'd dragged me away from the loving arms of my new bride. Once I'd had a few more, it didn't appear to bother me that my pillow was a pile of rotted corn husks and my mattress the cold hard ground. I passed out, you see. Seems even I, who can hold my liquor as well as any man, was quickly felled by that raw whiskey some farmer concocted in his barnyard still."

Pouring hot water over the herbs in the cup, Johanna composed her features and then carried the hot drink to him. She tried not to laugh at how badly his hands shook as he lifted the cup to his lips. He drained the contents in three swallows, then placed the cup on the floor.

"I'll just take that back to the kitchen," she stated quietly, aware that any loud sound made him wince. She bent down for the cup but was forced to drop it back on the floor when his hand shot out and grabbed her wrist. Within seconds, she found herself seated upon his lap, his arms wrapped tightly around her to hold her in place.

"You've found this whole affair highly amusing, haven't you?" his harsh voice rumbled in her ear. "I wonder if you'll think it's so funny when I'm done with you."

"You're behaving like a blamed fool," Johanna snapped, trying to squirm out of his hold, but his hand was like a manacle about her wrists and his arms were immobile as steel bars. She had no intention of shouldering the blame for something she'd had no means to prevent. "I don't see why you're angry with me for what happened last night. I was stolen too and taken outside in my nightclothes. I near froze to death."

"But you knew what was coming, didn't you? Looked forward to it as a reprieve from my love-making." He lifted her off his lap and set her to one side, trapping her between himself and the tall sides of the high-backed settle. One heavy thigh pinned down the faded material of her calico skirt and his arm formed a barricade in front of her. "I imagine you remembered that promise I made to you the day you proposed, to take you whenever and as often as I pleased. I intended to do just that, Johanna, make love to you over and over again, without interruption, but all along you knew that wasn't to be."

Her throat dried upon seeing the blistering censure in his eyes, and she quickly glanced away. He dropped his arm, then used his thumb and forefinger to lift up her chin so she was forced to look him full in the face. "I arranged for the children to be gone for several days," he informed her gruffly. "Brought out that basket of food so you wouldn't have any excuse for leaving my bed, but you didn't need one, did you? I heard you laughing when they dragged me away.

Imagine how I felt, knowing my loving bride preferred spending the evening with a bunch of drunken hooligans than with me."

She shook her head free, her blue eyes snapping angrily. "Those hooligans are our friends and neighbors! You have no call to insult them like that. Shivarees are a country tradition and it's not their fault you've got no sense of humor."

"You're right," he admitted, but she took no comfort in the obliging words. "Our neighbors didn't realize I wouldn't know what was coming. Only you were aware of that."

"I suppose I should have warned you," Johanna acknowledged grudgingly, prompting his short humorless laugh.

"Perhaps that little omission was deliberate," he suggested. "You knew what I wanted from you and were savoring the knowledge I wouldn't get it as soon as I thought I would." He released her chin, but took hold of her by the shoulders, his eyes burning into her face. "There are quite a number of things you haven't seen fit to tell me, but now that you're my wife I'm determined to cure that bad habit!"

"I don't know what you're talking about!" Johanna flared back. "Oh, I know what you want from me all right. You've made your lust for my body perfectly clear. Well, the day I proposed I told you exactly what I wanted out of this marriage."

"Aaah yes, I'm well aware of your reasons for marrying me." Tyler let go of her and leaned back on the settle, gazing toward the ceiling. Before saying more, he folded his arms over his chest, stretched his long legs out on the floor in front of him and crossed his ankles. "You wanted Berdine to have her David. You wanted another man around to help you work your farm. You wanted strong sons but will no doubt deny the pleasure we share in making them. But there's one reason you've left out, the most important reason of all."

"And what would that be?" Johanna asked, thinking he was about to make some other crude comment about her inability to hide her desire for him.

"You wanted to save yourself from prosecution."

"What?" she croaked, swallowing the huge obstruction that suddenly closed her throat. Surely, she couldn't have heard right.

"You're the blue-eyed scallywag that robbed me on the train," Tyler pronounced, his expression masked, but mockery gleaming in his fathomless eyes. "You knew if we were married I'd never turn you in, but what you didn't know is I found out about your little escapade quite some time ago."

Standing up, he walked to the mantle. He inserted his hand behind the clock, then, finding nothing, shrugged. "I see you've gotten rid of the evidence." She noted the predatory flash of white teeth beneath his mustache but couldn't do anything but stare. "I do hope you've put my service revolver in a safe place, Johanna, for I'm going to be very upset if it's not given back to me in the same sound condition in which it was taken."

Recalling the last time she'd found him leaning against the mantle, she realized when he had probably discovered her identity. It was the night of his barn raising. No wonder he'd behaved so strangely on the ride over to his farm. She paled to the color of chalk, then charged, "You've known about this ever since the night of the dance?"

"That's right."

Remembering what else had transpired that night, a tight knot of pain developed in her stomach, a churning nausea that made her feel ill. Humiliated tears welled up behind her eyes, but she refused to cry. He'd made love to her that night for the first time. She had thought his lovemaking a beautiful thing, would never forget how tenderly he'd taught her the ways of passion, but his tenderness had been nothing but a sham, a means of coaxing her past the walls of defense she erected against him. He'd been well aware of what lay behind her reluctance to get close to him and knew what she'd suffer once he took her into his bed. "That was the night you . . . you . . ."

"Made you my woman?" He brushed a stray lock of hair off of his forehead. "Indeed. That night I took into my bed a cunning little thief, who foolishly enjoyed behaving like a man, and I taught her why she should be eternally grateful she's a woman. I even married her, knowing full well that I couldn't trust her an inch. You see, I wanted a dutiful wife and I think we both know I now have the means to ensure you'll become exactly that."

Johanna jumped to her feet, her eyes flashing blue sparks of fury. "You've known about the robbery all this time and didn't tell me? You let my family suffer with the guilt of knowing we'd robbed a neighbor, another farmer like ourselves? We had to hold our breaths every time you uttered a word, and you enjoyed seeing us squirm, didn't you? That's the most low-down, mean and ornery thing I've ever heard in all my born days!"

Tyler looked as if he was considering whether or not there was any merit in her remarks, but then he shook his head, dismissing her ire. "I'd say you paid a very small price for committing such a serious crime. I could have had your whole family arrested but I didn't, did I? It was obvious to me that Fritz, Cordie and Amy were merely following your orders, and I doubt Berdine was aware of your plans until after you returned home with all my money. Isn't that true?"

"Yes," Johanna whispered, knowing there was no use in denying it. She had planned to tell him herself, beg him for forgiveness, but his accusations continued to rain down upon her head and she couldn't prevent the surge of temper that was building up inside her.

"Berdine probably wanted to give it back the night you found me on your doorstep but you wouldn't let her, would you?"

"That's right."

"You used the money to pay off a second mortgage taken out from the Kendall Bank."

She nodded. Obviously, he knew everything, every last incriminating detail.

"In order to make up to me for some of what you'd taken, Fritz came over whenever I called. Berdine sent over food as often as possible. Cordie and Amy spent hours digging roots out of my fields. Even you tried to soothe your guilty conscience by showing me how to plant my first crop of corn."

"That's not true." He had finally stated something that she could honestly deny. "We would have helped any new neighbor get started. People out here have to rely on each other. It's the only way we can survive. We're not vultures like you and yours, feeding off the meager profits we earn from our crops, getting fat off of our labors."

When Tyler ran his hand over his trim waist, then shrugged as if her words couldn't possibly be directed at him, she exploded. "You dog-eared dandy! I don't care what you do to me. I'm glad I robbed you! I only wish I'd taken more."

"You took nearly every cent I had with me," Tyler informed her calmly.

His indulgent expression fanned her anger to new heights and she cried, "When I saw you lying across that velvet divan, so drunk you couldn't see straight, I thought you were 'bout the poorest excuse for a man I ever did see. And . . . and I've had no reason to change my opinion ever since!"

All color washed from her face when he immediately straightened to his full height and took a step toward her. "Sure! Beat me! A cowardly drunkard like you probably gets real pleasure from hitting a defenseless woman."

There was no place for her to run, so she bravely held her position, glaring defiantly up at him as he approached. Rather than raising his hand to strike her, he placed his fingers over her mouth, and even that was done in a nonviolent way. His request for silence seemed almost polite and her eyes went wide with shock.

"Now," he began, once he was satisfied he had silenced her. He gave her a gentle push so she'd sit back down on the bench. "You've released all that pent-up emotion and that's fine, but we still haven't gotten to the heart of this matter. What I've been trying to tell you, Johanna, is that I'm prepared to keep this solely between the two of us. All I want is your promise that you've committed your last crime and that you'll try to make me a dutiful wife. If you can do that, I in return will make sure you and your family are well taken care of. No one but us need know about our little bargain. What do you say? Am I asking too much?"

Her total astonishment was written across her face and shone from her large eyes, but she still managed to give him an answer. "No, I . . . I guess not." A small shred of doubt furrowed her brow. "You mean I won't have to worry that you'll threaten me about this in the future? If I am a good wife to you, you won't tell anyone what we did? Not any of your friends? Not even your family?"

"My family are the last people I'd tell."

"Of course," she sighed sadly. "You wouldn't want them to know you'd saddled yourself with a thief."

She was too miserable to catch the pained expression that flickered in his eyes. Bowing her head as if accepting a life sentence being handed down by a judge, she mumbled, "You have my promise, Tyler. I'll try to be a dutiful wife to you and I'll never again do anything that could cast shame on the Heinsman name."

"The Kendall name, Johanna. Your name is Johanna Kendall and you'll answer to that until the day you die."

She could only nod, unable to prevent the single tear that slid from beneath her thick lashes and rolled down her cheek. Upon seeing it, Tyler's jaw went tight, and his teeth clenched. He forced himself to remain calm and keep his tone gentle. "There's no need to look like that, Johanna. I'm not a cruel man."

Again all he got for his effort was a meek nod. An angry glitter came into his eyes as he digested her opinion of him, then he spoke tersely, his words harsh, even though he had just claimed he was not a cruel man. "Why don't you begin your wifely duties by heating up some water for my bath? I reek of whiskey and God knows what else. I don't want to offend your sensibilities when I take you to bed."

"It's summertime. I can carry some towels to the river. That's where we bathe until it gets cold."

"I want a hot bath with plenty of steam," he said shortly. "The vapors will get rid of the last remnants of my unexpected inebriation."

Without any further words of protest, Johanna went to do his bidding. It was hard work and took quite a while for her to drag out the bathing tub, then carry in enough water from the well to fill it. By the time she had heated several large kettles of water on the stove and poured their steaming contents into the tub, she was sweating from both the exertion and the strain of holding her temper in check—no longer feeling as cowed as when she'd begun.

Tyler had not lifted one finger to help her yet had watched her like a hawk, as if waiting for her to complain so he could swoop down and berate her. She didn't understand the strange expression that came and went on his face while he stared at her, but she wouldn't risk arousing his anger further by asking about it. It was bad enough that she must endure being treated like a servant. She wasn't going to bring any more of his wrath down on her head. "It's ready, Tyler. I'll go fetch you some towels."

She crossed to the bedroom and went inside. The last thing she needed was for him to see desire gather in her eyes if she stayed and watched him disrobe. She was honest enough to admit that the mere thought of seeing him naked brought on a flush that wasn't caused by the heat from the stove. It didn't seem to matter that he appeared to enjoy humiliating her and would probably continue to do so. He affected her as strongly as ever.

She thought she had given him enough time to complete his undressing and get into the tub before she reentered the room but found he'd done no such thing. "Is something the matter? Isn't the water hot enough for you?"

"I need you to help me take off my boots."

"What?" She was incredulous.

"Are you going to help me?" he asked, a dangerous expression in his dark eyes, daring her to refuse. Did he want her to decline so he'd be justified in using physical force to convince her to comply?

"Certainly." She crossed the room, keeping her emotions under firm control. His reaction to her prompt courteous answer was so obviously disappointment that it did a lot to soothe her temper.

Bending down, she reached for his boot but he waved her back up. "Turn around," he ordered. "I'll show you how this is done."

After she'd endured the firm pressure of his foot pushing against her taut backside for the second time and the feel of his legs tightly wedged between hers as she pulled off each boot, she was dangerously close to venting her anger. She was absolutely certain he'd deliberately kicked up her skirts immodestly high just to embarrass her. By the look on his face, he'd thoroughly enjoyed his view of her bare calves and white drawers. "Will that be all?" Her words no longer conveyed a hint of courtesy, only her disgust.

Standing up, Tyler began unbuttoning his shirt. "For now, but once I'm in the tub you can come and scrub my back. I'd appreciate that very much." His grin was all male challenge, and although she hated herself she backed down. Flouncing away from him, she stomped back into the bedroom and slammed the door.

Hearing his chuckle, she shook her fist at him through the bedroom wall but didn't dare go back in the room. There was a series of loud splashes, then a contented sigh, and she was certain he'd finally installed himself in the tub. Feeling safe from any retribution, she called out, "Just because I agreed to be a dutiful wife doesn't mean I'll allow you to treat me like your own personal servant. If you want a lackey, you can go back East. Out here, a man can take off his own boots and scrub his own back."

"If I go East, you'll have to come with me," he called back. "Would you like a house full of servants,

Johanna? You'd always be dressed in the latest fashions from Europe—satin ribbons and ostrich feathers for your hair. You wouldn't have to worry about anything but which invitations to accept and which to turn down."

"You won't get me to that highfaluting place no matter what you do, so don't even try." Each word that tumbled out of her mouth increased her courage. "Look what living in Boston's done to you. A grown man who'd allow a woman to tend him in a bath. A dandy who needs help pulling off his fancy leather boots. Well, I don't want any part of your lily-livered city life. I'd choose Hemmington over Boston any day of the week. It's a place full of strong people who always earn their own way."

"And if they can't, they steal it from fancy citified dandies," Tyler boomed back, but there was little anger in his words.

Johanna was too carried away by her own outrage to mark his mild tone. "Why, you dog-eared blue blood! I suppose you'll remind me of that every chance you get! Well, that's just fine by me. I can recall a few things you'd rather I forgot."

When he didn't make another comeback, she went to the door and pressed her ear against the wood. She thought she heard him say, "Now, that's my Johanna," but knew she had to be mistaken. After that, all she heard was whistling, an enthusiastic rendition of the jaunty tune she'd sung the night before. Evidently, the men in his wagon had sung the same song and he'd picked up the melody. She mumbled an uncomplimentary phrase under her breath and trounced away from the door, commanding herself not to think about him any longer. She didn't know how much time passed, as she sightlessly gazed out the window thinking of nothing else.

"I'm finished. Would you like to take my place in the tub?"

Whirling around, Johanna found Tyler revealed in all his masculine glory, standing slightly inside the bedroom door. A hot blush rushed to her cheeks and she couldn't think of anything to say. Why did she let him affect her like this? Why didn't she look right through him as if he weren't there? But she simply couldn't and her traitorous eyes feasted on his bare flesh for much too long a time before she bit out, "I did bring you a towel. Have you no sense of propriety? My pa may have been a farmer but he never strutted around the house without a stitch on. It looks like we homesteaders have a better idea of proper behavior than you Eastern bankers."

Tearing her eyes away, she crossed to the bedroom and tore open the trunk that contained his clothes. After tossing a clean shirt and a pair of pants onto the bed, she stalked to the bureau and deposited several more of his shirts in the empty drawer that had once contained Berdine's things. She heard his bare feet padding across the room and assumed he was heading for the bed but learned her mistake when she felt his damp body pressing into hers from behind, pinning her against the bureau.

"So it isn't proper for a husband to stand naked before his wife," he murmured huskily, his breath warm on the sensitive skin below her ear. "Funny, I received the decided impression you very much enjoyed looking at me. Did you know that your eyes start shining and deepen to the color of a summer sea when you want me? And you lecture *me* on good manners. Johanna Kendall, surely it's most impolite to stare at a naked man and reveal such desire, then turn your back on him before he can do anything about it."

"Oh!" she gasped. The exclamation was a mixture of outrage and passion as he swept her hair to one side and began nuzzling the nape of her neck. His fingers nimbly undid the cut-steel buttons down the back of her gingham shirtwaist but she didn't move, paralyzed by the feel of his nakedness pressing against her.

She uttered a soft moan when his mouth drifted feather-light kisses along the straps of her camisole, then slid them down her shoulders. He kissed each new area of smooth flesh he exposed as he proceeded to strip her to the waist. When he reached in front of her and lifted one full breast into each of his hands, she couldn't contain her frantic sigh of pleasure. His fingers kneaded the soft flesh, while his mouth trailed over her shoulders, and down her spine. Leaving one hand to soothe the throbbing in her nipples, he used the other to unhook her skirt. He let it fall around her ankles and—within moments—the rest of her clothing occupied the same space.

When she felt his lips and tongue nipping a path from her hipbone across the twin curves at the bottom of her spine, slowly traversing toward her other hip, her head became too heavy for her neck to hold. As she leaned her forehead against the cool wood of the bureau, it was the only spot on her entire body that wasn't consumed by searing heat.

Straightening back up, Tyler again covered her breasts with both hands, then pulled her trembling body against his. "Oh, Tyler," she sighed, leaning her head against his shoulder and closing her eyes. She turned her face and accepted the kiss waiting to descend on her soft lips.

"Come, my Johanna." Tyler raised his head, bent slightly, then lifted her into his arms. "Let me show you that your blue-blooded husband is more than happy to tend a grown woman in her bath. I shall be your own personal servant. Between us, Blue Eyes, the only things that are truly proper are those that make us happy. We can concern ourselves with the proprieties when we aren't alone."

Since she had nothing to add to his huskily delivered remarks, her hands clinging around his neck, her head resting heavily upon his shoulder, he dropped a kiss on her forehead and carried her into the main room. "Your bath awaits, milady."

Chapter Sixteen

JOHANNA OPENED HER EYES AT THE FAMILIAR SOUND OF a cock crowing the dawn. As she'd done every morning since childhood, she stretched her body, preparing to rise, but instantly became aware that as of this morning, unlike any other, her life was irreparably changed. A man's tousled brown head rested upon her bare breasts and a muscled thigh, roughened with crisp dark hair, lay heavily across her slender legs. At the sight of Tyler's naked skin in contact with hers, her face grew hot and her whole body seemed to blush. She tried to move away but found herself trapped by a heavy arm pinning her long hair to the pillow.

A small gasp escaped her lips and she went rigid, staring down at her sleeping husband's face, unable to ward off the rush of erotic memories the sight of him unleashed. Asleep, his bold male features were contented, even the deep clefts beside his mouth were relaxed, a half smile tilting his firm lips. His lashes were long, thick and dark and a new growth of beard on his lean cheeks rasped her sensitive skin whenever he breathed, yet she didn't dare move for fear of waking him.

Her eyes roamed over him, much more aware of his nakedness than she was of her own. His broad chest, liberally covered with dark curling hair. His arms capped by bronzed, taut muscle. The sinewy power in his long legs. She couldn't breathe, astonished by the renewed desire that surged within her. It had been only a few hours since she'd fallen asleep in his arms, completely exhausted by his masterful lovemaking.

As if aware of her restlessness, yet still asleep, Tyler rolled to one side, his arm still trapping her hair but giving her a much more complete view of his unclothed body. Helplessly, her eyes strayed down his neck to his chest, then lower to his hard flat stomach. Yesterday he had taught her new lessons in passion, an education that had continued throughout the night. Under his expert tutelage, she'd discovered intimacies that went far beyond the boundaries of her imagination, and she'd been unable to do anything but yield to the devastating pleasure. Today, as she remembered exactly how total her surrender had been, her body burned with mortification. He'd begun by washing away the last of her defenses with the tender torment administered during her bath and by the time he'd finished acting as her servant, she'd given herself completely over to him, no longer worrying about the fact that he didn't love her.

Tentatively, she placed her hand on the smooth warm skin of his chest, her darkened gaze lingering on the virile part of him that he'd made part of her innumerable times over the past hours. As she watched, his manhood began to grow. Startled, her eyes flew to his. He was awake, watching her, the lopsided smile on his face belied by the gray smoke in his eyes.

"Johanna," he murmured drowsily, but the low timbre of his voice sent shivers across her flesh. Like a waking lion, he moved slumberously, rolling back toward her. His husky growl was that of a sated cat, yet there was hunger in his eyes.

Languorously, he kissed the corner of her mouth. Her hands fluttered protestingly to his shoulders, but with his first slight touch her eyes closed meekly in surrender. In the gray light, as if the dawn brought to mind no other daily responsibilities, he kissed her cheek and her ear, then nuzzled the lobe with his warm tongue. She cringed away from the tingling sensation, but he merely smiled at her, a slow, knowing smile that proved his memories of their night together were still fresh in his mind. For an instant, supreme male confidence and a challenging hint of triumph flashed in his eyes, but then his lashes drifted down to cover the expression.

"Good morning, Mrs. Kendall." There was a significant emphasis on the name they shared, but she was allowed no answering salutation. His mouth lowered over her lips. As he had taught her so well the night before, she lacked any means to resist but he didn't yet know what a fast learner she'd become. This morning he would discover what kind of weapons she had at her disposal and that his defenses were just as flimsy as hers. Her pride demanded no less and she arched against him, pressing her naked breasts to his chest as her arms rose by their own volition around his neck. Already, her body was on fire with a delicious need, and her fingers clutched his crisp, tawny hair, pressing his face even closer. Soon, soon she would show him the consequences of his expertise but until then . . .

She parted her teeth and tasted him. He tasted better than the elderberry wine her mother used to make each summer, like rich tangy ambrosia. She explored his mouth, seeking more of the intoxicating, the delectable taste that now belonged solely to her. An intense surge of female possessiveness overrode all other sensations. With or without love, Tyler Kendall was legally her man, and she had every right to savor the feel of his body—as much right as he had to savor hers. Forgetting everything else but this new sense of freedom, her hands ran hungrily down his back and over his taut buttocks. Maybe he did own her, but then she owned him as well.

At her ready response, she could sense the arrogant satisfaction in him and she smiled. Wait, Tyler, she silently commanded, just you wait. Last night she had been a helpless victim of his demanding possession, mindlessly buffeted from one climactic peak to the next. Today, however, he would learn how easily the reverse could also be true. She wanted to see his eyes on fire with passion, wanted *her* touch to drive him beyond caring about anything but his need for her.

She bucked him off her, but his offended grunt of surprise dissolved into a strangled gasp of pleasure as her soft fingers closed around his manhood. Her sleek supple body pinned his to the mattress as with feline deliberation she caressed him. Emboldened by the harsh tremors that rippled down his length, she became a wild kitten, provoking a beast much bigger than herself. Her breasts rubbed against his chest and she purred deep in her throat.

"Wh-what are you doing to me?" he faltered, rapidly losing the powerful strength in his limbs. "Oh God, Johanna!" His voice was trembling, uneven, as he felt her soft lips sliding down his throbbing flesh.

She wanted to be everything to him a woman could be. Aware that he was dangerously close to losing control, she kissed her way back up his body, then took his lips with wanton delight. Straddling his lean hips between her thighs, she taunted him with her soft breasts, rubbing them across his flat nipples as her lips and tongue explored his. After a long, demanding possession, she lifted her mouth away, staring into his desire-laden eyes. Her blond hair fell down around his shoulders like a shimmering wall of gold and she reveled in the fantasy of his capture. He was her husband, lover, partner—and she loved him.

"Johanna, let me . . . please," he moaned, his expression holding something akin to awe. She felt herself smile as his hands moved to her hips, urgently demanding that she ease the ache she had inspired.

"You're everything, Blue Eyes. Everywhere and everything."

Yes. That was what she wanted to be to him—his everything. She wanted him to see her image across their vast fields, in the blue skies, in each star in the heavens—everywhere. Lifting her hips, she took him inside herself, wanting to give and give and give until he'd never be able to forget it or her, no matter how long he lived. She accepted his groan of pleasure and didn't attempt to stop him as he reversed their positions and claimed her for a journey they could only take together.

Clinging to one another, they went somewhere beyond the highest cloud, where explosions of feeling blazed hotter than the sun, showering them both with golden mists of pleasure. Flying through space, she heard his voice calling out to her, "How I love you, Johanna. God, how I love you," and she wrapped her arms even more tightly about him to let him know she'd heard and would never let him go. She held on until the last convulsive shudder had faded away and they were again safe, drifting back to earth.

"Tyler?" It was a whisper that grew louder when she got no response. "Tyler, did you mean what you said?"

For a moment, he spoke only with his eyes, giving her answers she'd never expected to receive. His handsome features were open and honest, his lips parted in a gentle smile. "I gave you the words, my Johanna. Can you do the same?" He drew her up beside him, resting his head and shoulders against the carved headboard, watching her as she followed suit.

Allowing all of her feelings to shine forth in her eyes, she nodded. "I've loved you since forever."

Her reward was a devastating kiss that proved they had both spoken the simple truth when they repeated their marriage vows. Johanna was astonished. Finally able to speak, she asked, "But, Tyler, how can . . . why do you love me? I've robbed you, tricked you, practically forced you to marry me. I'm not your kind of woman at all."

"I can't count how many times I tried to tell myself that." Tyler grinned, shooing away the last of her fears with the tender look on his face and his next words. "But it never changed a thing. I couldn't seem to stop myself from falling in love with you." His dark eyes probed the blue depths of hers, "You see, Johanna, I've discovered you're exactly my kind of woman, the only kind I need or will ever want."

When he saw the tiny line develop between her brows, he reached out with one finger and smoothed it away. "You're feeling guilty again, aren't you? I recognize that look and this is the last time I want to see it. You know, if you hadn't insulted my masculinity the day you proposed, I would have told you then that I knew all about the robbery, probably right before *I* proposed to you. I don't condone what you did, and you'll never get far enough away from me to try anything so harebrained again, but I know what prompted you to do it."

He went on to tell her that, through David, he'd learned all about the deaths of her father and brother and her reasons for blaming the railroad. "There are a lot of injustices in the world, Jo. Maybe together we'll deal with them much better than we're able to do on our own. I know if I hadn't met you, I'd still be missing a part of myself I thought I'd lost forever."

"What?" Johanna stared into his eyes, perplexed by the deep vulnerability in their depths.

"It was the war," Tyler stated grimly, his features going hard as the memories returned.

Seeing the embittered look on his face, Johanna grasped his arm. "Tyler, you never have to speak of it again. I saw how you and David, two strong brave men, avoided talking about it the day you met. I love you and I want you to let me help you forget all the hurts."

"I think first I have to get it all out." Tyler placed his hand over hers, his fingers cold. "During the war, Johanna, I wasn't strong, nor brave. My father bought me a commission and I went blithely off to battle. I soon learned there was no more honor or glory in victory than there was in defeat, for all that came from either was the death of good men."

His gaze drifted up to the rafters, as if there he could look into the past, no longer aware of her presence beside him. "Following my lead, a whole patrol rode into ambush. Several men were killed, the rest captured. I spent almost a year in a prison camp, watching others die from starvation or illness or from being mistreated. I learned a very good lesson there. A man's background, social status, wealth—none of those matter when you're starving, when you're afraid you're the next man who's going to be beaten bloody. Nothing's more important than staying alive. The strongest of us killed off the rats that wanted our food and enforced a primitive justice that kept the weak from tearing each other apart. Every day was a fight for survival. I was beginning to prove to myself that I could cope with that ghastly place as well as the next man, when I was informed of my release. My wealthy father had somehow arranged my freedom in an exchange of prisoners. I was guilty of leading my men into ambush, saw them wasting away to bare bones in that prison, yet I was the one being given my freedom.

"I refused to go back to Boston, even though I was too weak to hold a gun. My parents were horrified, but I recuperated in an overcrowded army hospital until I was fit enough to rejoin my regiment. I spent the rest of the war fighting under Grant. I was never a great soldier, just a man doing what he must to survive, and for that I was given a medal for valor. When I went home after the war, I was greeted as some kind of a hero, but I knew the truth. I'd lived through the war because of my father's money. I couldn't stomach the false image they'd labeled me with, and I began, perversely, proving to them all that the exact opposite was true. I spent most of my time gambling and drinking. I can't remember how many nights I drank myself into a stupor and woke up unable to recall the previous day."

"Oh, Tyler." Johanna sighed sympathetically. "It must have been horrible, but . . ." Her voice trailed weakly away.

For the first time since he'd begun his explanation, he turned his head and looked at her. "But?"

She took a deep breath, not wanting to hurt him. "I . . . I don't know your parents, Tyler, but it seems to me they did the same as you."

"What?"

"Someone they loved more than anything was in prison and they did what they had to do. They fought for you in the best way they knew how. You're lucky they had the means to save your life. You can't feel guilty about it."

At first she didn't understand his smile, but then he explained. "So they did, Johanna. I understood that when I saw how a blue-eyed farm girl used every means she had to help her family, even risked robbing a train. I sure hope she no longer feels guilty. After all, she only did what she had to do at the time."

Hearing his teasing chuckle, Johanna pulled herself on top of him, laughing down at his startled face as she delivered a powerless blow to his midsection. "If you're so smart, why'd you leave Boston and marry up with a thief?"

"I heard somewhere that rehabilitated criminals make the best wives." He quickly forestalled more ineffective punishment by grabbing hold of her hands. Seconds later, he was off the bed and carrying her to the bureau. "I know you'd prefer a few more leisurely hours of pleasure in my bed but we've got work to do. It's way past milking time, love."

"Hmmph," Johanna grunted but nevertheless pulled open a drawer and removed some fresh clothes. Grumbling under her breath, she pulled on a pair of pants and a shirt. "This is what comes from marrying up with a farmer. Nothing's more important than the chores."

By the look on his face, she couldn't have bestowed a higher compliment. Her brows rose. "That wasn't intended as a compliment, Tyler Kendall."

"Well, I'm taking it as such," he retorted, white teeth flashing like a Cheshire cat's. "You didn't falter once when you called me a farmer."

"So?" she asked, not understanding.

"Hearing you call me that makes me think it's true. I've been working hard to prove I'm not going to quit but I've always sensed your doubt. That means a lot to me, Johanna. More than you know."

She could see that it did, but though she wanted a deeper explanation, he pulled on his boots and walked out of the bedroom. "Stop lagging, Johanna." His voice took on the same tone as hers: "Poor dumb animals don't wait for nobody, missus!"

Shaking her head, she remembered having once shouted those words herself and followed him out of the cabin. Once in the barn, they worked side by side, feeding and watering the animals, completing the milking and forking down bedding from the loft. Even though these were the same chores Johanna had done every day of her life, they now took on a new meaning. Tyler's smile was there to greet her as she poured milk into the large pails, his kisses interrupting duties she had once thought mundane. As she spoke softly to the animals, she heard his low rumbling voice doing the same, and several times she glanced up to meet his adoring eyes on her face, finding that some sweet endearment he'd delivered to the stock was intended for her. She highly doubted she'd begrudge doing chores ever again.

After they finished up in the barn, they enjoyed a simple meal they cooked together on the large cook stove. Seated on opposite sides of the table, Johanna barely tasted her food, content with watching him eat. "Why did you choose Nebraska, Tyler? I guess I still can't make sense out of you wanting to become a farmer."

"Good sense didn't come into it," Tyler agreed, taking a last swallow from his coffee cup. "Let's go for a walk by the river and I'll tell you all about it."

Hand in hand, they crossed the green grasses until they reached the riverbank. Without speaking, they both sat down to roll up their pant legs and remove their boots. "I don't think I'll ever find anything more enjoyable than wading," Tyler announced as he took her hand and led her into the water. "I know it leads to wonderful things. Unbelievable lovemaking . . . improper marriage proposals . . . I can't wait to see what will happen today."

Johanna found he could make her blush as easily as always and punished him for it by giving him a healthy shove.

"Hey!" The surprised exclamation was followed by a huge splash as he toppled sideways into the shallow water. He resurfaced in seconds but didn't look a bit offended by her unexpected retaliation. "Swimming! You have such grand inspirations, Mrs. Kendall. Let me help you take off your clothes."

She didn't have a chance to escape him and soon found herself completely naked, cavorting in the river with her equally naked husband. Inevitably, the good-natured splashing and play turned to more serious but far more enjoyable matters, and it was some time before Tyler carried his satiated wife to a soft grassy bed beneath the willow tree.

For a time, they just gazed upward into the vivid blue sky, but finally Tyler began the explanation he'd promised to give her during their meal. "I might have been behaving like a demented fool but I did know I was slowly destroying myself. If nothing else, I came out of the war with a strong sense of self-preservation. Every man needs a goal, and mine was to get away from the world I hated in Boston and find someplace where I'd have total peace. I chose Nebraska because I'd read about the rich farmland available and"—he gave her an apologetic look—"and because of my connections with the Western National Railroad, Nebraska seemed the best place to go. Little did I know that peace was the last thing I'd find out here."

The last was a challenge directed solely at her, but Johanna merely bestowed an impish smile and demanded he continue. Completely confident in his love, she laid her head down upon his shoulder, running her palm across his bare chest.

"When you're around I'm never safe," he scolded, then cleared his throat, and quickly stopped the provocative movement of her hand by trapping it in his own. He demanded with mock severity, "Do you want to hear more of this or not?"

"Of course I do," she replied, giggling. She moved slightly away but was immediately pulled back against him.

"Oh no, you don't," he growled. "You'll stay right here where I can keep a close eye on you." His intimate gaze traveled up and down her exposed curves until she decided they probably wouldn't complete their discussion unless she did something to distract him.

"You were telling me how you came to be on that train," she reminded. "As I recall, you were almost as helpless as a newborn babe. Couldn't even stand up to one half-grown man and two young girls."

"As *I* recall, I was almost murdered by a ruthless trio of gun-toting bandits."

She laughed. "Did we really come across like that? Willikins, all three of us were shaking in our boots."

The admission brought his sigh of relief. "That's nice to know. Every time I remembered that day, I wanted to wring your neck for making me look and feel like a defenseless fool. I looked into your blue eyes and all I saw was contempt. Imagine how I reacted when I discovered the woman I loved was the same person who'd ruthlessly aimed a gun at my heart, tied me to a chair and forced a gag between my teeth." He frowned, the memory arousing bruised feelings he'd long since rationalized away.

Sensing his state of mind, Johanna curled herself against his side. "I was scared to death just looking at you. You were so tall, so cruel-looking, and I knew with one false move on our parts you could have turned the table on us. When you reached for that little derringer, I almost died. Since then, I've been severely punished for my crimes. That day you dangled me over the edge of the loft, I was positive you'd recognized me and were going to drop me into the stall with the oxen. Then there were all those times you kissed me, and no matter what I did you made me respond. I was sure you knew that I was falling in love with you and you were laughing behind my back."

Her heartfelt speech restored his good spirits and he finished telling her what he'd planned, ending with, "After that day you came over to my place and let me kiss you, I was finished. All my plans went up in smoke. Instead of seeking ways to maintain my isolation, my goal became finding a way to make you part of my life. I was never more relieved in my life than the day you offered marriage. I was certain you didn't love me like I loved you, but I knew if I could get your name on a marriage certificate, I'd have plenty of time to bring you around." A vulnerable expression flitted across his face as he spoke, but it dissipated as he considered their present natural state. Casting her a lascivious gaze, he quipped arrogantly, "Didn't take me very long, did it?"

Not the least bit offended, Johanna dropped a quick kiss on his lips, wiggling her nose when the twitching of his mustache tickled her cheeks. She sat up. "Much too long to my way of thinking. If you hadn't been so nasty to me, I would have thrown myself at you long before now."

"I'll do my best to make it up to you."

By mutual consent, they both started getting dressed, reluctant to end their idyllic interlude but aware that the day was fast slipping away and there were many things that still needed to be done. Even though they were on a honeymoon of sorts, they were still responsible for the well-being of their stock and the crops they'd planted. "Maybe we should ask the rest of the family to come back early," Johanna suggested. "That way, they can do all the chores while you and I spend all our time 'wading.'"

"Not on your life," Tyler said firmly, reaching for her hand and tucking it into the crook of his arm as they began crossing the fields on their way back to the cabin. "Now when I start building a fine new house for my beautiful bride and the strong sons she's promised to me, I'll be happy for their help, but for the next few days I want to keep you all to myself."

Johanna was in total agreement with him, struggling to control the gigantic bubble of happiness that was swelling in her heart. "One day, you and I will stand here and look across our land, just like we're doing today, but our children will be standing by our sides. There may not be a lot of money in farming, Tyler, but you and I will be very rich."

He nodded, his love for her shining in his eyes. "My old gardener once told me that the Lord's promise was in every seed I planted. That's more than enough for me, Johanna Kendall. I really became a rich man the moment you came into my life."

Off in the distance, they could see the tall rows of ripening corn, golden wheat and sweet hay. Johanna stepped in front of her husband, leaned back against him and wrapped his arms around her waist. Tyler rested his chin on the top of her head, as together they gazed into the future and saw their laughing sons and daughters scampering through the tall prairie grasses, acre upon acre of growing crops, and themselves, working side by side, reaping a harvest of love.

Tapestry

HISTORICAL ROMANCES

Breathtaking New Tales

of love and adventure set against history's most exciting time and places. Featuring two novels by the finest authors in the field of romantic fiction—<u>every month</u>.

Next Month From Tapestry Romances

FIRE AND INNOCENCE
by Sheila O'Hallion
MOTH AND FLAME
by Laura Parker

POCKET BOOKS

Home delivery from Pocket Books

Here's your opportunity to have fabulous bestsellers delivered right to you. Our free catalog is filled to the brim with the newest titles plus the finest in mysteries, science fiction, westerns, cookbooks, romances, biographies, health, psychology, humor—every subject under the sun. Order this today and a world of pleasure will arrive at your door.

 POCKET BOOKS, Department ORD
1230 Avenue of the Americas, New York, N.Y. 10020

368